"COME TO BED WITH ME, LONGARM."

Angelita's voice dropped to a whisper. "I need you."

"You're just upset," Longarm said. "You'll feel different in the morning."

"No. I'm old enough to know what I want, Longarm." She hesitated for a moment, then went on. "I have been with men in bed before. Does that make you think less of me?"

"Not a bit."

Longarm said nothing more, nor did he make any move toward accepting Angelita's invitation. In a few seconds he looked up and saw Angelita standing beside him.

Angelita whispered, "You will not come to me, so I have come to you."

I0980955

Also in the LONGARM series
from Jove

━◆━ TABOR EVANS ━◆━

LONGARM

AND
SANTA ANNA'S GOLD

A JOVE BOOK

LONGARM AND SANTA ANNA'S GOLD

A Jove Book/published by arrangement with
the author

PRINTING HISTORY
Jove edition/November 1983

All rights reserved.
Copyright © 1983 by Jove Publications, Inc.
This book may not be reproduced in whole or in part,
by mimeograph or any other means, without permission.
For information address: The Berkley Publishing Group,
200 Madison Avenue, New York, N.Y. 10016.

ISBN: 0-515-06261-8

Jove books are published by The Berkley Publishing Group,
200 Madison Avenue, New York, N.Y. 10016. The words
"A JOVE BOOK" and the "J" with sunburst are trademarks
belonging to Jove Publications, Inc.

PRINTED IN THE UNITED STATES OF AMERICA

Chapter 1

Longarm looked out the window and shivered inwardly as the train pulled into the station. He had watched snow swirling past the windows of each of the three trains which had carried him south from Billings at a snail's crawl, but had not once seen the sparkle of sunshine for which he'd hoped.

In the Cheyenne depot he'd driven the chill from his bones with a sip or two of Tom Moore Maryland rye while he waited for the Union Pacific's daytime local to Denver, and finally had turned his head away from the white-drifted landscape only when the coach reached the crest rimming the little saucer-like valley in which Denver lay. Longarm took it as a personal affront that the snowfall was even heavier here in Denver than it had been in Montana or Wyoming along the way.

Old son, he told himself as the train squealed slowly to a halt, *you might as well pull up your britches and knuckle under to Jack Frost. It's wintertime now, and unless that case Billy Vail wired you about is someplace farther south than here, your butt's going to freeze off even if you was to put on two pairs of longjohns.*

Picking up his rifle and saddlebags, Longarm started for the coach door. Halfway down the aisle he got out of range of the heat cast by the squat cast-iron stove at the rear end of the coach and the icy wind from the open door whistled past his ears. After he'd alighted and started walking toward the depot, the howl of the Rockies' first big winter storm howled even louder.

Shunning the temptation to linger a minute in the half-warm air of Union Station, Longarm went on through and reached the street. Standing in the wind-tossed flakes he looked both ways for a hackney cab, but the street was bare of traffic. With an unhappy grunt, Longarm set his wide-brimmed tobacco-

1

brown hat more firmly on his head and turned up the collar of his coat to shield his ears. He tossed the saddlebags over one shoulder, tucked the butt of his rifle into the crook of his elbow, and started walking through the calf-high snow toward the federal building.

Although the halls of the big cut-stone building were warmer than the streets, Longarm's hands and ears and nose didn't begin to thaw until he stood in the outer room of the U.S. marshal's district office. The door to Billy Vail's office was closed, but even before Longarm could lay down his rifle and begin unbuttoning his coat the pink-cheeked little clerk told him, "Marshal Vail said you were to come right on in, if you got here before it was time to close."

Completely out of sorts with the world, Longarm touched a match to the long, slim stogie he'd slid from his vest pocket as soon as his fingers had gotten warm enough to feel anything, and acknowledged the clerk's remark with a nod. Leaving a stream of blue tobacco smoke in the air behind him, he opened Vail's door.

"Well, it's about time you got here," the chief marshal said, glancing up from his paper-strewn desk. "I looked for you a couple of hours ago. Come on in and close the door."

"I got here as fast as the train could bring me, Billy," Longarm replied. "Everything was running late all the way down here from Billings." He pulled the red morocco-uphol-stered chair he liked up to the corner of Vail's desk and settled into it.

"Your case up there is closed now, isn't it?" Vail asked.

"Sure." Longarm leaned back and puffed his cheroot.

"Well?" the chief marshal said.

"Well what, Billy?"

"You know perfectly well what, Long. Your report, damn it!"

"Oh, I can give you that real fast. There ain't a Lefty Clark gang any more. It's finished."

When Longarm returned his cheroot to his mouth and puffed it contentedly, Vail waited for a moment, then exploded. "Now, damn it, Long! You've been with me in this office for a long time, and every time you get back from an important case, dragging a report out of you is just like pulling your back teeth!"

"I don't know what else you need for a report," Longarm said innocently. "You sent me up there to Montana to get rid

2

of Lefty Clark's gang. Like I just told you, the gang's finished. There ain't any more of 'em left, at least not outside of jail."

"We go through this every time." Vail sighed in resignation. "And I don't know why I put up with it." He took a clean sheet of foolscap from his desk drawer and pulled his inkwell and pens a bit closer. "Go on, Long, tell me what happened. I've got to have a written report to send to Washington, even if nobody ever looks at it."

"You know, I got a pretty good hunch nobody ever does look at all the papers you send back East, Billy," Longarm said innocently. "It strikes me that all these damn reports don't do a thing but waste the time we could put to better use running down outlaws and killers."

"That might be true of cases that come to us direct," Vail agreed. "This one's different. It concerns important men, like Marcus Daly and Hearst and Tevis and that bunch. They've got more influence in Washington than we have, and if they ask for a report from the Justice Department, they expect to get it."

"Why don't you just wait and see if they ask, then?"

Vail shook his head. "I've told you before, Long. That's not the way it works. If I don't put a report in the file, some little snot-nosed pencil-pusher back in the Justice Department's going to find sooner or later that the Lefty Clark case never was officially closed, and it'll take six months for me to get all the paperwork straight."

Longarm suppressed the grin that started to show as Vail's griping continued. He had a hunch that his chief enjoyed the little scene they played out almost every time he closed an important case.

"Well, there's not an awful lot to tell, Billy," he began. "But if it's going to make you feel better, here's how it all happened. By the time I got to Butte, Lefty and his bunch had a four-day start, but that country up there's so rough I didn't figure they'd have all that much of a start, lugging almost three hundred pounds of money bags from the Anaconda payroll."

Longarm's hunch had been correct. He'd picked up the trail of the four heavily laden outlaws where they'd stopped first, at Murphy's Saloon, down the first slope of the Continental Divide where the trail ran through Pipestone Pass.

Murphy was a brawny redheaded Irishman with a fist-bent

3

nose and hands like small hams. After a ride that had taken a good part of the afternoon and most of the night, Longarm arrived at the saloon during the slack hour just before daybreak. He found Murphy alone in the barroom, and after exchanging half a dozen words with him Longarm knew the kind of man the saloon keeper was. He'd met the likes of Murphy before— men who couldn't seem to decide whether they were on the side of the law or the lawless.

"Now, look here, mister!" Murphy had blustered when Longarm asked about four men who might have stopped there four days earlier. "You can't expect me to remember every son of a bitch and his brother that puts up here for a night!"

"Oh, you'd remember these fellows, all right," Longarm replied calmly. "Four in a bunch, two packhorses, and both of the pack animals real heavy loaded."

Murphy made no pretense of even trying to remember. Almost before Longarm had finished speaking he was shaking his head. "I don't recall. They might've passed this way, they might not."

Longarm had encountered much smoother liars than Murphy, and knew that the saloon keeper would respond to only one kind of persuasion. He moved with the speed of a striking rattler. Wrapping a hand around the saloon keeper's brawny wrist, he gave the man's arm a quick twist that whirled him around. As the big Irishman turned, Longarm pulled the wrist up almost to his shoulder blades. Murphy fought to twist free, but Longarm's muscles were more than a match for the saloon keeper's bulk and brawn.

"Now, I know a man running a place like you got here wants to stay on the right side of the law," Longarm said quietly, but putting a bit more pressure on Murphy's arm as he spoke. "I didn't come looking for trouble, Murphy, but maybe if you jog your memory a little bit more, you can remember the fellows I was asking about."

"I—I guess they did come through," Murphy gasped. "Like you said, three or four days ago. And their pack animals was moving slow, even if it didn't look like they had all that much of a load on 'em."

"I'd imagine you heard them talking about where they was heading?" Longarm asked.

"They didn't talk much. I—I think I heard one of 'em say something about Three Forks."

4

Longarm felt the same glow of satisfaction that had swept over him a few nights earlier, when he'd filled an inside straight and pulled in a heavy pot during his regular poker game at the Windsor Hotel in Denver. He released Murphy's arm.

"That's better." Tossing a silver cartwheel on the bar, he went on, "I see you got a bottle of Tom Moore up there on your back bar. Pour me a drink out of it and keep what's left."

Pushing on through the breaking day, his progress speeded by the downsloping land, Longarm got to the Jefferson River in the late afternoon. Until he reached the river, one of the three streams that met to the northeast and formed the headwaters of the mighty Missouri, the trail ran through steep-walled gorges and canyons and along ridges from which there were few turnoffs. There'd been only a half dozen trails branching off, and none of these had borne the recent tracks of four riders and two overloaded packhorses.

When he reached the comparatively level and sparsely wooded valley through which the three streams flowed, Longarm moved more slowly. The main trail followed the Jefferson, and there were more turnoffs from it here, each one having to be examined carefully. At the third ford he encountered, Longarm found what he'd been looking for. At the water's edge, mingling with tracks that had been made earlier, he found the deeper than normal prints of the two packhorses. He forded the river and in the gathering shadows followed the faint trail that led him steadily east.

Dusk caught him at the edge of a thick stand of aspen. The leaves of the tall, close-growing trees were yellow now with summer's end, and were dancing their dervish flutter in the gathering evening breeze. It was as good a place as any to stop for the night, Longarm decided. The thin grass growing between the aspens would serve his horse, and he'd have shelter for the dark camp he would make.

Longarm dismounted, took a chunk of jerky from his saddlebag, and chewed it while he unsaddled. Working fast to beat the quickly falling darkness, he let the horse graze while he spread his bedroll and placed his saddlebags for a pillow. He finished the tough, chewy jerky and followed it with a fistful of parched corn, hunkering down on the edge of the bedroll. After a swallow of water from his canteen, Longarm took out a cheroot and a match, but as he was preparing to flick his thumbnail across the match head the dim figure of the horse caught his eye. The animal had wandered into the grove and showed no signs of stopping.

Hurrying after it, Longarm caught the beast, led it back, and tethered it for the night. He dug another match from his vest pocket and had not quite touched its head with his thumbnail when he saw a faint flicker of light through the trees beyond the aspen grove. The firelight filtered through the tree trunks made a few small gleams no bigger than a pinpoint, but Longarm's finely honed lawman's instinct led him to investigate. Taking his Winchester, he started through the grove on foot.

Moving silently, Longarm could smell the woodsmoke from the fire and hear the muttering of voices long before he reached the point where the aspens began to thin. He saw the dark forms of horses beyond the fire. There were several animals in a rope corral, but it was too dark for him to count them. All he could tell was that there were at least four horses, possibly more. The grove ended before he could see the fire clearly. He stopped in the thin cover of the tree trunks and moved from side to side until he could see the fire clearly. Two men were silhouetted against its glow. One of them was speaking, and now Longarm could hear him clearly.

". . . been back a long time ago," the man was saying. "How far is that place, anyhow?"

"Hell, don't ask me," the other one replied. "Lefty's the one that knows the country around here, not me."

"Well, I guess they're all right. But he ought've figured out we'd need more grub than we was carrying when we left."

Longarm knew he'd heard all he needed the moment the man at the fire said "Lefty." He slid the safety off the rifle and took a step or two further, stopped while the tree trunks still gave him cover, and called to the men at the fire.

"Get your hands in the air, you two!" he commanded. "I'm a U.S. marshal and I'm putting you under arrest!"

Before Longarm had said three words the pair outlined by the blaze were in motion. Swiveling around, they drew revolvers and were searching the shadows for a target.

"Drop the guns!" Longarm ordered. "You ain't got a chance!"

He had anticipated the outlaws' reaction and dropped flat in the few seconds before they opened fire. While the hot lead from their revolvers was whistling above his head, Longarm brought both men down with a slug apiece from the Winchester.

He waited a moment, watching the still forms of the outlaws, before standing up and starting toward the fire. He had just reached the bodies and was bending over the nearest, turning the corpse up to get a look at the dead man's face, when hoofbeats thudded in the darkness beyond the blaze and the sharp crack of a rifle shot sounded above the noise of the hoofbeats.

There was no cover except the trees, and Longarm knew he'd never make it to them. He dropped flat beside the body he'd just turned over and lay still while a second shot split the night. The hoofbeats had stopped now.

"You see him, Lefty?" a man's gruff voice called.

"He's laying there back of Slim," another replied. "You go around to the right. I'll go the other way, and we'll get him in a cross fire!"

Longarm had no choice but to hold his position. He strained his ears trying to hear the movements of the two men in the darkness. Only a few soft scraping sounds broke the stillness, and he could not locate their source. Longarm laid his rifle aside and slid his Colt from its holster. For what he was facing now, the quicker-shooting revolver was a better weapon.

A thunk of a boot toe hitting a stone sounded from the darkness ahead. Longarm rolled in time to avoid the pistol slug that thunked into the ground where his head had been. He fired at the flash of the revolver that had let off the shot, and a yowl of pain sounded through the gloom.

Longarm kept moving, whirling like a dervish as he angled toward the aspens. A shot cut the air close to him, and he let off a slug from the Colt, aiming by reaction at the air to the left of the muzzle flash. Longarm reached the trees, waiting for the shots that were never fired. He stood listening, but the silence was complete for several moments before a voice broke it.

"Lefty?" When there was no reply, the speaker repeated his call. "Lefty? You all right?"

When the question was not answered, Longarm spoke. "Lefty's dead. And you'll go with him if you don't drop your gun and get over by the fire where I can see you."

"Don't shoot!" the unseen man called hastily. "I'm giving up! I don't know who in hell you are, but even if I didn't have a slug in my gun arm I wouldn't take you on!"

Longarm waited until the man who'd surrendered was clearly visible in the firelight. Then he walked up and made his arrest.

"And that's about all there was to it, Billy," Longarm concluded. "I hauled the one that was still alive on down to Bozeman and left him at Fort Ellis, seeing as how the jail at Butte's as full of holes as a Swiss cheese."

"You won't have to go back there soon to testify?"

"Now, Billy, you know damn well old Judge Harris won't go up to Montana till the snow melts next spring. A judge's job's not like ours; they can pick and choose when they go someplace."

"You could've wired me when you closed the case," Vail said.

"No, I couldn't've, Billy. By the time I got into Billings and found your message waiting for me, all the wires were down. This damn snowstorm stretches clear on south all the way from Canada, maybe from the North Pole, for all I know."

"You won't have to worry about being cold where you'll be going on this new case," Vail said. He put aside the notes he'd made while Longarm talked and began searching through the papers on his desk, shifting them from one pile to another.

"I wouldn't mind a bit if you was to send me on a case that took me to hell." Longarm grinned. "Not if I could stay there long enough to get good and warm. But I figured I'd have a day or so of rest coming to me before I took out again."

"This case has already been waiting three days, Long."

"I guess you'll expect me to start right away, then?"

Vail cushioned his reply by saying, "I didn't get this one with the regular mail. It came on the direct wire."

Longarm knew what that meant. The direct telegraph line in the basement office of the Denver federal building to the Justice Department headquarters in Washington was used only when someone high in the department had an urgent assignment. Routine cases were sent by regular mail. He took out a fresh cheroot and with his steel-hard thumbnail flicked a match alight and touched its flame to the tip of the long slim cigar.

"If it's three days old now, another day won't hurt all that much, Billy," he said through a cloud of fresh smoke. "And I got to have a bath and time to get my clothes washed. I didn't stop day or night while I was chasing that bunch. If I was to take off my longjohns and stand 'em in that corner, they're so stiff they'd stay standing up without me in 'em."

"Well, don't try it," Vail said, smiling for the first time

8

since Longarm had come into the office. "All right. Take a day off, but be be ready to start the day after tomorrow. And you can leave your heavy underwear behind. You won't need it where you'll be going."

"You said something to that effect a minute ago." Longarm frowned. "Where'll I be heading for? Arizona? New Mexico? The Nation? They're about the only places I know—" He stopped short and looked at Vail with narrowed eyes. "Wait a minute, now. There's only one other place I know of where it'll be warm this time of the year. You mean I got to go to Texas again?"

"That's where your new case is." Vail nodded.

"Then I'll double in spades what I just told you, Billy. Do me a favor and send me to hell. I'd a sight rather go there than back to Texas."

Vail seldom laughed, but this time he guffawed. Then his face grew sober and he said, "It's going to take a while to tell you all about this case, Long. And you need to know right down to the dot over the last 'i' exactly what you'll be getting into."

"Go on. I'm listening," Longarm told his chief.

Vail shook his head. "It's just about time to close the office now, and I know you've had a rough couple of weeks. Take off whatever time you'll need tomorrow to get your gear in order, but come in late in the morning, after I've cleared away the mail. We've got some talking to do before you leave."

Vail's sober tone had its effect on Longarm. "You sound like this is some kind of a special case, Billy," he said.

"You could call it that, I guess." Vail nodded. "But I'll give you all the details tomorrow."

Longarm nodded and stood up. He turned to leave just as the office door opened and the little pink-cheeked clerk stuck his head in.

"Oh, Marshal Long," the young man said, "there's someone out here waiting for you. I didn't want to disturb Chief Vail while he was talking to you, but the man's been waiting quite a while, and he seems to be getting impatient."

Looking past the clerk, Longarm recognized a familiar face, but for a moment he couldn't associate it with a name. Remembering in the next instant, he said, "Hello, Duffey. I hope it ain't trouble that's brought you looking for me."

"It's not, Marshal," Duffey replied. "I've got a note here

for you." Reaching into his breast pocket, he took out a square envelope and handed it to Longarm.

There was no name on the envelope, and the note was so brief that Longarm read it at a glance.

"Is the storm going to be lucky? It's made me decide to stop over here until the weather clears. Duffey will bring you out if you can have dinner this evening."

A large, looping "J" was the only signature.

A smile was forming on Longarm's face as he looked up from the message. He said, "Just give me a minute to pick my gear up, Duffey. Then you and me will take a little ride."

Chapter 2

Gravel crunched under the wheels as Duffey turned the carriage off the brick-paved street into the semicircular drive that led to the Burnside house. The changed sound broke the chain of memory that had filled Longarm's mind during the long drive. The trip from the federal building had been longer than normal, as he'd had Duffey swing by his rooming house. The coachman had waited in front of the run-down house on the wrong side of Cherry Creek while Longarm took a half-minute whore's bath; a splash of rye whiskey on his palms and a quick rubdown to cleanse his skin. After that, he'd put on fresh underwear and a clean shirt and put his laundry out for the Chinese boy to pick up that evening.

In the swirling snow and fading light the ride back through town out to Sherman Avenue had been a slow one, giving Longarm plenty of time for memories. He'd gone back in his mind to the night almost two years before when he'd saved Julia Burnside from the unwanted attentions of an obnoxious and amorously inclined drummer on the Denver-bound Santa Fe Limited. The spark that had been ignited between Julia and Longarm during the remainder of the trip had burst into flame when they'd reached Denver.

Though soon afterwards Julia had moved to New York, where her widowed father had transferred his business operations, she still stopped at the family mansion when a trip west brought her back. Those trips had been few recently. More than six months had passed since Longarm had received one of the notes she always sent him announcing her arrival.

Now Longarm glanced along the front of the imposing mansion as he stepped out in the porte cochere and grimaced when he saw snowflakes filling the air so thickly that they hid the end of the mansion from sight. He stopped thinking about the weather then, for the door swung open and Julia stood silhouetted against the light from the entrance hall.

"Longarm!" she cried. She threw herself into his waiting arms and turned her face up to meet his lips. "Oh, Longarm!"

"You're a real treat to my eyes, Julia," Longarm said as they stood looking at one another after they'd broken the lingering kiss. "It's been a while since you was here last. And you get prettier every time I see you."

Julia's luminous brown eyes glowed as she gazed at him, her full lips parted in a smile that showed dazzling white teeth. She'd changed the style of her hair since Longarm had seen her last. Her shining raven-black locks were now arranged in a fringe of small curls that followed the curve of her smooth white brow and swept into a tight chignon at the nape of her neck.

She was a small woman; her head came only to Longarm's broad shoulders. She raised her eyes and leaned back to look up at him, then brought up her hands and cupped Longarm's chin with the palm of one while with the fingers of the other she stroked the longhorn curves of his full brown moustache.

"I still don't quite believe you're really here," she said. "I have to feel you to prove to myself I'm not dreaming."

"Oh, I'm real enough," he assured her. "But that don't mean I want you to take your hands away." He caught her slim wrist in one of his hands and pressed his lips to her palm. "I like to feel you touch me," He glanced down at her and smiled as he added, "And I like what I'm looking at, too."

Julia's dress was a simple one of soft crepe held only by a belt at the waist. When she lifted her head and arched her torso back the clinging fabric outlined her full breasts. They were rounder and even more generous than Longarm remembered.

She said, "It's been far too long a time. And I've been around stuffy young men who can't talk about anything except stock prices and what the bond market will be like the next day. While we're at dinner, you'll have to tell me what you've been doing since I was here last."

"Oh, what I've been up to ain't such a much," he said as Julia took his arm and led him from the hall into the adjoining sitting room. "Crooks and rascals get old as stocks and bonds after you see enough of 'em."

"Are you very hungry, Longarm?" Julia asked as they stopped in the center of the room. "Because if you are, we can eat now, in the downstairs dining room. My maid's going to serve us. I've already sent Mrs. Duffey to the servants' quarters, and Celeste will go up to her room as soon as we've eaten. Then we'll have the house to ourselves the rest of the night."

"Whatever pleases you," he replied. "I'd as soon stand here and look at you as eat the finest meal a cook could fix up."

"If you're not just flattering me—"

"You know I wouldn't tell you anything but the truth."

"Then why don't I tell Celeste to wait an hour and we'll have dinner in my sitting room upstairs?" she asked, looking at Longarm with eagerness in her eyes. "When Duffey didn't get back right away, I knew he'd found you and that you'd be here for dinner. But I've been getting more impatient by the minute, and now I've waited just about as long as I can stand to."

A coal fire burned with a soft red glow in the fireplace and gave Julia's bedroom its only light. She threw the quilted spread off the bed while Longarm took off his coat and vest and stepped to the bed to hang his gunbelt on the chair beside it.

Julia turned to Longarm while he was removing his shirt and buried her face in the brown curls that covered his broad chest. She sighed as she rubbed her cheeks on him, and the pressure of her body emphasizing the warmth of her breath on his bare skin began to bring him erect. Julia's hands went to his belt buckle and she raised her head to look up at him.

"I've been thinking about this minute since the train pulled into the depot last night," she said as her busy fingers made short work of unbuckling the belt and began on the buttons of his tight cord trousers. "Not that I didn't think of it before."

Julia pulled the trousers down and Longarm felt her warm hand on his swelling shaft, liberating it from his balbriggans to jut erect. She released him long enough to pull the bow of her belt loose and shrug her dress from her shoulders. It slid to the floor and a second shrug let the straps of her thin silken chemise drop to join the crumpled fabric of the dress.

Longarm bent to kiss her and Julia's soft, warm mouth opened to his tongue. While they held the kiss Longarm levered out of his boots and pushed his pants and balbriggans to the floor. He bent to kiss her unthrust breasts and under the soft caresses of his lips and tongue Julia's body began trembling gently.

"Oh, Longarm!" she whispered, the urgency of her tone

13

carried in her uneven breathing. "If you knew how many times I've dreamed about being back in this room alone with you, you wouldn't make me wait! And I can't wait any longer, damn it!"

Grasping Longarm around the waist, Julia whirled him around. He felt the weight of her small body pushing him backward and yielded slowly, letting her move him to the edge of the waiting bed, finally falling on the mattress on his back.

Julia got on her knees above him, her thighs straddling Longarm's groin. She raised her hips and her soft hand closed around his erection, guiding it. Longarm did not move to help her as she lowered her body slowly. He lay back, looking up into her smiling face, as he felt the the swift engulfing of moist pulsing warmth when Julia dropped with frantic haste and impaled herself on his rigid upthrust shaft.

"Oh, lovely, lovely!" she gasped as she sank down. "Nobody but you can make me feel the way I do right now."

In the instant before her lips met his, Longarm said, "I sorta like the way you make me feel, too, Julia."

For a few moments they both lay quietly, lost in the sensual pleasure that surged through their joined bodies. Julia was the first to stir. Her breasts were pressed against the matted curls on Longarm's chest; she shifted her shoulders from side to side, shivering softly at the rough hair rasping against the tips of her rosettes.

She soon found that this was not enough. She began a slow, almost imperceptible rotation of her hips that brought a soft purring sigh to her lips. Longarm lay quietly, letting her set the pace of their pleasure. He slipped his hands between their close-pressed bodies and cupped Julia's generous breasts in his palms. She shivered at the caresses of his hard finger-tips on her nipples.

Julia's soft sigh became a moan, and Longarm remained motionless while the rotation of her hips gradually grew faster until she was writhing frantically above him, her body gyrating on the rod of rigid flesh that bound them together. Julia's back arched, and she bent her head, her lips seeking Longarm's.

Their lips met and their tongues joined. Longarm clasped his hands around Julia's softly firm buttocks and pulled her down still further, holding her while she shook in a final, frantic quivering. She cried aloud, and for a long moment poised rigid and motionless, then finally relaxed. With a long, contented sigh she sank down, her body growing limp, until she lay quietly, her head resting on Longarm's muscular chest.

After a few moments had passed she whispered, "I stole that one from you. But I remember how long you can hold on, so I didn't think you'd mind."

"You know I don't," he told her. "But tell me when you've rested long enough."

"Who said I needed to rest?" Julia smiled. "How can I rest, as long as I feel you filling me the way you are?"

Longarm clasped his arms around Julia and brought her up from the bed with him. He stood motionless for a moment, long enough for Julia to entwine her fingers around his neck. Then he turned and held her suspended while he leaned slowly forward and lowered her until she lay on her back on the soft bed.

Crouching above her, Longarm caressed her breasts softly, his callused hands brushing lightly across the soft mounds with their dark pink protruding tips. Julia reached up to stroke his cheeks, her fingertips dancing over his lips and running down the cords that began to stand out in his neck as their caressing was prolonged. At last Longarm's eyes questioned her in the flickering light of the fireplace, and she nodded.

"Of course," she said. "Now, if you're ready, too."

"I'm always ready for you, Julia," Longarm replied.

He moved gently at first, with deliberate strokes, long and slow. Julia lay quietly, her eyes veiled, a dreamy smile on her full red lips. Bit by bit, tension crept back into her muscles. Her hands on his face moved faster and at last she grasped his shoulders and pulled Longarm down to join her lips to his.

Longarm stroked faster as their tongues probed, and Julia's hips began to rear up to meet his downward thrusts. They moved together in a rhythm that grew faster with the passing minutes, Longarm pacing his thrusts to match Julia's mounting excitement. Her body was tense and quivering now, and as she began to writhe in one quick heaving roll after another they broke their kiss.

Julia's head arched back, her soft neck a smooth white column in the glow of the firelight. Her head began rolling from side to side, and her fingers clenched on Longarm's wide shoulders as she levered herself up to meet his lunges. She locked her legs tightly around Longarm's hips, trying to pull him deeper as he thrust into her, and Longarm shortened his

15

strokes while he increased their speed, stabbing with quickened thrusts into Julia's soft, eager body. She clung to him, short throaty groans bubbling from her lips.

"Don't ever stop, Longarm!" she gasped. "Even if I beg you to, don't stop!"

"Don't worry," he assured her. "It'll be a while before I let go of you."

Julia's writhing grew more and more frantic. Her groans became sharper and burst from her throat in a mounting crescendo. Longarm held himself firmly in control while he speeded the tempo of his lunges. He kept thrusting deeply until Julia jerked in a final flurry of mad abandoned threshing. She screamed softly, then the scream grew louder as she mounted to her climax and with a last loud cry stiffened and clung to him. Longarm thrust hard and held himself pressed into her firmly until Julia sighed with a low gasp of contentment and went limp.

Even then, Longarm did not stop his deep, slow thrusts. He moved more deliberately now, burying himself gradually, and Julia opened her eyes at last and looked up at him.

"Oh, yes," she sighed. "And even if I didn't ask you, I'm glad you remembered not to stop."

"I always keep my promises," Longarm told her.

Julia raised her head to kiss him, but this time kissing was not enough for her. She closed her teeth on Longarm's lip and bit down gently before moving her mouth over his corded neck and broad shoulders, nibbling gently, rubbing her soft face on his warm, smooth skin. Longarm kept up his deep deliberate thrusting until Julia sighed and lay back. She spread her thighs wide, opening herself fully to his penetrating shaft.

Longarm's body was demanding now that he share in Julia's pleasure. He responded to her excitement and let himself mount with her as her hips rose and fell in time with his hard downward lunges. When Julia's final climactic scream rang in his ears he loosed his control and jetted while she clung to him as he drained in a series of shuddering spasms.

They lay with closed eyes while their shivering subsided. After long minutes ticked away in the dim room, Julia stirred. She opened her eyes and looked up, offering her lips to Longarm for a soft, slow kiss to seal their gratification.

"What a wonderful way to start an evening," she sighed. "I could lie here with you forever, Longarm."

"We'll stay this way as long as you want to, Julia," he said softly in her ear. "It's early yet, and we've got the whole night ahead of us."

"Yes," she whispered softly, "and I intend to make the most of every minute of it."

On the wall of Billy Vail's office the clock was chiming ten when Longarm walked in. The chief marshal looked up from the sheaf of papers he was holding and scanned Longarm's bronzed, freshly shaven face, the smooth drape of his black string necktie, and the newly pressed creases in the sleeves of his long Prince Albert coat. Vail nodded approvingly.

"You look a hell of a lot better than you did when you left here yesterday, Long," he said. "I'm glad to see you were smart enough to get a good night's sleep instead of sitting in that all-night poker game with your cronies at the Windsor."

Longarm kept his face expressionless as he replied, "I just just couldn't think much about playing cards last night, Billy."

"I'm glad I didn't ask you to leave today," Vail went on. He held up the fat stack of documents he'd been inspecting. "The papers on this case just got here from Washington in the morning mail. I've been going through them since I came in, so pull up a chair and we'll look at them together."

"Can't you just tell me about the case the way you always do?" Longarm asked. "You know I ain't much good at paperwork."

"I'm afraid not. I've run across a few things you need to study for yourself. Now sit down and let's get started, or we'll be here all day."

Longarm pulled the red morocco-upholstered chair up to the desk and settled down in it. He said, "You know, Billy, I sure don't feel good about having to go back to Texas. Seems like I always get into some kind of a ruckus down there."

"I'd be happy if Texas was the only place you got into a ruckus," Vail said with a smile.

"Trouble's awful easy to get into with all them Ranger pals of yours," Longarm went on. "It looks like me and the Texas Rangers just rub each other the wrong way."

"Now, you know the Rangers are a crack outfit, Long," Vail said. "You just happened to be on the other side once or twice."

"From what I've seen of 'em, the Rangers have only got

17

one side to any case they handle. That's their side."

"That's nonsense!" the chief marshal snorted. "You know the Texas Rangers are a crack law-enforcement outfit. They get their man, they've got guts, they're fair, and they're honest."

"Oh, I grant you all that, Billy," Longarm replied. "But you left out one thing about 'em."

"What's that?"

"They carry a pretty mean grudge, too. They're just like a bunch of elephants. They never forget a man who's once got crossways of 'em."

"Now, just because you've had a few run-ins with the Ranger force doesn't give you any right to run them down."

"Oh, I wasn't running down your old buddies, Billy," Longarm said quickly. "But I got an idea I'm the number one man on their hate list."

"Well, you've got to admit you've always held your own when you've tangled with them, Long. But I'll tell you one thing. After serving with them so many years, I'd like nothing better than to go and work with them on a case again. Not that I'm running our own outfit down, you understand."

"Oh, sure." Longarm slid one of his long slim cigars from his pocket and started to strike a match, but before he'd flicked the match into flame said, "You know, Billy, that ain't a bad idea you just had."

Vail looked up from the file he held and frowned. "What idea?"

Longarm grinned. "Why, you go to Texas and leave me here."

"Now you know damned well—" Vail began before he saw the smile on Longarm's face. He snorted and gestured toward his desk, where stacks of wanted flyers, heaps of loose correspondence, and a double pile of fat blue-covered files bound with red ribbons lay. "If it wasn't for this, don't think I wouldn't go!" he finished.

"Well, my offer still stands," Longarm said.

"And I still say no." Vail pushed aside some of the papers on his desk to clear a place for the file he still held. He put the thick blue folder down and opened it. "Now, here's what this case amounts to. You're going down to Texas to look for a bunch of gold coins that have stirred things up lately. It's—"

"Billy," Longarm broke in, "I hate to butt in when you're

18

telling me something, but ain't it the Treasury Department's job to handle any cases that have to do with money?"

"Only if it's United States money."

"And these gold pieces ain't?"

"No. They're Mexican coinage, twenty-peso gold pieces, all bearing an 1836 date."

"Why can't the Mexican government look out for itself, Billy? How come we're going to catch a bunch of crooks that've been counterfeiting Mexican money?"

"These gold pieces aren't counterfeit, Long. They're real enough. That's the trouble."

"You know, the more you tell me, the less sense it makes. If it's real money, why're we going after it?"

"Because it's circulating in Texas. Most of the coins have shown up in San Antonio."

"You know, that's a real nice town, Billy. The only thing wrong with it is that it's in Texas."

"Forget about Texas!" Vail snapped.

"I'd be real glad to, only you just got through telling me how tickled I oughta be to go down there."

Vail was still angry. "I don't give you many direct orders, Long, but I'm giving you one now. I don't want to hear any more jokes about Texas. Is that clear?"

Longarm realized he'd almost ridden a good horse to death. He said quickly, "I'm sorry, Billy. I guess I let my big mouth run away with me. Go on. I won't josh you any more."

"Good. Now, there's more than gold coins involved in this case. Forget the gold; it's not that important. The real point is that there've been two Treasury men killed while they were investigating those damned gold pieces. You're going to Texas to clear up a double murder."

Chapter 3

"If you say so, Billy," Longarm said, his voice flat.

Vail waited for him to continue, but Longarm simply sat and looked at him across the desk. After a moment, the chief marshal said, "Well? No questions, Long?"

Speaking slowly, choosing his words carefully, Longarm said, "Oh, I got a lot of questions, Billy, but I don't see how I can ask 'em without getting you all riled up again."

"I won't get riled. Go ahead. Ask your questions."

"When you started telling me about this case, you said me and the Rangers wasn't going to get mixed up. Then you told me about the Mexican gold pieces, and right afterwards you said I was to forget about 'em. Am I right so far?"

"Yes." Vail nodded.

"Well, now it looks like I'm going to Texas to investigate a double murder. Billy, how in hell can I investigate a murder case in Texas and not get mixed up with your Ranger friends?"

Vail smiled thinly. "When you put it that way, it doesn't make much sense, does it?" He thought for a moment, then went on. "Let's see if I can get you straightened out. You see, Long—" Vail stopped, frowned, and started again. "Those two Treasury agents were sent to Texas to find out about the Mexican twenty-peso pieces, because the story was going around that they were from Santa Anna's gold hoard. Does that help you to understand what this case is all about?"

Longarm's brows were drawn together in a puzzled frown. "You mean the Santa Anna that massacred all them fellows at the Alamo? Jim Bowie and Davy Crockett and all the others I heard so much about when I was a tad?"

"Yes. The same one."

"But, Billy, that happened a long time ago—forty or fifty years back. If I remember rightly, Santa Anna's dead."

"Oh, he's dead, all right. But he's supposed to have left this gold—"

"You mean the twenty-peso Mexican gold pieces, I guess."

"Of course. They're what started this whole damned mess," Vail replied. "He left the gold, or he's supposed to have left the gold—" He stopped again and slapped his hand on the desk so hard that the pink-cheeked young clerk came bursting in from the outer office. Vail stared at the clerk for a moment and demanded gruffly, "What in hell do you mean breaking in on us this way? Don't you know enough to knock?"

"But—but, I thought—" The youth's cheeks were no longer pink, but ashen.

"I don't give a damn what you thought! Get out!" When the shaken youth had gone, Vail turned back to Longarm and asked, "Now, where were we?"

"You just said Santa Anna left a lot of gold somewheres."

"Well, it's almost certain that he did, but the Treasury's got a suspicion that somebody's found it now."

"So that's why we got two murdered Treasury agents and a lot of old twenty-peso pieces popping up in San Antonio?"

"Exactly," Vail agreed. "Except that the gold pieces are new, even though they are dated over forty years back. Now, the thing about this case—" Again he stopped and shook his head. "Damn it, Long, now you've got me all twisted up!"

"Well, I'm glad I ain't the only one," Longarm said. "It don't make me feel so silly if you're mixed up, too."

Vail sat silently for a moment, scratching his chin. Then he said, "I think I see a way to straighten all this out for you. Wait just a minute." He leafed through the papers in the blue folder he was holding and extracted several closely written pages. Handing them to Longarm, he said, "Here. You sit right where you are and read these over for yourself. I'm going out for a breath of fresh air to see if it'll clear my head."

For a moment after Vail left, Longarm sat staring at the pages in his hand. They were buff-colored sheets with blue lines from the standard tablets found in every federal office. The writing was in black ink, in the rounded Spencerian style the public schools taught. It was very clear and easy to read. With a sigh, Longarm lighted a fresh cheroot and began reading.

A superscription in parentheses headed the first page. It read:

Extracted verbatim from archives of the Republic of Texas, holograph document signed by Gnl. Sam Houston, date of April 26, 1836, titled "Report to the Congress of the Republic of Texas on Events Subsequent to the Battle at San Jacinto River."

On this day, the confusion following the battle having subsided and stragglers of the Mexican forces having been pursued and assembled under guard, I instructed my adjutant to bring Gnl. Santa Anna to my tent. My wounded leg being much improved, I had been able to frame details of the terms of the Mexican surrender. This was my second conversation with Santa Anna. The first was immediately after his capture at the end of the battle as stated in my Report of 22 pox., a quite terse exchange in which he agreed that his forces would lay down their arms.

On Santa Anna's arrival, and the usual exchange of courtesy, I informed him that he must accept my terms of surrender without amendment, both in his capacity as Pres. of Mexico and Gnl. of the defeated army. Further, I informed him that he would be held personally responsible for the discipline of his forces while the surrender was carried out and during his retreat to Mexico. The Gnl. agreed without argument to my stipulations. He was a dispirited and defeated man.

Thereupon I presented my terms to Santa Anna. These were that (First) his forces give up all arms, military and personal: rifles and bayonets, pistols, cannon and field pieces, swords and daggers, but be allowed to keep their knapsacks and personal knicknacks; (Second) that his forces be assembled in an area of my selection, to remain there under guard, and that they maintain military discipline until such time as he could organize them in retreat, which was to be carried forward in the best military fashion; (Third) that as Pres. and Gnl. he must at once hand over to me the war chest and other treasure carried by him, which I was at this time seizing in the name of the Republic of Texas, not as spoils of war, but as reparation for the ravages caused to civilians by the actions of his forces.

These terms are contained in the attached document signed by Santa Anna as Gnl. and Pres. I do not consider

22

them to be either punitive nor generous. I put much thought into framing them, it always being in my mind that our Republic and Mexico must as soon as possible come to terms by which we could share our common border in peace if not amity, and resume commerce between us.

Gnl. Santa Anna accepted the First and Second articles. He demurred at the Third, but without rancor. He argued that his army must sustain itself during a long retreat and mentioned that without funds to purchase rations his men would be tempted to loot during their long march back to the Rio Grande.

Recognizing the validity of Santa Anna's argument, I agreed that the escort accompanying his men on retreat would be provided with funds from the Mexican war chest to buy rations as needed.

Santa Anna then raised the question of the treatment I would accord him personally. I informed him that my personal sentiment notwithstanding, my intention was that he be given the respect due to his official station as Pres. and Gnl.

Santa Anna asked that he be provided a carriage suitable for himself and a female companion. He had himself, he said, been suffering a malarial fever which weakened him greatly and had prevented him from exercising command of his troops and had contributed to his defeat. I deemed his request reasonable and agreed. Santa Anna's female companion, as hitherto mentioned, had been allowed to remain with him after his surrender on the 21st prox. I had not seen the woman and did not wish to, but on consideration agreed that the Gnl. would be allowed to keep his personal carriage and horses.

I then informed Santa Anna that our conversation was ended, and demanded immediate surrender of the Mexican war chests and ordered him to accompany the platoon already detailed to seize and bring the chests to my tent. He agreed at once and left with the platoon commanded by Lt. Perry.

On return of the platoon carrying the four chests containing Santa Anna's funds, I discovered to my disappointment that the treasure was far less than the sum anticipated. From searches of the Mexican soldiery and interrogation of the paymasters, I had determined that Santa Anna's war chest had originally contained what they described as a huge quantity of twenty-peso gold coins designed to commemorate his anticipated conquest, hence these bore the date 1836. Each coin contained one Troy ounce of gold. and as they were struck by a private mint in the U.S. there is no question of the purity of the metal or its possible debasement.

Knowing how the wars with Mexico have drained our Republic's treasury, and depreciated the value of our money in the U.S. and elsewhere, it had been my hope that Santa Anna's war chest would provide the Republic with a desperately needed sum of hard money.

I was greatly taken aback when the chest were opened and found they contained only paltry numbers of coins. In the first chest there were 629 coins, in the second, 810, in the third, 542, and in the fourth only 381. In all, the number of the coins totalled 2362. The face value of the coins in Mexico would thus be 47,240 pesos, and at the last rate of exchange with which I am familiar, $23,620 in U.S. money, or $141,720 in the currently depreciated currency of the Republic of Texas.

While the sum is a substantial one, it is far less than the amount I had confidently expected to recover. I suspect there is some treachery involved in this discrepancy and have assigned Col. Goldsmith and Maj. Wyatt to conduct an investigation

Rubbing his chin thoughtfully, Longarm laid the last page of the report aside and picked up the next sheaf of documents. It contained fewer pages than the first, but he saw that it was another excerpt from a later report made by Sam Houston to the Texas Congress. This one was dated April 28. Longarm read:

I must regretfully state that since my Report of 26 prox., there has been no progress made in resolving the discrepancy between the rumors that Santa Anna's war funds were far greater than the sum contained in the four appropriated chests. Both Col. Goldsmith and Maj. Wyatt have pursued their investigation diligently, but with no success, nor have I been able to sift any believable facts from the rumors the Colonel and Major have reported to me. There are five rumors which recur frequently:

(First) That the chests were never as full as the rumors said they were.

(Second) That disbursements made to the soldiery at San Antonio de Bexar left the chests badly depleted.

(Third) That Santa Anna ordered large sums to be given as bribes or rewards to certain citizens of San Antonio following the storming of the Alamo.

(Fourth) That Santa Anna brought six chests from Mexico instead of the four delivered to me, and that the two missing chests were buried for him to recover later.

(Fifth) That the gold pieces were placed in the barrel of a cannon, its mouth sealed with molten lead, and the cannon sunk in the San Jacinto River; some reports name Buffalo Bayou as the place in which the cannon was sunk.

None of these rumors has what I deem the ring of truth, but I hereby offer my opinion as a guide to the Congress should it wish to pursue further investigations:

As to the first rumor, this seems most plausible than any, for gold multiplies rapidly in rumors and idle talk of soldiers.

As to the second, Mexico's soldiers are paid much less than even the pittance paid those of our own Republic. While Santa Anna's force was large, more than 4000 strong in its initial muster, you will recall from my battle Report of 22 prox. that he had lost some 800 men at the beginning of my engagement here. By no stretch of the imagination could a sum as large as was rumored to exist be depleted as greatly as was the sum I seized.

As to the third, I have no comment. This is a matter which the Congress must determine to investigate or ignore.

As to the fourth, the number of chests was almost certainly four. There were four paymasters, each tallying the payments due to 1000 men.

As to the fifth, there was no time for either of these moves to have been carried out. Santa Anna would not have ordered his war chest buried before the battle here, as he was confident of victory, and there was no opportunity during or after the end of fighting to have either buried the gold or concealed it in the ridiculous manner the rumor mentions, sealed in a cannon bore.

There is only one other matter of concern to be included. Santa Anna and his defeated army has begun its march home. The Gnl. was in a state of depleted strength at his departure. He was barely able to walk, and it was necessary for his female companion to help him into the carriage. We shall not be troubled by him again. As to the woman, I say nothing more.

I await the pleasure of the Congress in receiving orders to dismiss my brave soldiery so that they may return to peaceful pursuits.

There were only two more pages in the sheaf of papers Vail and instructed Longarm to read. He picked up the first. It was a letterpress copy of a single paragraph, and was on official Treasury Department stationery. The superscription identified it:

Treaty of Annexation, U.S.A. Republic of Texas
Article XXVII. Navigable waterways: All bays, estuaries, channels between mainland and islands, and all navigable rivers or navigable sections thereof, and all canals or channels now in existence and notwithstanding prior title or usage shall henceforth be the domain of the United States of America, and subject to its exclusive jurisdiction under existing and future statues, laws or ordinances.

Pinned to the sheet was another letterpress copy, this one on Justice Department stationery:

Re your query regarding the attached, it is our opinion that Article XXVII clearly gives Treasury full and undisputed claim to any "treasure trove" discovered in Texas' navigable waters.
Corps of Engineers confirms that both the San Jacinto River and Buffalo Bayou are in this category.

Longarm put these sheets on top of the other ones he'd read. There were still some papers in the blue folder and he picked it up. He was holding it still unopened when Vail returned.

"If you're through reading the papers I gave you, I'll put them back in place," the chief marshal said, taking the folder. "The rest of what's in here is confidential. Not that I've got any objection to you reading it, Long, but you know how damned picky those Washington lawyers can get."

"Sure." Longarm took out a cheroot and lighted it.

Vail settled into his chair and looked across the desk at his deputy. "Well?" he asked. "Does the case make sense to you, now that you've read what old Sam Houston wrote?"

"Oh, I got sense enough to figure out the part about the gold, Billy. I didn't get much connection between that and the stuff about the rivers, though."

"That's just A-B-C," Vail said. "If somebody has found the gold Santa Anna might have hidden—if it really was sealed up in a cannon bore and dumped in the river or the bayou— it goes into the U.S. Treasury. If it was buried on land, it belongs to Texas. The Treasury Department's just covering their asses."

"That's an awful lot of ifs." Longarm frowned.

"You know damned well there are ifs in any case!"

"Sure. But this one has got more than most. Now, let's see if I finally got it all straight. Maybe Santa Anna left a big pile of gold someplace down in Texas. Maybe somebody's just found it. Maybe the gold belongs to Texas, maybe it belongs to the federal Treasury. The Treasury Department sent some fellows to make sure where it was found. They got killed. This case I'm going on is to—" Longarm shook his head.

Vail interrupted. "You were going right down the line for a minute. What made you stop?"

"I guess I'm going to make you mad again, Billy, but I don't see any way around it," Longarm said soberly. "There's just one thing pops into my mind. It don't matter how much I juggle it around, it comes out the same way."

"Get to the point," Vail said. "I won't get mad."

"Maybe you don't look at it the way I do, but it's plain as day to me that if there was all them gold pieces and it turned out they really belong to the Treasury, then the most likely ones to've killed them Treasury men was some of your Ranger friends."

Vail's face began to grow red. Obviously struggling to control his temper, he asked, "What makes you say that?"

"If the gold belongs to the Treasury, then Texas stands to

lose it. And if Texas was out to keep it, they'd have to keep the Treasury men from reporting to Washington. And who'd they have besides the Rangers to stop 'em?"

"Just exactly how do you figure that?"

"Well, who the hell else *is* there?"

"Nobody knows! Why, they could have been killed by . . ." Vail stopped, his face now betraying his anger.

"Go on, Billy," Longarm said quietly. "Who else could have done it? It sure as sin wasn't Santa Anna. He's dead."

Vail did not answer for a long minute, while the flush faded from his face. He said quietly, "The Rangers didn't find those gold pieces, Long. Somebody else did. My guess is that the Treasury operatives were killed by whoever found it."

"I don't imagine them two dead Treasury men went around saying what their business was. But it'd be easy for the Rangers to find out, wouldn't it? For all you know now, they might've been looking for it before the Treasury men got to Texas."

Vail's voice revealed the strain he was under and the anger he was suppressing. "The Texas Rangers aren't hired killers, damn it! Sure, they'd shoot a dangerous fugitive, or an outlaw trying to escape. But they're not cold-blooded murderers!"

Longarm said, "I'm sure sorry I stepped on your sore toes, Billy, but you asked me, and I told you how it looks to me. Now, if you feel like you don't want to send me on this case— the way I feel, and all—why, that's up to you."

"It's not like you to shy away from a case." Vail frowned.

"I didn't say I was shying away or begging off," Longarm said quickly. "I just want you to know the way I look at it."

"All right." Vail nodded. "Now I know, and it doesn't change my mind a bit. It's your case, Long. You've got all the information I can give you on it. And I want you on the train tomorrow morning, on your way to San Antonio!"

Chapter 4

A South Texas twilight, the long dusky glow that lasted for an hour or more during the weeks between autumn and winter, was beginning to darken the cloudless sky when Longarm alighted from the train at the I&GN depot on the west side of San Antonio. He stopped on the station platform to get his bearings. Though he'd made enough visits there to remember the town's general layout, he could see at a glance that some changes had taken place since his last trip.

To the west, where green farm fields had spread earlier, new houses now stood beyond the tracks and lined freshly graded streets almost as far as Alazan Creek, a mile away. A thin line of new business buildings bordered the railway yards to the east, but between the depot and the distant twin towers of San Fernando Cathedral, which marked the beginning of the long-settled downtown section, he saw that no change had taken place in the district where most of San Antonio's Mexican population lived. Between the the tracks and the cathedral lay an expanse of small *jacales*, shacks and shanties huddled together along unpaved streets that were little more than alleys.

A growl from his stomach jogged Longarm's memory as well as his appetite and he recalled the square where each evening the chili queens presided over their small stalls. Longarm searched his memory, but could not think of the name of the square. With his bedroll on his shoulder, his saddlebags in one hand, and his Winchester in the other, he walked the few steps to the line of hackney cabs that stood beside the station.

"There's a place between here and town where I've had a few real tasty meals when I was here before," he told the hackman. "I was wondering if it's still there. It ain't a restaurant, just a big open place where you sit down—"

"Haymarket Plaza," the cabbie broke in. "Hop in, mister."

"If there's a decent hotel between here and there, maybe I could get you to stop and wait while I get a room and drop all this loose gear before I eat," Longarm said. "I ain't so sure I'll need to stay right down in the middle of town."

"There's the Occidental House," the hackman replied. "It's new and clean, and a lot of drummers stop there now. Costs you a lot less than the Menger or one of the hotels downtown, too."

"That sounds all right," Longarm said. "Just pull up there long enough for me to get signed in and drop my stuff, then we'll go on to that Haymarket place."

Freed of his load after registering at the Occidental House, but hungrier than ever, Longarm stepped out of the hackney a quarter of an hour later and surveyed the busy scene. Daylight still hung on, a narrow slice of deepening blue, but while the twilight was about to surrender to darkness, Haymarket Plaza was lighted by half a hundred lanterns hung on low poles spaced with no apparent pattern in an open area the size of a city block.

In the soft yellow glow that spilled from the lanterns faint, wispy smoke rose from the food stalls, carrying through the air the spicy aroma of red peppers, onions, garlic, and hot cooking fat. The evening was just beginning, but the aisles between the cooking stalls that dotted the plaza were filling fast. The stalls themselves were severely utilitarian. Most of them were simply three wide planks set on trestles to form a U-shaped counter, with the enclosure in the center occupied by the low charcoal stoves covered with sheet-iron grills on which two or three big pots usually stood.

Longarm looked at the nearest stalls. All of them had a few customers standing at the counters holding thick bowls from which they spooned up chili con carne, red beans, or a mixture of the two. They peeled the cornhusks from tamales and ate them out of hand, or craned their necks forward to avoid the rich red sauce that dripped from tacos each time they took a bite.

Toward the center of the plaza, Longarm saw that a few of the stalls had benches or chairs for their patrons. Deciding he'd eaten too many meals standing up, Longarm began working his way through the crowd, inspecting stalls where seats were provided.

As nearly as Longarm could tell, there was little difference between the food served at the different stalls. He stopped at the first one that had chairs along its counter and sat down. The overly buxom chili queen presiding at the stove greeted him with a smile that was followed immediately by a sales pitch in a mixture of English and Spanish.

"Ah, you know where to find bes' food," she said. "What you like, *señor?* Bowl chili, *un dimy*, chili *con frijoles*, a neeckle more. Maybeso you like tamales? Four for neeckle. You wan' tacos, they two for neeckle. I got enchiladas, they two for neeckle *con queso*, neeckle apiece *con carne*."

"All of it sounds good," Longarm told her. "Maybe I better try some of everything."

"Oh, you wan' *comida completa! Chili con frijoles, dos tamales, un taco, una enchilada*— all jus' a quarter. An' plenty tortillas, all you wan', they go with *la comida*."

"That sounds just about right," Longarm agreed. He dug a twenty-five-cent piece from his pocket and laid it on the counter. "Go ahead and dish it up."

While the chili queen turned to the stove and began filling a thick plate with food, Longarm surveyed his surroundings. The crowd on the plaza was growing steadily thicker. People were arriving on foot from all four of the streets leading to it. He saw no unescorted women, though there were many family groups and a large number of men by themselves or with a companion or two. Most of the women wore black rebozos, some as shawls, some as head covering and shawl combined.

Longarm's inspection of the crowd was broken by the chili queen when she stepped from the stove to the counter and put a heaping plate of food down in front of him. The plate was large, and the deep red serving of chili con carne that covered half of it looked to him to be as big as an ocean. A mountain of beans formed a dam down the center, dividing the chili from the corn-husk-encased tamales, the crisp tortilla filled with meat, and the second tortilla, which was rolled into a cylinder and covered with a sauce of even brighter red than the chili.

Picking up the quarter Longarm had placed on the counter, the chili queen put in its place a saucer piled with tortillas and said, *"Comerse, hombre. A buen gusto."*

Longarm attacked the food, spooning in mouthfuls of the spicy chili between bites of the taco. When that was gone, peeled the cornhusk from a tamale and ate it before tackling the enchilada. By the time he'd eaten most of the chili and beans and the cheese-filled tortilla roll and had started eating

31

the second tamale, he was feeling full. He ate more slowly, chewed his bites longer, and was considering leaving the remainder of the food when he felt a small, almost imperceptible tug on the skirt of his long black coat.

His first thought was that he'd been chosen as a target by a pickpocket, and Longarm dropped his right hand to his revolver butt as he swiveled his head to look behind him. He saw no one. The gentle tugging was repeated, and he looked down. The woman who stood behind his chair was old and small and so stooped that he had not seen her with his head at normal eye level. The skirt of the rusty black dress she wore dragged the ground, and her face, framed in the folds of a black rebozo, was seamed with wrinkles on top of wrinkles. Only her eyes did not show her age. They were coal-black and gleaming brightly in the network of deep lines that surrounded them.

"Please, *señor*." The old woman's voice was a reedy, rasping whisper. *"No tengo dinero, y tengo mucho hambre.* You don' eat tortillas, you geeve me them, no?"

Longarm's knowledge of Spanish was slight indeed, but he understood the two or three key words, and the rest of her plea was plain enough. He said, "Well, I sure ain't going to be able to handle any more grub. Take the tortillas and welcome, lady."

"Ah, gracias, señor!" she wheezed. *"Dios recompensarle!"*

By straightening up as best she could and stretching to her utmost, the old woman could reach across the counter to the tortillas. Her hand was closing on the saucer when the chili queen turned from serving a customer and saw what was happening. With speed surprising in one of her bulk, she darted across the stall in time to grasp the crone's wrist just as it closed on the tortillas.

"Ladrona!" she cried. *"Bruja! Dejarse!"*

"Now, hold on!" Longarm said. "The old woman asked me if I was going to eat them tortillas, and I said I wasn't. But if they was part of the supper, like you said, then I paid for 'em. If I don't want to eat 'em, I got a right to give 'em to her!"

"You don' ondestan, *señor!*" the chili queen snapped. "Thees Juana, she ees all time beg, all time steal."

"Maybe she's got to, just to stay alive." He turned to the old woman. "Juana—that's your name, I guess?" She nodded and he went on, "If you want the tortillas, go ahead and take 'em." Then he told the chili queen, "Giving her them tortillas won't cost you nothing. Don't grudge her a little bit of grub."

"*Juana es bruja, señor,*" the chili queen said. She still held the old woman's arm. "Weetch! She breeng you the bad luck!"

Longarm understood *bruja*. He remembered Clarita, who'd claimed to be a witch, and the eerie demonstration she'd given him to prove her prowess. He said, "I'll take my chances. Let her have the tortillas." He looked at the paper-thin corn cakes, already beginning to curl up as they cooled, and a thought struck him. "Look here, I'll do better than that. Dish her up the same supper I had. I'll pay for it."

"You make beeg mistake," the chili queen warned.

"Well, I don't reckon it'd be the first mistake I ever made," Longarm said. He took another quarter from his pocket and laid it on the counter. "Here's your money. Now, go on and fix her up a good meal."

Muttering in rapid-fire Spanish under her breath, the chili queen went to the stove and began filling a plate. Longarm said to Juana, "Come on and sit down. You won't have to eat them dry tortillas. I'm going to buy your supper.

"*Oigame!*" she said. "*Dios benedice, señor! Gracias, mil gracias!*" She saw that Longarm did not understand, and said, "I am to owe you more as thank you, *señor.*"

"You don't need to thank me. It ain't such a much, buying you a meal. And I guess you need one."

"You got name, *señor?*" she asked.

"Sure. It's Long. But folks mostly call me Longarm."

"*Brazolargo?*" Juana frowned. She shrugged. "*Cualquier.*"

With Longarm's help, Juana scrambled up into the chair next to his. When she was seated, her chin was only a few inches above the counter. The chili queen, her lips compressed in open disapproval, slapped a food-filled plate in front of her and moved quickly away. Juana tore a tortilla into quarters and used the triangles as spoons to scoop up mouthfuls of beans and chili. She kept her eyes on Longarm while she ate.

Longarm lighted a cheroot and puffed on it. He wanted to go about his own business, but he had an idea that if he left he'd be exposing Juana to any retaliation the chili queen might take. The stall's proprietress had ignored them after serving Juana's meal. She kept herself busy attending to the wants of other customers.

After she'd eaten half the chili and most of the frijoles,

Juana ate more slowly. She produced a cloth bag from somewhere in the folds of her dress and between bites slipped into it the enchilada, the taco, and the tamales. Her eyes, shining like wet obsidian marbles, darted in quick flicks from Longarm to the chili queen, as though she feared one of them might try to stop her. She held up the filled bag.

"You don' care I take thees?" she asked.

"No. I bought it for you. If you want to save something to eat later on, that's up to you."

"Why you do thees, *Señor Brazolargo?* All I am ask ees the tortillas you don' eat."

"Oh, I guess it's because I been hungry a few times. I know what an empty belly feels like."

"You are hear Luzita say I am *bruja?*"

Longarm nodded, and asked, "Are you?"

"Quien sabe?" Juana shrugged. "I see theengs."

"Things that're going to happen?" he asked.

"Si." She looked at him, her old face sober, and said, *"Tal vez* ees happen, *tal vez,* ees not. *Es en los manos de Dios."* Then she frowned and asked, "You got no scare from me, no?"

"Why'd I be afraid of you? I ain't hurting you none."

Juana nodded. "Ees so. But *la gente,* they scare from me."

"People get spooked when they don't understand things."

Juana studied Longarm's strong, rugged face and said, "You are brave man, *Señor Brazolargo.* But ees—" Suddenly she stopped, shook her head, and fell silent.

When she did not continue, Longarm said, "Go on. You were about to tell me something."

"You wan' I tell you what I see from you?"

"If you see something up ahead, I might as well know about it," he told her, smothering a smile.

"Bueno." Juana's eyes slitted and she began to sway in the chair. "You go to *un castillo,* no?"

"A castle?" Longarm frowned. He shook his head. "Not that I know of."

"Si, si!" Juana insisted. "You go! Ees so plain I see *castillo!* But ees not all. I see men weeth guns. I see—" She stopped suddenly, and her voice grew tense. *"Senor! Cuidado! Hay hombres malos acerca ahorita! Cuidao, cuidao!"*

"Well, now, I try to be careful all the time, Juana. It's the best way I've found to stay out of trouble."

"Cuidado ahorita!" she said, her voice urgent.

"Sure. Now, if you're through eating, I guess I'll mosey on and go about my business."

Longarm stood up and stepped away from the chair. As he moved, a gun barked from somewhere in the crowd, and a slug tore into the chair's wooden back, ripping through it and splintering the crosspiece against which Longarm's shoulders had rested only seconds earlier. The bullet traveled on, hitting one of the pots that stood on top of the stove. A stream of liquid spurted from the pot and spread across the stove's sheet-metal top, raising a cloud of steam. Around the stall shouts and screams rose, and the people in the vicinity began scurrying away.

Longarm had hit the ground before the slug struck the pot. He drew as he went down. Clutching the butt of his Colt, he lay on the packed earth of the plaza while his eyes searched for the source of the shot.

Another report cut the air, and a second slug whistled past him, traveled under the counter, and struck the stove, sending a shower of sparks and bits of burning charcoal flying. This time Longarm saw the flash of flame from the muzzle of a revolver, but the counter and stove of the adjoining stall hid the man who'd fired it.

Crawfishing along the hard soil, Longarm found cover behind the stove in the adjoining stall and raised his head cautiously, his revolver ready. A half-dozen stalls away, a distance of perhaps twenty yards, he saw the back of a man pushing his way through the milling crowd. It was the only back he saw. Everyone else was facing in his direction. That the man was running, or trying to run, was the only clue Longarm had, but it was all he needed. Leaping to his feet, he began shouldering through the excited, chattering spectators and started in pursuit of the would-be assassin.

Half a dozen times he caught fleeting glimpses through the milling crowd of the man he was trying to follow, but he never succeeded in getting a really clear look. The light was uneven, with pools of brightness where the lanterns of the stalls hung on their posts and big areas of obscurity between them. The crowd was still shifting around, but when the people in Longarm's path saw the Colt in his hand and the grim set of his jaw, they hurriedly stepped aside.

During the brief periods when Longarm had a reasonably good view of his quarry, he'd noticed some vague familiarity in the running man's movements. As he pushed ahead, he searched his memory for some hint, some half-forgotten association, that would identify his assailant. He'd gotten none by the time the man ahead reached the end of the plaza—and, what was worse, the gap between them had increased. He caught a glimpse of the man running into one of the streets that led to Haymarket Plaza, and sped after him.

In front of the running man, Longarm saw the dark street, with gaslights spaced far apart, long stretches of blackness between them. He broke into a run. To shoot the fleeing man would have been easy, but Longarm could still hear footsteps ahead, booted feet thudding on the baked dirt of the street. He strained his eyes, trying to catch sight of the unknown man when he would be silhouetted in the glow of the distant streetlight.

Absorbed in his pursuit, Longarm had overlooked what might lie behind him. The shot that roared from the darkness at his back and the ugly droning of hot lead whizzing past his ear took him by surprise. In instant reaction he dropped to the ground, whirling as he fell, and when a second shot followed the first he was ready to reply.

He aimed to the right of the spurting muzzle blast and his Colt barked twice. He rolled the instant he'd triggered the second shot and the slug that plowed into the ground where he'd been lying missed him by inches. There had been no muzzle blast visible from the direction he'd been aiming when that shot was fired. Longarm realized that the man he'd been chasing had doubled back in the darkness, setting a trap for him. If the second man had held his fire a few moments longer, the trap would have succeeded.

Old son, them fellows know their business, Longarm told himself as he crawled in the darkness away from the position he had just occupied. *Them shots have been too quick and too close for comfort. Now, that means they're either soldiers or lawmen or hired killers, and you got to use a little bit of skulduggery if you expect to save your bacon.*

Without changing his position or interrupting his train of thought, Longarm went through a routine made familiar by long use. Reaching into his coat pocket, he took out two cartridges. Working by feel, he ejected the cases of the spent rounds from the Colt's cylinder and slid in the fresh loads.

Now, he told himself, *let's see about trimming down the odds a little bit.*

Longarm slid his derringer from the vest pocket in which he carried it. Without taking time to release the snap that connected the derringer to his watch chain, he held the ugly little snub-nosed gun in his left hand and raised his arm, the watch on its chain dangling at his elbow. Twisting his wrist, he aimed in the general direction from which the last shot had come and fired one barrel of the derringer.

From across the street a shot barked in reply. Longarm was ready. He leveled the Colt in his right hand at the area to the right side of the red-streaking muzzle blast and fired twice. He rolled at once, but no shot came from the blackness facing him, nor did gunfire sound from his right, where the man who'd been tailing him had taken the potshots.

Patiently, Longarm waited. He knew that the type of men he'd deduced were after him were probably as familiar as he was himself with the tricks and ruses of professional gunmen. The silence, in its way, was louder than the shots. The night was now so still that the ticking of Longarm's watch was loud in his ears, but still he did not move.

A new noise broke the stillness. It was the clanging of a bell, and it grew quickly louder. Soon moving lights flashed into sight at the end of the street where it opened into Haymarket Plaza. They illuminated the fronts of the shacks and shanties facing the street, but the wagon stopped before the lights could reach the area where Longarm had dueled with the two invisible gunmen.

In a moment the silhouettes of half a dozen men appeared against the lights of the wagon. They wore domed helmets and the long coats that even in the dark identified them as policemen. All of them had revolvers in their hands, and several carried bullseye lanterns. Longarm holstered his Colt and replaced his derringer and watch in their pockets. He lay still and waited for them to reach him.

Chapter 5

As the policemen moved into the dark street, they split up. Leaving their wagon in the middle of the narrow thoroughfare, half of the men started forward along the side of the street on which Longarm lay, while the others went to the opposite side. Both groups advanced slowly, hugging the fronts of the houses as they edged ahead, flashing their lights into the narrow gaps between the closely clustered shacks. In the blackness, the light from their small bullseye lanterns illuminated the ground only a few feet ahead of them.

On the side of the street where Longarm lay, the squad had covered only a few paces when he heard one of them exclaim, "Hey! Wait a minute! That looks like somebody laying in the street in front of that house ahead."

A few moments later, another one said loudly, "All right, the rest of you can come on up now. It's a dead man, all right."

Longarm could follow the men's movements by the light of their lanterns as they gathered around the body of the man who had appeared from nowhere to fire at him. He got only a quick glimpse beofre the officers closed around the recumbent form. Then, no matter how he craned and twisted his neck, he could see nothing but the policemen clustered around the corpse.

Longarm was anxious to see the dead man's face, but he realized quite well that any movement he made could have serious and possibly fatal results. As yet, the San Antonio policemen had no idea what sort of fracas they'd gotten into, and until they'd figured out what had happened, they were understandably edgy. He'd seen men who had moved unthinkingly get shot by accident in comparable situations, so he remained motionless.

"Any of you fellows know him?" one of the policeman asked.

A chorus of nos met the question. Then another said, "He ain't going anyplace, that's for sure. We better catch up with Donovan's bunch; they're getting ahead of us."

Their lanterns flashing, throwing reflections from the panes of windows now and then, the policemen started forward again. On the opposite side of the street, the other group was now almost directly across from the spot where Longarm lay, but they were concentrating on the gaps between houses and the area directly in front of them.

They went past Longarm without having seen him, but he was discovered very quickly when the group that had stopped to look at the corpse approached. The beam of one of the bullseyes flashed across him, and the policemen holding the lantern raised his voice.

"Damned if there's not another body here! And he looks like a white man!" the policeman called.

"I ain't dead," Longarm said calmly, holding himself quite still, looking up at the pistol muzzles covering him. "Not by a long shot. And I'd take it kindly if you'd get that light outa my eyes."

One of the policemen stepped up and felt around Longarm's waist. He found the butt of the Colt and yanked it from its holster. "All right, mister," he said. "You can get on your feet now, and tell us what the hell's been going on here."

Before Longarm could move or speak, a shout went up from the men across the street, announcing that they had discovered the second body.

"We got a live one over here!" the policeman who'd found Longarm shouted to his companions. "But he still hasn't told us what all the shooting was about."

"I ain't had much of a chance yet," Longarm pointed out. "But you can tell your friends across the street that they won't find any more bodies laying around."

"How the hell do you know that?" one of the others asked.

"Because I shot both of 'em," Longarm said quietly. Then, realizing that he was at a disadvantage as long as he was lying on his back, in the silence that had followed his announcement he filled his voice with conviction and told them, "My name's Long. Deputy United States Marshal, out of the Denver office."

"If that's the truth, I guess you got a way to prove it?" the policeman who still stood over him asked.

"All the proof you need," Longarm replied. "Just don't get

39

nervous, now. I'm about to take my wallet out of my pocket."

"Go ahead," the officer told him, without moving the muzzle of the revolver that was pointing down at Longarm.

Moving his hands slowly and carefully, Longarm took out his wallet and flipped it open to show his badge. The policemen put their heads together as they inspected it.

"All right, Marshal," the one who'd taken charge said. "I suppose we can take your badge as proving you're who you say you are. You can get up now."

Rising to his feet, Longarm returned his wallet to his pocket and extended his hand for his Colt.

"I'll ask you to do without your gun till Sergeant Donovan gets over here," the policeman told him. "I don't think I need to tell you why."

"No. I'd be doing the same things you have, was I in your place," Longarm replied. "And, to save you asking, I didn't shoot these two fellows until after they tried to gun me down back there on Haymarket Plaza. I didn't know they was after me, or even that there was two of them." He stopped, then went on, "If it's all the same to you, I'll save my breath. Then when your sergeant gets here, I'll just have to tell about it once."

Men from the second group of officers had begun trickling across the street by now. One of them came up just in time to hear what Longarm had said.

"I'm Donovan," he announced. "Go on, tell us about it."

To observe the formalities, Longarm showed Donovan his badge and then, as tersely as possible, described the surprise attack on him at the chili queen's stall, his chase of the man he'd seen running from the plaza, and the shootout on the dark street that had followed.

He concluded by saying, "Now, I'll save you asking if I know who them dead men are. All I saw of the one in the plaza was his back, but there was something about the way he was moving that give me the idea I'd seen him before. I never did see anything of the other one but the muzzle, blast from his gun."

"And you killed both of 'em just shooting at their gun flashes?" Donovan asked skeptically. "By God, now, that's some kind of shooting! I don't believe there's a man . . ." The police sergeant paused and frowned. "Hold on! The name on your badge is Long, and I know a U.S. marshal's badge when I see one. And you're out of Denver. Why, hell, you must be the fellow they call Longarm!"

"Some folks call me that," Longarm admitted.

"From the yarns I've heard about you, I figured you was just somebody people had made up," Donovan said. "Like—well, like old Mother Goose, or a storybook like we had when we were kids."

"Sorry to disappoint you, Donovan," Longarm told him. "I'm alive and real enough. You can see that for yourself. But if you're not satisfied, you can send a wire to my chief, Billy Vail, and he'll wire back that he sent me here on a case."

"Oh, I had in mind asking the captain to let me do that, as soon as we get back to the station," Donovan replied without cracking a smile. "You'd better tell me what kind of case you're on, though, just to make sure. I suppose this shooting has some connection with it?"

"I can't guarantee it does," Longarm replied thoughtfully. "I was sent down here to look into the murder of two U.S. Treasury agents. They'd come from Washington to check up on a cache of Mexican gold old Santa Anna's supposed to have left in Texas after Sam Houston whipped him at San Jacinto. I can't say whether these two gunhands I tangled with are connected with my case or not, until I get a look at 'em."

Donovan nodded. "If they are, it'll help. Suppose you take a look at them and see if you know who they are."

Longarm and Donovan walked side by side to the nearest body, followed by the rest of the police squad. The corpse lay facedown, and Longarm turned the limp form over. He gazed at the face of the dead man, a wide face with thick lips above a heavy jaw and a wide, flat nose framed between high cheekbones. Memory brought the dead man's name back quickly.

"I know him, all right," Longarm told the police sergeant. "His name's Esquivel. He was one of Diaz's *rurales*. Me and him tangled some time back, when I was on a case along the border."

"A *rurale*?" Donovan said, disbelief in his voice. "They're not supposed to come on this side of the border, any more than our Rangers are supposed to cross over into Mexico."

"Unless somebody's pushed San Antonio quite a ways west or moved the Rio Grande east, this fellow didn't pay much

41

attention to them rules," Longarm said dryly.

"What kind of run-in did you have with this Esquivel across the border?" the sergeant asked.

"A pretty good one. The *rurale* outfit he belonged to was in cahoots with a bunch of crooks on this side of the river, and before all the smoke settled it wound up in a right fair fracas. A bunch of the *rurales* got killed, so I reckon when Esquivel spotted me on Haymarket Plaza he figured he'd get even."

"Well, let's go look at the other one," Donovan said. "I'd bet before you look that he'll turn out to be a *rurale,* too."

Though Longarm was reasonably sure he recognized the second man, he could not put a name to him. As he told Donovan, when he'd been on the case in Mexico where he'd first encountered the *rurales,* he'd been too busy fighting them to memorize their names and faces for future reference.

Donovan nodded. "I don't see that there's any reason for us to hold you, Long," he said thoughtfully. "Even if your badge didn't cover you, this Esquivel and whoever the other fellow is started the shooting. All you did was defend yourself. But if you'll drop in at headquarters tomorrow and have a talk with Chief Black, I'd take it as a personal favor."

"Sure," Longarm agreed. "If you need me before I show up, I'm staying at the Occidental House."

Before returning to the hotel, Longarm revisited Haymarket Plaza. The early evening supper rush was over by now. There were only a few late diners finishing their meals, and half the stalls had already been knocked down and taken home by their owners. The stall where Longarm had eaten was gone, and when Longarm asked at the closest neighboring stall about the chili queen, all he got was a blank look and a series of head shakes.

He walked around the plaza for a few minutes, but Juana had vanished, too. His questions about the ancient *bruja* met the same kind of blank stares and head shakes.

Two days of travel, the night between them spent trying to snatch forty winks in a rattling day coach, had strained even Longarm's iron constitution. When his inquiries at Haymarket Plaza continued to meet a wall of passive resistance, he decided he'd done his duty.

There were no hackney cabs in sight, so he started walking back to the Occidental House. Halfway to the hotel, the bat-wings of a saloon caught his eye. He pushed through and bought a bottle of Tom Moore. In his room, Longarm puffed on a cheroot and sipped from the bottle of Maryland rye while he cleaned his Colt and derringer and reloaded the two weapons.

A lazy soak in a tub of hot water in the bathroom down the hall put him in the mood for bed. After a nightcap and a final cigar, he turned off the gas in the chandelier and stretched out luxuriously. He was asleep in two minutes and slept through the rest of the night like a baby.

In the cold morning light, Longarm fingered the stubble on his cheeks while he looked at his dirt-stained coat. He told himself, *Old son, all the wallowing around you done on that street last night sure didn't help much. What you better do right after breakfast is get fixed up to look halfway decent. Likely the clerk downstairs knows where there's a place to eat and a barbershop close by.*

Stopping at the desk to inquire, Longarm was greeted by the clerk with a broad smile. The man said, "Good morning, Marshal Long. If you don't mind waiting just a moment, the manager would like to have a word with you."

Before Longarm could reply, the chubby, smiling manager came bustling out of his office. He seized Longarm's hand and began pumping it. "I'm Fred Johnson, Marshal Long, and I can't tell you how glad I am to meet you. Please accept my apologies. I'm sorry that we—"

"Wait a minute, now," Longarm interrupted with a frown. "I can't figure what you feel like you got to apologize for. I didn't make no complaint about my room."

Ignoring Longarm's interruption, Johnson went on, "I'm sorry we didn't recognize you when you signed in last evening, but we had no idea that a United States marshal as famous as you are would choose our modest accommodations instead of going to one of the big hotels downtown. Now, I've arranged to move you to a larger, more comfortable room with a private bath, and—"

Longarm raised his voice. "Hold on here!" The surprised hotel manager stopped with his mouth open. Longarm said with a frown, "How'd you know who I am? I don't recall putting down anything but my name when I checked in."

"Why, of course you didn't!" Johnson beamed. "I'm sure you assumed that we knew who you are, and I regret that we didn't recognize your name at once. Now, there'll be no charge for your accommodations, of course. We want to—"

"Will you listen to me a minute?" Longarm broke in. When the manager fell silent, he went on, "I don't know where you got the idea that I'm some kind of high-muckety-muck, but wherever you got it, you're wrong. I just do my work."

"And very important work it is, too," Johnson said. "Keeping down the lawless element, and things of that kind. But, as I was saying—"

"Will you listen to what I'm trying to ask you?" Longarm said, not trying to hide his irritation. Johnson's flow of words stopped once more, and Longarm went on, "What I want to know is where you got the notion that I'm some kind of nabob."

"Why, it's all in this morning's *Express*. Your name and what you did last night take up almost the whole front page," the hotel man replied.

Longarm's jaw dropped. "The hell you say!"

"Oh, it's all there," Johnson assured him. "I have a copy in my office, if you'd like to look at it."

A few moments later, Longarm was staring with mounting anger at the morning edition of the *San Antonio Express* spread out on Johnson's desk.

WEST SIDE SHOOTOUT! proclaimed the banner headline that ran across the top of the front page, and below it, in italics almost as large, *Famous U.S. Marshal Kills Mexican Gunmen in Midnight Gunfight*.

As he read the story below the headlines, Longarm's anger reached the boiling point. He saw any hope that he might have had of conducting a quietly anonymous investigation vanishing in a sea of printer's ink. While the story had only the sketchiest of details, it gave away his case very thoroughly. Everything of importance was there: the midnight gunfight, the suspected connection of the two dead men with Diaz's *rurales*, Santa Anna's gold cache, the murdered Treasury agents.

Nor was that all. From somewhere the *Express* reporter had dug up a number of details of Longarm's own history. The newsman had pulled out all stops in painting Longarm as a combination of King Fisher, Ben Thompson, Captain McNelly, Heck Thomas, and a half dozen other lawmen, with a few overtones of Bat Masterson and Wild Bill Hickock thrown in.

"Wait till I get my hands on that damned Donovan!" Longarm gritted between clinched teeth, slapping his palm on the hotel manager's desk where he'd spread out the newspaper to read it. "He'd oughta had better sense than to spill all this to some little pip-squeak reporter who don't know his ass from a hot rock when it comes to what oughta go into a newspaper and what oughta be kept out of it!"

"I'm sorry our newspaper's upset you, Marshal Long," Johnson said when Longarm's explosion subsided. "But I'm sure if you go to see the editor and tell him what the trouble is, he'll do his best to make it right."

"Did you ever know anybody who could put an egg she's laid back into a hen?" Longarm asked. He crumpled the newspaper into the semblance of a fold and tucked it under his arm. "I'll be back after a while. If this damn yarn's scared any of the crooks I'm after and they come running to find me to give up, just tell 'em to sit down and wait."

Longarm's temper had cooled a bit by the time he reached police headquarters and was shown in to Chief Black's office. Black took the initiative, and in doing so dissolved most of what remained of Longarm's anger with his first few words.

"If you're looking for Donovan, you're looking for the wrong man, Long," he said quietly, after a glance at Longarm's grim face. "The only thing you could blame him for was not going to your hotel last night and telling you that there was a reporter for the *Express* waiting here when the flying squad got back from the West Side. All the reporter had to do was look at the blotter and listen to the men who made that run when they were talking among themselves."

"You mean to sit there and tell me you let reporters have free run of your headquarters, Chief?" Longarm asked.

"I've never been able to figure a way to keep them out," Black replied. "The police commissioner's an elected official in San Antonio, Long."

Longarm grunted. "It figures, I guess. That makes him a politician, and all he's got on his mind's getting reelected."

"Did you ever see a politician who didn't butter up to the press?" Black asked. Longarm smiled grimly and shook his head. The chief went on, "When I complain to the commissioner about reporters being underfoot and printing information that ought to be kept confidential, he just reminds me that police headquarters is a public building."

"I guess I was a little bit out of line, coming storming in here," Longarm admitted. "Now the story's out, there's not any way to call it back."

"None that I can see," Black agreed. "Now, I'm sorry as hell for what happened, and I'll do anything I can to help you in whatever your case is. I don't know much about it, but if you need a hand from me or my boys, all you've got to do is tell me."

"I'll take you up on that right now," Longarm said. "Them two Treasury agents that got killed—I guess your force handled the case. I'd like to know whatever you've turned up on it."

"That's the one thing I can't do for you, Long," the chief replied. "My men were pulled off that case before they ever got started looking into it. Pulled off by the Texas Rangers."

"There's bound to've been some talk—" Longarm began.

Black shook his head. "The Rangers don't talk to us about their cases, Long. When they come in, we're shut out."

"I've run into their shutouts before." Longarm nodded.

"If I do hear anything . . ." Black began.

"Sure. I'll be around town a while, long enough to follow up on what few leads I got," Longarm told him. He stood up and extended his hand. "And if I'm going to catch up with what's already happened, I better not waste any time. If you hear anything, you know where I'm staying."

In the hackney going back to the Occidental House, Longarm took stock. Aside from the scanty information given him by Billy Vail, his only fresh lead was the presence of Esquivel and his companion. There was no doubt in Longarm's mind that the two had been sent to San Antonio when rumors of the discovery of Santa Anna's gold reached Mexico. As soon as word of their death got back, gold-hungry Diaz would certainly send other *rurales* to replace them.

Well, even if it gags you some, old son, it looks like you're going to have to go beg the Rangers to let you in on what they've dug up, Longarm told himself. *And if they don't feel like passing anything on to you, you'll just have to do some digging of your own.*

Still frustrated and out of sorts when he got out of the cab at the hotel, Longarm started across the lobby and was halfway to the stairs when the desk clerk hailed him.

"Marshal Long! There's a—a man in that chair over in the corner who's been waiting to talk to you," the clerk said.

Longarm looked in the direction of the clerk's nod. The man who was waiting was anything but an appealing sight. He wore a battered, shapeless slouch hat of tattered felt, remarkably disreputable duck jeans, and an equally disreputable and mended Prince Albert coat cut in the style of a generation far earlier than Longarm's. His tobacco-stained white beard had not been combed or trimmed for at least a year. It sprouted wildly in all directions and reached halfway down his chest.

When he saw Longarm crossing the lobby toward him, the man stood up. He was as tall as Longarm, and considerably bulkier.

"You'd be that fellow Long the paper was full of this morning," he said. "If you're here looking for Santa Anna's gold, I reckon I'm the man you need to talk to."

Chapter 6

Longarm studied the oversized, bewhiskered man who faced him and asked, "What makes you so sure about that?"

Pulling his hamlike hand from his coat pocket, the bearded man opened it and showed Longarm a gold coin lying in his palm. He tilted his hand to let the coin slide up to his fingers and framed it between his thumb and forefinger. Then he held it up to Longarm's eyes.

Countless nights at the poker table enabled Longarm to keep his face expressionless while he looked at the golden disc. It bore the same emblem he'd seen on the national Mexican shield, an eagle with a serpent clutched in its talons, and the legend 20 PESOS. The old man flipped it over. Longarm saw the bust of a man wearing the high-crowned cap that until recently had been the official headgear of Mexican army officers and the date 1836.

"This is what you're lookin for, ain't it?" the man asked.

Longarm had no intention of giving away the fact that until now he'd never seen even one of the coins that composed Santa Anna's gold hoard. He countered the question with a suggestion. "Maybe you'd better tell me where you got that," he said to the man.

Guffawing gustily, the bearded stranger shook his head. "I might tell you if we can strike a deal, but not until then."

"What makes you think I'd want to strike a deal with you?"

"Because I know some things you don't. Things you ain't likely to find out unless I tell 'em to you."

"That's real interesting," Longarm told him. "But finding things out is part of my job, and I'm supposed to be a pretty fair hand at it."

"Look here, Long. I put myself out to come here and talk

to you," the man said. "If you don't feel like listening, that's your bad luck."

"Oh, I didn't say I wasn't ready to listen," Longarm told him. "But before I go on any further, who'd I be listening to?"

"Me, first of all. After that, it'd be pretty much up to you what to do."

"I listen to a man better when I know his name."

"Brown."

Still studying the bearded giant's face, Longarm observed quietly, "Brown's a name like Smith and Jones. A lot of people answer to it, and it's hard to tell one from the next." He met the stranger's eyes and added, "Not that I'd have any trouble picking you out of a crowd."

"First name's Jim. But I answer best to what most everybody calls me. Two-toe."

"Sounds like there's a story behind that," Longarm smiled.

"Oh, sure. I lost all but the first two toes on my left foot when I got caught in a blizzard where I was gold mining up in Dakota Territory, and they got frostbit."

"You've been around a spell, I take it?"

"You don't have to look twice to see that, Long. Sure, I done a lot of things in my day. Back when the wagon trains was rolling, I guided a little bit. Fit Injuns, hunted buffalo, scouted for the Army. Been about most everyplace a man might wanta go. Come down here where it's warm when I got tired of having my butt froze off, and been here ever since."

"All right, Two-Toe." Longarm nodded. "Let's talk. But this ain't the best place for it. We'll go up to my room."

As Longarm led the way to the stairs, the desk clerk called, "Marshal Long, Mr. Johnson's had your luggage moved to Room 214. Here's the key."

Taking the key, Longarm led the way upstairs. Two-Toe Brown followed him with a peculiar shuffling gait. The new room was bigger than the one Longarm had occupied originally, and through an open door on one side he saw the rim of a bathtub. Two-Toe Brown was inspecting his surroundings with a curiosity that was equal to Longarm's.

"Damned if you federal marshals don't do right well by yourselves," Brown grunted. "This sure beats the room I live in."

"It beats the one I live in up in Denver, too," Longarm said.

"But that's neither here nor there. Sit down, Two-Toe, and tell me how you came by that twenty-peso gold piece."

Pulling down his lower eyelid, the old man asked, "You see any green there, Long?" When Longarm did not answer, but turned away and sat down in the nearest chair, he went on, "I don't do any talking till we make a deal."

"What kind of deal?"

"How big a share I get outa what gold we find."

"You're sorta quick to talk about 'we,' Two-Toe," Longarm said dryly. "I don't remember saying anything about us being partners."

"I don't reckon you did, at that," Brown admitted.

Longarm went on, "Maybe you don't understand all you need to about this gold. It don't belong to me."

"Anyplace I've ever been, gold belongs to whoever finds it."

"I don't hear you calling it your gold, Two-Toe, so I take it that you ain't found it yet. Have you?"

Longarm watched the old man closely. When Brown's jaws clenched and he gulped and delayed in replying, it was a pretty good signal to Longarm that his blind shot had hit home. To hide his impatience, Longarm took out a cheroot and lighted it. Brown was still staring at him when he released the first puff of blue smoke from the long, slim cigar. Finally the old fellow spoke.

"Lemme put it to you this way, Long," he said. "Mebbe I don't know right to a tee where the gold is, but I know the man that does."

"You'll guarantee he does?" Longarm asked.

Two-Toe Brown hesitated a bit longer this time, then said, "Hell, no, Long! What kind of damn fool do you take me for?"

"Maybe the same kind you take me for," Longarm suggested.

"Now wait a minute!"

"*You* wait a minute," Longarm said sternly. He could see plainly the point to which Brown was trying to steer their conversation. "Let's get something straight. I just work for old Uncle Sam, I don't talk for him. That gold belongs to the U.S. government, and even if I wanted to—which I don't—I can't give away a penny of it."

"I ain't talking about *giving!*" Brown retorted. "Nobody I can remember ever give me a damn thing. And I ain't begging, neither. What I'm saying is, if I lead you to that gold, I intend to get paid."

"You mean a reward?"

"I don't give a shit what you call it, just so I get what's due me for leading you to the gold."

"What about this other fellow, the one you said knows where the gold is?" Longarm asked. "He'll expect a reward, too, I imagine."

"I'd imagine so." The old man nodded.

"Suppose there was just one reward paid out," Longarm said thoughtfully. "Would you split it with this other man?"

"If it's big enough," Brown answered promptly.

Longarm nodded, then explained, "I work for the Justice Department. The Treasury's the part of the government that's after Santa Anna's gold. If I was to turn it up, all I could do was turn it over to them."

"Looks like I misread that newspaper piece, then. It made you out to be jick, jack, and joker in the game."

Longarm could see what might be his best clue to the gold slipping away. "The Treasury pays rewards to folks that recover government property. I know that," he said quickly.

"How high you figure they'd go?"

"That'd depend on how much you and your friend can turn up. Nobody's going to be damned fool enough to say how much until the gold's counted. Suppose you was promised a thousand-dollar reward, but you could only come up with maybe a hundred dollars' worth of them gold pieces. How much chance do you think you'd have to collect that thousand?"

Two-Toe nodded slowly. "Not much, I'd imagine."

"Not any," Longarm amended.

They sat silently, eyes locked, each trying to outwait the other. Longarm could almost smell Two-Toe Brown's eagerness to feel the weight of the coins he'd receive as a reward for having been instrumental in recovering the gold. He waited patiently, and his patience was repaid when Brown broke first.

"What about a percentage?" he asked.

In the few reward arrangements to which he'd been a witness, Longarm had observed that the Treasury Department lawyers who handled such matters were more inclined to agree to a percentage than to a flat sum paid to an informant.

"I'd say that's your best bet," Longarm agreed. Anticipating the next question, he added, "Five percent—maybe seven."

"I had ten in mind."

"You might get that much, but I wouldn't bet on it."

Having yielded the first time, Two-Toe found it easier to do so the second. He waited only half as long this time before nodding. "All right. Seven or five—we got a deal."

Longarm would not lie, even though he knew the truth might send Two-Toe Brown off in a storm of anger. "It's not a hard and fast deal yet, Two-Toe," he said. "I'll do my best for you when the chips go down, but remember what I already told you—I can't give you any kind of guarantee."

"Suppose I was to say a flat five percent?"

"I'd still have to tell you the same thing."

For a long minute, Two-Toe's rheumed, age-filmed eyes drilled into Longarm's gunmetal-blue ones. At last the old man broke off his stare.

"Even when I don't like hearing what a man tells me, I'd a heap sight rather have him tell me the truth than lie," he said. "All right, Long. Whatever the percent turns out to be, we got ourselves a deal."

"Maybe we better have a drink on it," Longarm suggested.

"Hell, that's the best offer I had since old Running Buffalo threw in an extra squaw for a half-chewed plug of terbaccy," Two-Toe replied. "Go on and pour."

As they sipped their Tom Moore, Longarm asked Two-Toe, "You mind telling me how you got mixed up in this business about Santa Anna's gold?"

"I don't see why I shouldn't. I got into Dakota Territory prospecting a good while before the rush begun up there, and hit good pay dirt. I come out with a pretty good-sized poke, when you count the nuggets and dust I'd been squirreling away and the cash I got when I sold my claim." Two-Toe paused to sip.

"And I'll bet you decided to retire," Longarm prompted him.

"You hit it right. Figuring how old I was, I had enough to keep me the rest of my life, so I just decided to find a place where it stays warm, and settle down."

"Which is why you picked out San Antonio?"

"Pretty much. I was here before, in my rambling days, and I remembered how it warn't too wet and not too dry and not too hot and not too cold. Well, to cut it short, I run low on cash money a little while back, and had to start selling some gold."

Brown stopped and coughed. Longarm took the hint. He got up and refilled their glasses, saying sympathetically, "Talking's a dry business, Two-Toe, but I need to hear everything you can tell me before I make any sort of move."

"Sure." The old man nodded, swallowed half his drink, and went on, "Now, that was real fine gold we dug up there, Long—pure as God made rain in springtime. Well, when I finally made up my mind to sorta settle down here in San Antone, I had to have me a grubstake."

"So you started selling the gold you'd saved?"

"Sure. I sold off a pinch here and another one there, and pretty soon one place tried to cheat me, and then another one begun to cut corners. But there was one fellow always give me honest weight and didn't try to shave what I had coming. So I stopped going anyplace but his."

"He'd be the one that you got the Mexican gold piece from, then?" Longarm asked. When Brown nodded, he went on, "How'd he happen to pay you off in Mexican money?"

Somewhat sheepishly, Two-Toe replied, "I guess you'd say he dickered me into it. You know anything about gold, Long?"

"A little," Longarm answered noncommittally.

"Well, an ounce of fine gold's worth twenty dollars anyplace in the country. Has been for as long as I remember. Except fine gold's too soft to make into money, so at the mint they add a little copper and silver to it. That makes it harder."

Longarm nodded. "I know about that, Two-Toe. I been to the U.S. Mint in Denver a few times. But they add that to the full weight of the gold."

"Sure." Brown nodded. "Only it makes the coins harder to melt, and what you got when they're melted don't assay pure."

"What difference does that make?"

"About two dollars an ounce, when you're selling melted gold coins," the old prospector replied. "But Mexican coins is pure gold, and they assay full weight."

"I still don't see what difference that makes." Longarm frowned.

"It makes a lot when you're selling. You see, Long, on this sid of the border, folks don't trust Mexican money."

Longarm was beginning to see the picture now. "So your

friend had trouble getting rid of them Mexican twenty-peso pieces, and made you a deal," he said. "You taken 'em and melted 'em down and sold the gold and kept the difference. Am I on the right track?"

"Right down the middle."

"Why didn't your friend melt 'em himself? Why'd he need to pay you money he could've kept?"

Brown snorted, the disgusted reaction of the professional to the inept or amateur. "Hell, he didn't know a miner's crucible from a pickax. Besides, folks around San Antone don't trust Mexicans any more'n they trust Mexican money."

"Meaning your friend couldn't sell even melted-down gold himself, I take it?"

"He'd found that out before he made a deal with me," Two-Toe replied. "The banks and jewelry stores he tried wouldn't pay him full weight. But they knowed me. I'd sold gold to most of 'em. So him and me, we made our dicker."

"How many of them twenty-peso pieces have you melted down for this friend of yours?" Longarm asked.

"Hell, I ain't kept any tally, Long. I'd say something over a hundred, give or take a half dozen."

"I don't suppose he told you where he was getting them?"

"Nary a word. And it wasn't because I didn't ask him."

"Did it ever strike you that there was something crooked about what you and him was doing?"

Two-Toe took his time answering. He sipped from his glass, looked thoughtfully at Longarm, then said, "All I figured was that he didn't want to pass them coins, Long. And as for what I done—well, I don't know of any law that says a man can't melt down some old gold pieces if he wants to."

Longarm rubbed his chin. "I guess that's right, when you come down to it. No, I'd say you're clear, as far as the law's concerned, Two-Toe."

"I'll drink to that, if you'll pour again," Brown said.

Longarm refilled their glasses. After he'd returned to his chair, he lighted a cheroot and asked, "What kind of business is this friend of yours in, Two-Toe?"

"He calls hisself a *cambiador,* which means a money changer, but what he's really got is a pawnshop."

"You feel like telling me his name?"

"You'll meet him soon enough. Plenty of time for that."

Longarm decided there was nothing more he could learn

from Two-Toe Brown at this stage. He tossed off the rest of his Tom Moore and stood up. "One thing I've learned, Two-Toe," he said. "There never is enough time to let any go to waste. Drink up, and let's go see your friend right now."

By the time Longarm and Two-Toe Brown left the Occidental House, the morning was well along toward noon. The old prospector waved aside Longarm's suggestion that they hail a hack and led him in the direction of Haymarket Plaza. They reached the area of huts and shanties, and Longarm followed the bearded giant into the twisting maze of narrow, unmarked streets that wove through the shacks like a lopsided spider's web.

There was no rhyme nor reason to the layout of the area. Its higgledy-piggledy streets were lined with dwellings, closely spaced, with other small houses behind them visible in glimpses through the narrow walkways between the shacks. A few large, imposing houses rose behind high adobe walls like islands, with shanties that were barely head-high and seemed about to collapse from the weight of their roofs snuggled up to the walls. There were a few stores, all small, bearing hand-lettered signs: ROPA, ABARROTES, FARMACIA, EMPENADOR, and some saloons with fanciful names: CANTINA ALEGRE, EL LORO PURPURA, but wherever Longarm looked, the district reeked of poverty.

So did the few people who were abroad. Most of them were either very young or very old, and Longarm guessed that all the able-bodied residents, men and women alike, were at work, the men as laborers, the women as maids or cooks in the prosperous homes that surrounded the *barrio* the way a sea surrounds an island.

Longarm kept his bearings as best he could by watching the tall towers of San Fernando Cathedral, visible most of the time in the clear, sun-bright air above the low roofs of the dwellings. He was pretty sure that he could find his way out of the maze when Two-Toe Brown stopped in front of a small brick building, neater than most of its neighbors, with sturdy bars set in front of opaque glass panes in its two small narrow windows. On the door was a sign: CAMBIADOR Y EMPENADOR.

"This is it," Two-Toe Brown said.

He opened the door and led the way inside. Following him, Longarm took in his surroundings with a quick, experienced glance that missed nothing. There was very little to see. Two straight chairs stood against the wall on one side of the room.

A counter spanned the space from front to back on the opposite side. On the counter was a thick ledger and a gold scale.

Behind the counter a man was sitting. His plump, unlined face did not match his hair, which was snow-white. He looked up and peered at Longarm and Two-Toe through gold-rimmed spectacles.

"This here's Felipe Aguierre, Long," Brown said. Turning to the man behind the counter, he went on, "Long's the man I was telling you about, Felipe. He's the fellow that's going to get the government to buy all of Santa Anna's gold."

Chapter 7

After Two-Toe Brown had completed the introduction, neither Longarm nor Aguierre made any acknowledgement of the other. They examined one another silently, in quick evaluating glances, until their mutual silence began to become oppressive.

"*Señor* Long," Aguierre said at last.

"Mr. Aguierre," Longarm replied, determined to be as reticent as the money changer.

Turning to Brown, Aguierre asked, "You are sure you have made no mistake, my friend?"

"Damn it, Felipe, you're frettin' like an old woman!" Brown replied. "After me and Marshal Long chinned for a while, I seen he's the kinda man that'll play square with us."

"And did you tell him why we have discussed the matter of surrendering Santa Anna's gold to him?" Aguierre asked.

"I didn't come flat out with it," the whiskered giant replied. "I figured we'd better all be together afore we started to talk about chapter and book."

Longarm broke in on the dialogue between Brown and Aguierre. "That's something I been wondering about ever since your partner come calling on me, Mr. Aguierre," he said. "You two being ready to settle for a slice when you could have the whole pie didn't make much sense to me. I figured that was your business, and I wasn't about to upset no apple carts by asking too many questions."

Aguierre looked at Longarm again, studying his rugged face. Then he said, "Marshal Long, just a short distance from here, you were attacked last night by two *rurales*. You are fortunate that your skill with a gun was greater than theirs, or we would not be talking here now."

Longarm shook his head. "I don't see what that's got to do

57

with anything. Them *rurales* were trying to pay off an old grudge they had against me."

"And did it not occur to you that their seeing you on the plaza was a coincidence, a matter of chance which had nothing to do with their real mission?" the Mexican asked.

"Sure it did. Them fellows didn't have no way to know I was going to be here in San Antonio."

"They have been here for a week." Aguierre paused and with a bitter grimace added, "My friends and I were the real targets of their pistols. Your encounter with them was an accident."

"Well, I didn't see how they couldn've come looking for me, seeing as I didn't know my chief was sending me here until a day or so before I left Denver," Longarm said. "But why'd they be after you and Two-Toe, Mr. Aguierre?"

Aguierre sighed. "It is hard to explain these things to someone who does not know the history of our country, Marshal Long. Santa Anna's gold means little to me, but it means a great deal to a cause for which I am fighting."

"I guess you better try to explain," Longarm said. "Because you're right, Mr. Aguierre. I sure don't understand."

"Very well." Aguierre thought for a moment before he went on. "You must realize first that the wars Mexico fought against Texas and against your country were small ones."

When Aguierre paused, obviously trying to find the best way of explaining, Longarm said, "They didn't seem like such little wars at the time."

"Ah, but they were, compared to the war between races which has been going on in Mexico for three hundred years," Aguierre replied. "You see, Marshal Long, my family is called *guachapine*. We are descended from the Spaniards who defeated the *Indios*, and from the nobility of France, who came to Mexico with Maximilian. It was not until Hidalgo defeated and ousted the French invaders that the *Indios* took control of my country."

Aguierre paused again, and Longarm said, "That was before Santa Anna fought Texas, if I recall rightly. What's it got to do with his gold?"

"Be patient," Aguierre said. "Santa Anna was one of us—a *guachapine*— but after Texas defeated him he sold his sword to Juarez and the *Indios*, then betrayed them. He came back to us, but turned turn traitor again and went back to the *Indios*

58

when Porfirio Diaz siezed power. But honor was not known to Santa Anna. When he died, he was ready to turn against Diaz, trying to overcome the distrust of us *guachapines* and rejoin us. But even though Santa Anna offered us the gold he had stolen after the Texans beat him, we would not have accepted him."

"Sounds to me like there was a lot of crisscrossing going on down there," Longarm observed.

"There still is." Aguierre nodded. "The war between the *guachapines* and *Indios* still goes on in Mexico, Marshal Long. I am here as a fugitive from Diaz. There is a reward on my head; I would be shot at once if I returned to Mexico. My people must have Santa Anna's gold before Diaz's men find it and seize it."

"I guess I can see where it all makes sense," Longarm said. "You figure it'd be better to turn the gold over to the Treasury and send whatever reward you get back to your friends than to risk having Diaz's men beat you to it."

"Of course." Aguierre nodded. "This is why we have sought your help. But you must be paid for your services, Marshal Long. Now, I am sure you have discussed your terms with my colleague, or he would not have brought you here."

"I don't follow you, Mr. Aguierre." Longarm frowned.

"Your fee," Aguierre said. "It is important that we understand one another on that matter, above all."

Longarm replied, "If I don't misread what you're saying, you want to know how big a bribe Two-Toe's offered me."

"Bribe is a very harsh word, Mr. Long." The Mexican smiled. "It has an ugly sound. In my country we have a better word. We call it *la mordita*—the little bite."

"Marshal Long didn't—" Two-Toe began.

Longarm interrupted him. Without raising his voice or betraying his anger, he said, "I don't take bribes by any name you want to call 'em, Mr. Aguierre."

"But that is not possible! Are you not an official of the government?" Aguierre's white eyebrows rose and his voice showed his surprise. "A marshal is a federal official, is he not?"

"Why, that depends on what you call an official," Longarm replied. "I work for the government, sure, but all I am is a sorta hired hand." He paused, then added, "Oh, I know there's some men working for the government who ain't above taking

59

money under the table. I just don't happen to be one of 'em."

"If we do not pay you, how are we to be sure we can trust you?" Aguierre asked. "You must accept something from us!"

"All I want is just what me and Two-Toe agreed on," Longarm said. "My job's done when I hand Santa Anna's gold over to my chief up in Denver."

"He's giving you the real straight of it, Felipe," Brown said. "We'll get a percent of the gold back from the U. S. Treasury, but Long wouldn't cut hisself in for a penny."

"That gold don't belong to me or to you," Longarm reminded Aguierre. "It don't belong to Mexico, neither. Santa Anna was supposed to've handed it over to Texas, but that was before Texas joined the United States. I ain't sure whether it's going to the federal government or to Texas, but that's for them to decide. All I'm after is to get it back."

An instant after he'd finished speaking, Longarm wished he could recall his words. He'd seen the frown grow on Aguierre's face as he tried to explain his position, and realized belatedly that Aguierre knew quite well that if Texas received Santa Anna's gold, not a penny of it would go to Mexico. Before Longarm could think of a way to correct his error, Aguierre broke in.

"*Señor* Long." He frowned. "I do not understand what you mean when you say that you do not know where the gold will go. Is there a question regarding its ownership, then?"

"Oh, there's likely to be some fuss kicked up by Texas when I hand the gold over to the U. S. Treasury," Longarm replied easily.

"But we will receive a share, a percentage, as Two-Toe has said, regardless of who does get the gold?" Aguierre asked.

Longarm suppressed a sigh as he answered. "Like I told your partner, you can look to the U.S. Treasury to pay you something if you hand Santa Anna's gold back to them. But I work for the U.S. government, Mr. Aguierre, not for Texas."

Two-Toe said impatiently, "Long's telling you the exact same thing he told me, Felipe. I figured it's the best deal we're likely to get."

"Will you then personally guarantee that you will deliver the gold to the federal government?" Aguierre asked.

Longarm shook his head. "That's something I can't promise. If my chief says I got to hand it over to Texas, I'll have to do what he tells me to."

"You see now why I said that you must accept the *mordita*," Aguierre said. He smiled. "You drive a shrewd bargain, Marshal Long, but I understand why you waited to negotiate your fee until you could bring me and Two-Toe together."

After the violence that had erupted around him the night before and the frustration that followed exposure of his mission in the newspaper, Longarm's patience was very thin. Aguierre's insistence was jangling his nerves anew.

"I'll talk just as straight as I know how to, Mr. Aguierre," Longarm said. "All along, I've been trying to tell you as plain as possible that I didn't come here looking for money or anything else for myself. There ain't any kind of deal you could offer me that'd change my mind. Now, if you want to hand over Santa Anna's gold to me, I'll deliver it to the United States government. After that, it's outa my hands."

Without hesitation, Aguierre shook his head. "Then we have no way to reach an agreement."

"Now, hold on a damn minute!" Two-Toe Brown exploded. "How about me, Felipe? You figure on cutting me outa the deal, too?"

"There is no deal to cut you out of," Aguierre snapped.

"Damn it! I need that share you promised me!" the big man shouted. "Why in hell you think I been going along with them piddling little dabs you been handing out? Can't you tell when a man's busted and too old and tired to work any longer?"

"Just a second, Two-Toe," Longarm broke in. "What about that yarn you handed me back at the hotel—that you'd made enough money off your mine to keep you for the rest of your life?"

"I was lying, Long. Sure, I had a little bit when I pulled outa Dakota Territory, but nowhere near what I made out I had."

"Why'd you think you had to lie?" Longarm asked.

"Because I learned the hard way that nobody's gonna listen to a crippled old bum that's broke and begging." He whirled to face Aguierre. "A man'll do most anything to get his hands on what he needs to keep him going. If you won't deal with Long, I sure as hell will!"

Before Longarm could move to stop him, the bearded giant had pulled an old-style Bowie knife from beneath his coat. The knife had a blade a foot or more long and as wide as a man's flattened palm. Moving with surprising speed in spite of his odd shuffling gait, Brown started toward Aguierre. He carried the Bowie knife in a manner that showed he'd fought with it before, holding the grip in his big fist like a sword hilt, at hip level, the blade's edge down, parallel to the floor, the needle-sharp tip extended.

Longarm had seen men go berserk before. Now and then, old scouts and trappers and miners, men who had endured and survived extreme hardships for years on the Western frontier, were seized by sudden and often unprovoked fits of madness which led them to kill at the slightest provocation, often for no reason at all.

Longarm's hand swooped by instinct for the butt of his Colt, but when he saw Brown's broad back he did not complete his draw. The idea of backshooting an anger-crazed old man who had no weapon except a knife rasped against Longarm's grain. He let his hand drop from the Colt. Leaping on Two-Toe's back, he wrapped his arms around the big man's upper arms and massive chest.

Before Longarm could clasp his fingers in a secure grip that would immobilize the demented frontiersman, Two-Toe spread his heavily muscled biceps sideways, like wings, and broke Longarm's embrace. Spreading his legs when he felt himself sliding off the giant's back, Longarm landed on his feet, but badly off balance.

Longarm's leap diverted Brown's attention from Aguierre. He began turning when he felt Longarm land on his back, and as he turned he started to bring up his knife hand, the wicked blade shimmering in the light that seeped through the nearly opaque windows. Struggling to steady himself, Longarm drew his Colt, still hoping that he would not be forced to fire.

Longarm was just raising the hand holding the Colt when the back of the Bowie knife's blade struck his wrist as Brown raised his knife hand. The heavy blade struck a nerve that lay under a thin layer of flesh. Longarm felt a burst of agonizing streaks of pain dart up his arm like lightning flashes. The stabbing pains caused him to open his gun hand involuntarily and the Colt clattered to the floor.

Two-Toe's hand had been deflected only slightly when the Bowie knife struck Longarm's wrist. He lunged forward, bent on completing his knife stroke. Longarm dropped to the floor as the huge blade swept around in a slashing stroke that would have cut him deeply.

Despite his age, Two-Toe Brown had not lost his skill. He reversed the sweep of the blade with a twist and brought it down like an ax as Longarm landed sprawling on the floor. As the blade descended in a chopping slash that would have taken his arm off at the shoulder, Longarm rolled like a cat.

Instead of slicing through flesh and bone, the knife cut into the floor. For a moment Brown wrestled the knife's grip, trying to free the deeply imbedded blade from the board it had split. Longarm's Colt was out of reach, so during the moment while Two-Toe was trying to free the knife blade, he reached into his vest pocket for his derringer.

Longarm discovered that his right hand was still numb. Try as he might, he could not force his fingers to close around the stubby little gun. He brought his left hand up, and this time he succeeded in grasping the derringer.

Brown had freed his Bowie knife beofre Longarm's hand closed on the derringer's butt. Longarm looked up to see the giant standing over him, the knife poised for a downward slash. He raised the muzzle of the derringer, but before he could trigger the weapon a shot barked from across the room.

Two-Toe Brown's massive frame jerked at the impact of the slug, but he did not fall. With the deep, fearsome roar of a hurt animal, he turned and started toward Aguierre. Longarm held his fire, waiting for Brown to crumple to the floor, but though the revolver in Aguierre's hand barked a second time, and Two-Toe's feet faltered as the bullets tore into him, he covered the few feet that still separated him from Aguierre and brought down the Bowie knife in a slashing cut.

Swaying like a huge tree felled by the woodsman's ax but reluctant to fall, Two-Toe Brown stood tottering in front of the counter while Longarm leaped to his feet. Just as Longarm stood erect, Brown lurched forward and collapsed across the counter in front of Aguierre.

Longarm had seen many men die, and he knew at once that Brown was dead. Aguierre had slid from the chair in which he'd been sitting, and Longarm hurried around the end of the counter. He looked down at the fallen man.

Aguierre lay against the door of a squat black safe that stood below the counter. The Bowie knife was buried in his shoulder at the base of his throat. Spurts of bright arterial blood from his severed jugular vein were staining the blade and the starched collar of Aguierre's white shirt, but he was still conscious.

"El loco." Aguierre gasped. *"Me ha matado."*

Longarm said nothing as he dropped to one knee. Looking at the wounded man at close range only confirmed what he'd known all along. There was no way he could help Aguierre. Any effort to stop the flow of blood by pressure would choke the man. He could only look on while Aguierre's life drained away with each fresh spurt of blood.

"Oigame, Long!" the dying man wheezed. *"Es claro que— tu es hombre honorable. Hallase—el oro de—Santa Anna antes de—los cabrones de Diaz! Hacele—"* Suddenly Aguierre's mind cleared in that moment of superhuman strength and clarity of mind that so often comes to men in the last few seconds before death. His voice was surprisingly strong as he said, "You have not understood me."

"I savvied most of it," Longarm assured him. "You want me to find Santa Anna's gold before Diaz's men do."

"Yes. Go to—Buffalo Bayou. Find my—nephew. Jorge— Montero. Tell him—tell him—"

Aguierre's last vestiges of strength had been exhausted by his effort to speak. His mouth opened and closed, but only a few garbled wheezes came out. They ended within seconds as his life finally drained away and he slid from the chair to the floor.

Longarm got to his feet. For a moment he stood motionless, looking at the two bodies. He frowned at the safe while he slid a cheroot from his vest pocket. It was crushed and bent after his scuffle with Two-Toe Brown, and he rolled it in his fingers to restore its shape before lighting it. By the time the long slim cigar was drawing well, he had decided what he must do.

Pulling Aguierre's lifeless form aside, Longarm tried the locking lever on the safe's door. It yielded and he swung the door open. There were a half dozen fat envelopes on one shelf and on the bottom of the safe lay a large bag. He pulled out the envelopes and found them unsealed, but when he examined the papers they contained he found the writing that covered them was all in Spanish.

Longarm tucked the envelopes into a pocket of his coat and turned his attention to the bag. He knew what it contained as soon as he felt its weight. When he pulled the drawstring and looked inside and saw the glow of gold, he nodded. He took out one of the coins. It was, as he'd been positive it would be, one of the 1836 twenty-peso gold pieces.

64

Well, old son, you found part of Santa Anna's gold, he told himself, *even if it ain't much. There's maybe sixty or seventy of them coins here, and that's not more'n a fleabite on what there's supposed to be. But it's a start.*

Placing the bag on the counter, he slid the unwieldy bulk of Two-Toe Brown to the floor and explored the pockets of the dead giant's coat and trousers.

Aside from the gold piece Brown had shown him at the hotel, the pockets held less than two dollars in U.S. coinage. The only other item was a bent and faded daguerreotype in the coat's breast pocket. The image was so dim that he could barely identify the subject as female. His face stony, Longarm replaced the picture in the dead man's pocket.

On leaving the building, he locked the door and slid the key into his pocket. Then he walked unhurriedly back to the hotel, assembled his belongings, and checked out of his room.

In the hackney cab taking him to police headquarters, Longarm's stomach reminded him that the noon hour had passed long ago without receiving its usual refilling. He ignored the message, and though its urgency did not diminish, continued to ignore it while he talked with Police Chief Black.

"When I left here this morning, you said if I needed a hand from you, I'd get it," Longarm reminded Black. "I sure hope you wasn't just being polite."

"I wasn't," the chief replied. "What happened, Marshal? Another shootout?"

"You could call it that, I guess. I didn't kill nobody this time, though."

"What's on your mind, then?"

"Did you ever run into a big fellow called Two-Toe Brown?"

"Oh, he's a town character." Black smiled. "Harmless, I'm sure. Why? Has he caused you some trouble?"

"No. But him and a Mexican fellow named Felipe Aguierre killed each other a little while ago. If you want to pick up their bodies, they're in Aguierre's office over on the West Side." Longarm put the key to the office on Brown's desk.

"What's your interest, if you didn't kill either of them?" Black frowned, looking at the key.

"They pushed into my case. I was there when they had their fracas. I locked the door because I wanted your men to be the first ones in the building." Longarm took out a cheroot and lighted it while he waited for Brown's next comment. When

65

it came, it was what he'd hoped it would be.

"What do you want me to do?" the chief asked.

"Play it with a soft pedal as much as you can. Be sure my name ain't in any of the damn newspapers in connection with it."

Black nodded. "That's easy enough."

"And I got one more favor to ask you. I guess you got a private safe of your own. Most police chiefs I know have one."

Black nodded. "Yes, I have. You want to leave something in it?"

"If it won't put you out none." Longarm laid the package of 1836 coins beside the key.

"You'll want a receipt, won't you?" Black asked.

Longarm shook his head. "Not for this bundle. Just take care of it for me till I get back."

"Be glad to." If Black was curious as to the contents of the package, he did not betray it. He went on, "I feel like I still owe you, Long. If there's anything else—"

"Thanks, but there won't be. I'll be out of town in an hour, and if we're both lucky there won't be any need for those two killings to bring me back."

Chapter 8

"I'll be real obliged if you'll tell me the easiest way to get out to Buffalo Bayou," Longarm told the attendant at the livery stable across the street from Houston's MK&T depot.

When his train had pulled out the evening before, Longarm had relaxed with a feeling of relief, glad to be leaving behind the frustrations which had dogged him in San Antonio. He knew that picking up a trail in a city that size, with its mixed population, had been nothing more than good luck. In Houston, which was a town of only fifteen thousand locating the man named by the dying Aguierre should be a lot easier.

Longarm's mood had improved still more after a full night's sleep at a hotel near the depot, and a good breakfast. Now, as he stood waiting for the liveryman man to finish saddling the deep-chested bay he'd rented, Longarm felt a great deal better than he had the previous day. He was not even impatient when the liveryman finished tightening and buckling the saddle cinch before answering his question.

"How far down the bayou you plan on going?" the man asked.

"That depends on where I find what I'm looking for."

"Well, which side you need to be on—north or south?"

"If I knew that, I wouldn't be standing here asking you a lot of questions," Longarm replied. "Does it make a difference how far east I go, or which side of the bayou I'm on?"

"Maybe it don't matter to you, but it does to me, mister," the liveryman replied. "It's my horse you'll be riding."

"I'm paying you for the use of the horse," Longarm pointed out. "Where I ride and what I do when I get there's not any affair of yours."

"You're a stranger to these parts." The man nodded wisely.

Longarm's good mood was finally fractured. He snapped,

"Look here, do you aim to rent me this critter or not? I'd imagine there's another livery stable close by where I can get a good horse, if you ain't interested."

"Now, don't get riled up, friend," the man said. "Just let me explain something to you."

"Go ahead. I'm listening."

With the air of one who had repeated a familiar explanation many times, the liveryman said, "Mister, that damn bayou snakes around for right onto twenty-five miles before you get to the bay. Here in town, for maybe three, four miles farther on, you can just about step a horse across it wherever you want to. Then it widens out and the bottom's mud ten feet deep. You try crossing anyplace after the crick starts to spread out, and you'll hurt a horse making it fight through that mud."

"There's no bridges across it?"

"Nary a one, not after you get outa town. Once Buffalo Creek widens out into the bayou, the only way you can get across is to go plumb down to Morgan's Point on the bay. There's a ferry there. They'll haul you and the horse across in a boat."

"That's a long day's ride," Longarm said.

"Well, now, if you'll tell me what you're looking to find, maybe I can help you figure out how to get there," the liveryman suggested. "There ain't a hell of a lot a man could be after in that stretch of country between here and the bay. Just a farm or two, and a few bunches of Meskin squatters' shanties."

"Them shanties, are they bunched up pretty good?"

"They mostly are. There's about three, four places where they're right thick. The Meskins calls 'em *caserias.*"

"Which side of the bayou is most of 'em on?"

"I guess I'd have to say the south side, especially after you get close to the place where old Sam Houston wiped up on Santa Anna and the Meskin army. The north bank's mostly salt marsh, once you get a few miles outa town."

"That place where the battle was—how far is it from town?"

"Around twelve, fourteen miles. There's clumps of them shacks all along there, back from the bayou."

"I'm obliged." Longarm nodded, threw his saddlebags over the horse's rump, laid his bedroll on top, and tied them down with the saddlestrings. While he worked, he told the liveryman, "I'll take good care of your nag, friend. Like I said, I might

68

keep it just for a day or two, but don't get worried if it's a week."

"You're paying for it," the liveryman said with a shrug. "As long as you get it back in fair shape, it don't much matter when."

There were paths on both sides of Buffalo Creek as it wound sinuously through the downtown section of Houston, and Longarm kept to them, turning out for the frequent narrow bridges, barely wide enough to accommodate a single carriage. A mile from the livery stable the houses began to thin out. They were built back from the creek and stood farther apart.

He rode now through open country, a featureless, flat plain. The ground was bare in spots, covered in others with a knee-high growth of reedy grasses, dotted with a few groves of sprawling live oaks and broken by an occasional expanse of tilled fields surrounding a farmhouse.

Another mile and the creek began to grow wider, and Longarm decided he'd reached the point at which it became a bayou. The current grew more sluggish as the waterway spread out. Soon the current became a barely perceptible ripple of motion that hardly stirred the foul-smelling scum and the rotting debris of civilization the creek had carried from town to the spreading surface of Buffalo Bayou.

Though the morning was neither warm nor cool, the sky was cloudless and the sun bright. As it climbed higher in the windless morning sky the smell from the scum and debris on the water grew progressively stronger. With no breeze to carry the smell away, it very quickly permeated the air. The earth became soft and so spongy that now and then the horse sank fetlock-deep into the saturated soil.

Longarm saw no reason why he should continue to stay close by the stagnant waterway. The bayou was the only geographical feature visible in that flat and sparsely wooded land, and if by some unlikely chance he should lose sight of it, he was sure he could find it by its smell alone. He turned the horse and, when he could no longer smell the bayou, put it back on a course roughly paralleling its bank. He let the animal set its own pace and pick its own way, with only an occasional touch of the rein to keep it headed east.

A bit more than an hour's ride from the edge of Houston, Longarm encountered the first of the squatters' shanties. There were two dozen or more of them, huddled close together as though for mutual protection against an unfriendly world. In Mexico, the huts would have been called *jacales,* built by driving tree limbs or boards into the ground, plastering the chinks between them with mud, and putting on a roof of any material at hand: pieces of tin or sheet metal, canvas, boards with slats covering the cracks.

A gaggle of half-naked children played in the open area between the *jacales* and the bayou. When he saw no adults in the narrow passages between the huts, Longarm reined over to where the children were playing. The play stopped as he approached and the youngsters formed a straggling semicircle as he drew closer to them. He stopped a few feet from the group.

"Any of you tads talk English?" he asked. The blank stares that greeted his question gave him the answer. He tried his very sketchy Spanish. *"Aqui es el hombre, Jorge Montero?"*

"No se, señor," one of the children piped.

"Montero," Longarm repeated. "Jorge Montero."

"No se, señor," another of the youngsters echoed.

Longarm sat looking at the children for a moment, trying to decide whether to try another question or move on, when a woman's voice sounded from the huts. Longarm turned to look and saw that the woman stood at the edge of the clustered huts. She wore a shapeless dress and an apron. Her hair was streaked with gray and her face deeply lined.

"De quien busca?" she called again.

Longarm toed the horse into motion. The woman waited for him to approach, then asked, "You look for somebody, maybe?"

Touching the brim of his hat with a forefinger, Longarm stifled a sigh of relief. "I'm trying to find a man named Jorge Montero. He's supposed to live along the bayou someplace around here."

Shaking her head, the woman said, "He don' leeve here, *señor.* I don' know heem."

"There's some more . . ." Longarm hesitated for a moment. "More of these little towns up ahead, I guess?" he finished.

"Ah, si," she replied. "Three, four more *caserías.* You look more, maybeso you find heem."

Longarm rode on. The soft, spongy earth extended in an even wider belt from the bayou now, and the second settlement

70

was a good half mile back from the water's edge. It was only half the size of the first, and there were fewer children playing around the tiny hovels, watched over by an ancient Mexican woman. She reminded Longarm of Juana. Her stature was small, her face deeply seamed, and her head covered with a black rebozo. She spoke no English, but when Longarm kept repeating the name of the man for whom he was looking, her face finally brightened.

"Montero?" She nodded and pointed east. *"Ah, si, creo que conozco. Siga derecho, a la proxima casería."*

Longarm understood the gesture, if not all the words. He resumed his ride along the bayou and just before noon sighted the third of the settlements. It stood well back from the bayou, which beyond the settlement curved gently to the north. It was even smaller than those at which he'd stopped earlier, but while most of the dwellings were the same type of shacks he'd encountered at his former stops, a number of them could be classed as houses. Some of the more substantial ones were built of milled lumber, and three or four had even been painted.

There was the usual group of children playing at the edge of the houses, and Longarm breathed a sigh of satisfaction when one of them recognized the name Montero.

"Ah, Montero, si, si," the youngster replied, nodding vigorously and pointing to one of the more substantial houses near the opposite edge of the *casería. "El señor Jorge vive ahi, en la casa verde."*

There was no sign of life around the green house to which the youngster had pointed. The windows were curtained, the door closed. Longarm swung out of the saddle and knocked. A dark-haired woman in her middle twenties opened it and began talking at the same time.

"He descubrido mas oro, Jorge? Es lo mismo razon que desea a la casa a esta hora," she said briskly. Then she lifted her eyes and saw Longarm, and her mouth formed into a O of surprise. She went on quickly, "I am sorry. I mistook you for someone else. Please excuse me."

"No harm done, ma'am," Longarm told her, doffing his hat.

Although her English was perfect and unaccented, Longarm would have known at a glance that she was of Mexican ancestry, for she wore the kind of costume he'd seen many times

71

below the border. Her loose blouse had a scoop neck threaded with a ribbon. It was pulled in at the waist by the folds of a long, full skirt with an embroidered hem.

She was not, he thought, beautiful, or even a very pretty young woman. Her nose robbed her of any claim to beauty. It jutted like a crag from the bridge and descended in a straight line to flaring nostrils. Longarm noted the rounded chin and full lips, the large, lustrous brown eyes and high cheekbones. Her hair was thick, black, and glossy, and was pulled back from a high oval forehead. It was caught at the nape of her neck with a gold clasp and streamed straight down her back to her waist.

"We have so few visitors—" she began, then stopped short. "But that doesn't matter. Are you looking for someone?"

"Matter of fact, I am. One of the youngsters back by the trail said this is where Jorge Montero lives."

"Yes. It is. He isn't here at the moment, though. I am his sister. Angelita is my name. Perhaps I could help you?"

"My name's Long, Miss Montero. Custis Long, deputy United States marshal outa Denver."

Longarm had not expected his words to bring the reaction they did. Angelita Montero paled and her eyes opened. A worried crease appeared on her brow.

"A United States marshal?" she gasped, then recovered and went on. "Why on earth are you looking for my brother? I'm sure he's done nothing wrong."

"Just to ease your mind, Miss Montero, I didn't come looking for your brother to arrest him. I got some news that—"

Angelita Montero recovered quickly. The frown vanished and was replaced by a smile. She said, "Please excuse me, Marshal Long! I apologize for being so lacking in courtesy that I'm keeping you standing outside our door. Do come in, where we can sit and talk more comfortably."

Angelita opened the door wider and Longarm followed her into a square, bare hall. She indicated a door, and he went into a moderate-sized room, dim because the heavy drapes at its windows reduced them to glare-free translucent panels. The room was sparsely furnished: an upholstered divan, three or four straight chairs, a table on which stood a large, ornate oil lamp. There was no carpet on the floor.

"Perhaps you'd like one of the chairs better than the divan,"

72

Angelita suggested. "I've noticed that men who wear a gunbelt don't seem comfortable on it."

"You got real sharp eyes, Miss Montero," Longarm said. He laid his hat on the floor beside a chair and sat down. "I don't recollect any other lady I've run into ever noticed that."

Angelita sat on the sofa facing Longarm. "I'm afraid you're going to have a long wait if you want to see Jorge, Marshal," she said. "He doesn't usually get back until the late afternoon."

"Well, I come quite a ways to talk to him, and it's a long ride back to Houston. So I guess I'll wait, if you don't mind."

"Of course I don't."

"It'll be nice just to sit without moving for a while," Longarm said. "Seems like all I been doing lately is travel."

"If you rode out from Houston this morning, I would imagine you're hungry, Marshal. I was just thinking of having my lunch. I'd be delighted if you'll join me."

"Now, I don't want to put you to a lot of trouble—"

"It won't be any trouble at all. But please don't expect a fancy meal. I'm heating a pot of *cocido*—that's a meat stew, if you aren't familiar with Spanish dishes—and there's plenty for both of us."

"Well, it's right kind of you to ask me, and I'll be real pleased to sit down with you," Longarm said.

"I know that most men like a drink before they eat, and I enjoy a glass of wine myself. Can I offer you a glass of *tequila,* or *aguardiente,* Marshal?"

"If it won't offend you, Miss Montero, about the only liquor I got a real taste for is Maryland rye whiskey. I just happen to have a bottle out in my saddlebags, and if you don't mind, I'll step out and get it."

"Of course I don't mind. While you're getting the bottle, I'll set out some glasses and see how the *cocido* is doing." As they went into the hall, Angelita added, "Leave the door ajar, Marshal. It has a spring lock on it."

Except for her remark, Longarm might not have noticed the lock, but he inspected it as he went out. It was an unusual type to be found on a residence door, with a latching button that kept it from being unlocked with a key from the outside. He noticed, too, that the door was unusually thick, and when he went back into the parlor and gave the windows a second look, he saw that there were two layers of curtains, one of them

73

between the glass pane and a set of iron bars, the other draped over the bars on the inside to hide them from the room's occupants.

Angelita returned, carrying glasses and a bottle of wine on a tray. She put the tray on the table beside the bottle of Tom Moore and said, "Would you like for me to pour your drink, Marshal? Or would you prefer to do it yourself?"

"Why, if you'll just put a few swallows in a glass for me, it'd be real fine."

"I didn't ask if you took water with your whiskey," she said, pouring whiskey for Longarm and red wine for herself.

"No, thanks, Miss Montero. But, with your permission, I'll light up a cigar."

"Of course. And lunch is ready, whenever you feel like eating." Angelita returned to the sofa and sat down. She sipped the wine and said, "You mentioned that you were from Denver, Marshal Long. I'm not hinting for information, but it seems strange that your government should send you to Texas, when I'm sure there are other federal officers closer. Whatever it is you want to talk to my brother about must be very important."

"Well, I don't have anything to do with picking out the places where I get sent," Longarm said. "My chief just tells me what he wants me to do, and I do my best to handle the job, whatever it might be."

"That's how it is with Mexico's *rurales*, I've heard." Angelita nodded.

"I've run into them *rurales* a few times," Longarm said, his voice flat and without expression.

Angelita was silent for a moment. Then she said, "From the tone of your voice, I gather that you don't have much admiration for the *rurales*. Isn't your job much the same as theirs?"

"They ain't the same at all," Longarm said emphatically. He saw that the conversation was taking a direction he wanted to postpone until Jorge Montero returned. Swallowing the remainder of his drink, he went on, "I'll take you up on what you said a minute ago, Miss Montero, about eating whenever I'm ready. Seems like this whiskey's stirred up my appetite."

"Why, of course. I'm hungry myself."

They stood up and Longarm followed Angelita through the hall into a small dining room. The table was set for two. She indicated the chair on the opposite side of the door through which they'd entered.

"If you'll sit there, Marshal Long, I'll go to the kitchen and bring in the *cocido*."

Angelita went around the table and disappeared through the door centered in the wall. Longarm took the chair she'd asked him to occupy. A napkin folded into a peak was in his plate. He picked it up and was shaking out its folds when he heard a small noise behind him. He started to turn, expecting to see Angelita returning from the kitchen.

His half turn brought his cheek into contact with the cold steel muzzle of a shotgun. He could see the twin barrels from the corner of his eye.

"You will please sit quietly, Marshal Long," a man's voice said. "I will not hesitate to blow your head off if you try to draw your pistol. Angelita, take the marshal's gun from its holster and give it to me."

Chapter 9

Longarm did not make the mistake of moving. He sat frozen while Angelita reached around from behind him and slid his Colt from its holster.

"Don't make the mistake of moving when I do, Marshal Long," the man holding the shotgun warned. "I'm going to come around the table where I can watch you while we talk, but if you lift a finger, I'll shoot."

"I ain't no more anxious to die than the next man," Longarm replied levelly. "And the only reason I came here is to talk."

Longarm breathed more easily when the cold muzzle of the shotgun was removed from his skin. He obeyed the command to sit still, remaining motionless and silent while the other man stepped around the table, still keeping him covered with the gun.

He was already sure that the man was Jorge Montero, and did not need the confirmation that came when he saw the family resemblance he bore to Angelita. Montero was several years older than his sister, and though his nose had the same craggy configuration, it was not as prominent as hers. His black hair was brushed back straight from his forehead. He wore the blue cotton shirt of a laborer with a red bandanna knotted around his neck, and farmer's overalls. Longarm noted that his hands and the cuffs of his shirt-sleeves were stained with fresh dirt.

Without taking his finger off the trigger, Montero rested the shotgun on the table, its muzzle only inches from Longarm's chest, and sat down in the chair Angelita had placed for herself.

"You are a wise man," he told Longarm. "Please remain very still while we talk of why you have come here looking for me."

"I told you already," Longarm replied. "I came to talk to you, if you're Jorge Montero."

"Of course I am. Who would you expect me to be?"

Longarm saw that Montero was still tense. He was also very much aware of the danger involved in sitting with the muzzle of a shotgun almost touching his chest, a shotgun with a tense finger on its trigger. He wanted the minutes of danger to pass before he went on to the main purpose of his visit.

"Your sister and me was about to have a bite to eat," Longarm said quietly. "I don't mind putting off eating, but if we're going to have a long palaver, I'd like to have a smoke. I don't suppose you'd object if I get out a cigar?"

"I'm sure you understand why I do not yet trust you fully, Marshal Long," Jorge replied. "I do not want to deprive you of your cigar, but neither do I wish you to move." Without taking his eyes off Longarm, he said, "Angelita, the marshal will tell you in which pocket he carries his cigars. Please take one out and hold a match for him. Better still, light it for him, as you used to do for our father."

"I carry my cigars in my top left vest pocket," Longarm said. He followed Montero's example, and did not shift his eyes from the man opposite him. "I got matches in my right-hand coat pocket."

"Take out only the cigar," Jorge said quickly to Angelita. "Get a match from the kitchen. As long as my finger is on the trigger of this shotgun, I do not want you close to him any longer than is necessary."

Angelita leaned over Longarm's shoulder and took out one of his cheroots. Longarm heard her footsteps as she went back to the kitchen. When she returned, she stood to one side of him while she pierced the end of the cigar with the match stick, struck the match, and puffed the cheroot until its tip glowed. Then she put the cigar into Longarm's mouth and stepped away.

Longarm nodded. "Thanks," he said. He puffed on the cigar for a moment and then, talking around it, went on, "You want me to start out by telling you what brought me here, Mr. Montero, or would you rather ask me some questions? Whichever way you choose, you'll hear the same story."

"Go ahead and talk," Montero invited. "If I have any questions, I'll ask them."

"I guess the best place to start it telling you how I came to know where to look for you and your sister. Your uncle over

77

in San Antonio told me you were living here."

Behind him, Longarm heard Angelita gasp in surprise and say, *"Tio* Felipe?"

Montero's brow puckered into a frown. "You know my uncle, then? Don Felipe Aguierre?" he asked.

Longarm nodded. After a moment's wait, he decided there was no kind or easy way to break the news to the Monteros. He said, "I hate to tell you this, Mr. Montero, but your uncle's dead."

Under her breath, Angelita said, *"Madre de Dios! Jorge, preguntale como—"*

Montero shook his head, the frown still on his face. He snapped, *"Esparate,* Lita!" His eyes fixed on Longarm, he said, "I do not believe you would lie about a matter such as this, Marshal. It would be too easy for me to find out the truth."

"I told you the truth," Longarm said. "And, to save you asking, I'll tell you that I was there when a man named Two-Toe Brown killed Mr. Aguierre with a knife. I tried to stop Brown, but I couldn't."

Angelita broke in again. *"Este hombre, este Brown, Tio Felipe he cuentemos de el, acordarte."*

Jorge nodded, still looking at Longarm, and asked, "Were there others there besides you and Brown?"

"No. It was Brown who took me to see your uncle."

"And how did you meet this man Brown?"

"If you'll let me reach in my coat pocket, I'll show you a page outa the San Antonio newspaper. It'll explain things a lot faster'n I can tell you. Or have your sister take the paper out, if you'd rather."

"Take out the paper, Marshal Long. I trust you that far."

Longarm took the page from the *San Antonio Express* out of his pocket and spread it on the table. Angelita moved around to read the newspaper over her brother's shoulder. Longarm waited motionless until they had finished reading.

"If you're ready to listen now, I'll tell you what happened after that," he said.

"Go on." Jorge nodded. "Until I hear the entire story, I will wait to ask the questions that are already in my mind."

As quickly as he could without omitting any important details, Longarm sketched the scene in Felipe Aguierre's office. He concluded, "So that's how it all happened, Mr. Montero, even if there's not any way I can prove it, with your uncle and

Brown both dead. About the only proof I got is in my pocket, if you'll let me reach in and get it out."

When Montero nodded, Longarm took out one of the twenty-peso gold pieces he'd held back from the bag in Aguierre's safe. He laid it on the table.

"This proves nothing," Montero said.

"Oh, I don't argue that. All it proves is that I got my hands on it some way or other. It's up to you to judge whether I told you the truth about how I come by it."

"Creo que el es verdico, Jorge," Angelita said quietly.

"Si, este lo creo mismo." Montero nodded. "If you understand Spanish, Marshal—"

"I don't, except a word or so now and then," Longarm replied. "But, from the way you sounded, I figure you believe I am telling you the truth."

"Yes. But only for one reason."

"What's that?"

Tapping the somewhat tattered newspaper page, Montero said, "This. There is no better way you could have convinced Angelita and me of your good intentions toward us than by showing us this paper. If the *rurales* are your enemies, we are your friends."

He lifted the shotgun from the table and leaned it in a corner, then thrust his hand out. Longarm grasped it in a firm grip, and the two men shook hands.

"Well, I'm glad that's settled," Longarm said.

"No more than I am," Jorge replied. *"Bienvenida,* Marshal Long. *Nuestra casa es suyo."*

"Not that I blame you for being gunshy about me," Longarm told them. "You folks not knowing me from Adam's off ox."

"There are more reasons for our suspicions than you know now," Angelita told Longarm. "And I'm sure Jorge will want to tell you about them. But when he came back from the battlefield so unexpectedly, we were getting ready to have lunch. I'll set another place, and we can talk while we are eating."

While Angelita was in the kitchen, Longarm told Jorge, "I don't generally get taken by surprise the way you done to me a while ago. I'm right glad we're both on the same side now."

Jorge shrugged. "Surprising you was not difficult. I saw your horse when I came up to the house. It was not a horse that belonged to a friend, so I became suspicious. I came quietly in by the back door. When Angelita came into the kitchen, we arranged our movements. You see, we were not sure of your intentions."

"You figured I was coming to arrest you?" Longarm asked.

"Arrest or kill—how were we to know?"

"U. S. marshals don't go in for murder, Mr. Montero. Sure, we'll shoot when we got to, but we don't backshoot nobody."

"We could not know that. In Mexico, our family has had experiences with the *rurales*. We feared the force to which you belong might be like them. They kill on Diaz's command, or without it, if they meet someone who opposes them."

"Take my word for it, Mr. Montero, our men ain't any ways like the *rurales*. I brushed up against them before that shootout in San Antonio, and they come off second best. That's why them two tried to kill me."

"It is the best recommendation you could have offered."

"Is it good enough to get you to believe what I told you about your uncle—what he said before he died?"

"Perhaps. There have been things—" Montero broke off as Angelita came in carrying a steaming pot, then said, "We will eat before we talk more of this matter of Santa Anna's gold."

Angelita dished up the *cocido,* a tasty mixture of beef, rice, onions, and tomatoes. Longarm's breakfast had been very early, and he ate hugely. They talked in generalities during the meal, breaking the barriers that had been between them, getting acquainted. When their hunger had been satisfied and the table was cleared, Montero glanced across at Longarm, a questioning look on his face.

"Shall we talk now?" he asked.

"Talk's what I been waiting for," Longarm replied.

"Very well. First I must ask you a question. How much do you know of the history of Santa Anna's gold?"

"I read a lot of General Sam Houston's reports that he sent to the Texas Congress right after the battle he fought with Santa Anna back in 1836," Longarm answered. He gave them a brief but complete account of what he'd read. Then he decided the time had come to open the real discussion he'd been planning during the meal. "We're pretty near where that fight happened, Mr. Montero. Soon as I found out where you were living, I figured that's why you picked this place out."

"I would have trusted you less if you had not said that." Jorge smiled and added, "If we are to be friends, it is time that

80

we dropped formalities between us. Please, call us Jorge and Angelita. And surely you have a name by which your friends address you?"

"A lot of my friends call me Longarm. If it suits you to call me that, go ahead."

"Very well," Jorge said. "Yes, Longarm, we are living here for a reason. You know that this is part of the battlefield over which our people and the Texans fought. It was not a neat battle, from what I have learned. And my authority is as good as General Sam Houston. Our grandmother was the mistress of Santa Anna, the one to whom General Houston referred to as 'that woman.'"

Longarm's jaw dropped. "You mean to say that General Santa Anna was your granddaddy?"

"No. No, indeed. She bore Santa Anna no children. And he was a cruel man with women, Longarm. Grandmother left him soon after he returned with his army to Mexico. A few years later, she married our grandfather."

"But I'd imagine you heard a lot about Santa Anna from her," Longarm said.

"We certainly did." Angelita smiled. "Not only from Grandmother when she was alive, but from our father."

His voice carefully casual, Longarm asked, "Well, have you found the gold you been looking for here?"

"I suppose I should have told you sooner that we've been looking for it," Jorge said. "General Houston's suspicion was very shrewd, but not quiet shrewd enough."

"Maybe you better explain that to me," Longarm suggested.

"Houston was right about some things," Jorge said. "There wasn't any gold sealed in a cannon with melted lead and thrown into Buffalo Bayou."

"But there was more gold than Santa Anna turned over to Houston?"

"Oh, of course," Jorge replied. "Santa Anna fooled Houston twice. Houston was wrong when he wrote in his report that there hadn't been time for Santa Anna to hide any of the gold after the fighting was over and before he surrendered."

"That's the gold you been trying to find," Longarm said.

"Yes." Angelita nodded. "Grandmother said that Santa Anna and his orderly buried it. Then he shot the orderly."

"Well, from what I've heard about Santa Anna, that's about what he'd do, all right," Longarm said thoughtfully. "But didn't your grandma remember where they'd buried the gold?"

Jorge shook his head. "She didn't know, but it was somewhere close to Santa Anna's tent. She said they weren't gone long enough to have carried all that gold very far."

Longarm shook his head. "I ain't running down your grandma, but I don't see how her yarn hangs together."

"In what way?" Angelita asked.

"Houston must've put guards to watch Santa Anna. And I never seen a general yet that didn't have more than one flunky hanging around him. They'd have known what he was doing."

"I didn't include all the details of Grandmother's story," Angelita told Longarm. "Santa Anna had already buried the gold when he surrendered. He saw his soldiers running and throwing down their guns, and realized very quickly that he wasn't going to beat the Texans. So he sent all the officers on his staff to join the fighting. Then he and his orderly buried the gold."

"Close to where Santa Anna's tent was, you said." Longarm was silent for a moment. Then he asked, "I don't guess she could remember where the tent was pitched?"

"She didn't know," Angelita replied. "All she remembered was that from the tent she could see the bend of the bayou where it turns north. She wasn't sure how far the tent was from the bayou. I don't suppose she'd notice a thing like that, though I'm sure Santa Anna made a map of the place in his mind."

"And never told anybody whereabouts, of course." Longarm took out a cheroot and lighted it before he said, "I guess I'd have kept my mouth shut, too, if I'd been him." He exhaled a puff of blue smoke and went on, "Jorge, you said Santa Anna fooled Houston twice. What was the other time?"

Before her brother could reply, Angelita broke in. "Of course he did! A minute ago, when you told us what General Houston had written about Santa Anna being too sick to walk and his legs being so weak that Grandmother had to help him into his carriage, I had a hard time keeping myself from laughing, the way Grandmother always did when she told us that part of the story."

"You mean Santa Anna was play-acting for Houston?"

"He certainly was. There was nothing wrong with Santa Anna's legs. He could hardly walk because he had so many money belts strapped around his body, and bags of coins tied under his clothes. Grandmother did, too, but she wasn't weighted down as heavily as Santa Anna."

82

"What happened to that gold, then?" Longarm asked. "Did your grandma and Santa Anna get back safe with it to Mexico?"

"We don't know what happened to it, Longarm," Jorge said. "As many times as she must have told about having to help Santa Anna into the carriage, she would never finish it. She said the rest of the story was for somebody else to tell."

"Don't that seem sorta peculiar?" Longarm frowned. "I'd've thought the best part of a yarn like that was how they managed to get all that gold home, if they got it there at all."

"She was always laughing so hard about fooling Houston that she didn't finish the story." Angelita smiled, remembering.

"You're sure she and Santa Anna got back to Mexico with it?"

"If they hadn't gotten the gold back to Mexico, I don't believe Grandmother would have thought the story was so funny," she replied.

"Well, that makes sense," Longarm agreed. He turned to Jorge. "You been doing an awful lot of work, I guess. Swinging a shovel ain't one of my favorite jobs."

Jorge held up his hands, heavily callused, and said, "It wasn't easy at first. But you can see I've gotten used to it."

"Ain't your neighbors kinda curious about all the digging you been doing, Jorge? If I was you, I'd worry about them. Ain't it occurred to you some of 'em might be here to spy on you?"

Jorge shook his head. "There are only our friends among them. Do not worry about them. They will not betray us."

"I guess you know best," Longarm said. "You'd know better'n me. But you got a hard job, because as near as I've found out, that battle spread out over quite a bit of territory."

"It did, yes. And it was fought a long time ago, almost fifty years. Of course, all I have been able to do is to move on from one old grave to the next. The only landmark I've had to go by was the bend in the bayou."

"Land changes, too, in fifty years," Longarm said thoughtfully. "Even if you'd had a starting point, it might not've helped much."

"About the only thing I've been able to do is to find places that still show signs of something having been buried. You know how easy it is to notice a spot where the earth has sunk in."

Longarm said, "Sure. But places like that around here would

83

mostly be old graves, I'd imagine. Soldiers buried in a hurry after the battle, right where they died. Digging into old graves wouldn't be exactly to my taste."

"Nor to mine," Jorge told him. "I've disturbed a lot of bones. It hasn't always been possible for me to tell whether the man buried was a Mexican soldier or a Texan, but I've said a prayer over each of them and reburied them all."

"Well, I'll give you credit, Jorge," Longarm said. "You sure ain't one to give up easy."

"Oh, I've thought about giving up more than once," Jorge confessed. He looked from Longarm to Angelita, his face breaking into a triumphant smile. "Today I was glad I didn't. I'm very sure that I've finally uncovered Santa Anna's gold."

Chapter 10

For a moment, both Longarm and Angelita stared openmouthed at Jorge. Then Angelita said angrily, "And you haven't told me until now?"

"How could I?" Jorge asked. "Until now, we haven't been sure about Longarm. For all I knew when I came in, he could have been an agent of Diaz."

"One thing's been bothering me, Jorge," Longarm said. "All along, I just figured you had Santa Anna's gold, and here you say you just found it. Where'd your uncle get that bag of gold pieces that was in his safe in San Antonio?"

"That was all the gold we had until now, Longarm," Jorge replied. "The gold has been a secret our family has been careful to keep. We didn't know exactly where it was hidden, just the general area. We did not want all of Mexico looking for it."

"How about Santa Anna himself?" Longarm asked. "He ain't been dead long. Weren't you afraid he'd dig it up?"

Jorge shook his head. "No. Santa Anna has either been in exile and watched very carefully, or has been president of Mexico since he hid the gold. When he was an exile, he was guarded carefully by the government. When he was president, there were always too many people around him to give him a chance to reclaim it."

"But now you've found it!" Angelita said excitedly. "Where, Jorge?"

"In one of those graves east of the *casería* I told you of several days ago, Lita. I worked through the morning and dug up four of the five graves by noon. I found nothing but what most of them contain: bones and some buckles and buttons and pocket trinkets that hadn't rotted away. I was ready to give up and come back here to the house to eat, but I decided to dig up the fifth grave to save having to go back there later."

"Wait a minute, Jorge," Longarm broke in. He looked at Angelita. "The two or three times you went back to the kitchen, you were looking for Jorge to come home, right?"

"Yes, of course," she replied. "Jorge and I had already planned what we'd do if anybody but one of the people of the *casería* came to the house while he was gone."

"I walked right into your trap," Longarm admitted. "You'd do for a man to tie to, Angelita."

"If that's a compliment, thank you, Longarm. Now, I'm dying to hear the rest of Jorge's story."

Jorge continued. "I dug up the fifth grave." He turned to Longarm. "These aren't deep graves, you understand. There's not more than a foot or two of earth on top of most of the men the soldiers buried."

"I been in a war, Jorge. I've seen dead soldiers buried in shallow graves after a battle," Longarm said.

"Well, the fifth grave didn't look any different from the others," Jorge went on. "I cleared away the dirt around the skeleton and was just about to cover it up again when I saw the top of a bag—a leather pouch—sticking up below the ribs. I pulled it out, and when I felt how heavy it was, I knew at once that it was full of coins." Reaching into his pocket, he took out a handful of the twenty-peso gold pieces and spread them out on the table. "Like these."

Longarm and Angelita stared at the coins gleaming against the white cloth, but made no move to touch them. The gold pieces were darker in hue than the others Longarm had seen, due to their long interment, but they bore the familiar design of Santa Anna's hoard.

"I take it there was more'n one bag?" Longarm asked.

"There were fifty bags in all," Jorge said quietly.

"Fifty!" Angelita exclaimed. "But, Jorge, we never dreamed there would be so many!"

"I counted to see how many coins there were in the bag I took out," Jorge told them. "There were five hundred."

Longarm was stirred by the same excitement that had brought Angelita's exclamation, but he did not betray it. "If them other bags has all got the same amount in 'em, you found an awful lot of money, Jorge," he said evenly.

"I didn't stop to count the coins in the other bags," Jorge said. "But I lifted them and looked inside. As nearly as I could tell, they weighed the same, and were just as full."

"That is a lot of money," Longarm said.

"After I'd covered up the grave, while I was walking back to the house, I tried to add it up, but I couldn't." Jorge smiled.

"It oughta be easy enough to figure," Longarm said. "You just go by the rule of ten. Fifty bags, at five hundred gold pieces to the bag, that'd be—let's see—" He shook his head. "No, it can't be that many. I added a naught too many."

Angelita smiled. "There are twenty-five thousand gold pieces in that grave."

Longarm's forehead furrowed as he concentrated on the mental arithmetic he was doing. "Twenty Mexican pesos is worth ten U.S. dollars. That'd figure out at—" He shook his head. "I ain't used to big figures like this, but I make it to be a quarter of a million dollars. And that is a whole lot of money anyplace!"

In Mexico, the gold pieces would be worth half a million pesos," Angelita said. She turned to her brother with a triumphant smile.

"That's a small amount compared to the treasure Diaz can command," Jorge said soberly. "But, for our people, it's a very big sum indeed!"

"Hold on a minute, Jorge!" Longarm said. "Ain't you forgot the deal your uncle and me worked out?"

"To hand the gold over to you, and let you give it to your country's Treasury?" Jorge frowned.

"That's what Mr. Aguierre figured was the best thing to do," Longarm replied.

"I haven't forgotten," Jorge said. "But, in Mexico, those coins are more important to our people, Longarm."

"Provided you can get it back across the Rio Grande without the *rurales* jumping you and taking it off your dead bodies," Longarm replied soberly. "Or the Rangers arresting you and grabbing it for Texas. Mr. Aguierre figured it was better to keep part of that money than to risk losing all of it. It's like the bird you caught and the one that's still in the bush. You open your hand to catch the one in the bush, and lose the one you got for sure."

"Not quite," Angelita broke in. "We have the gold. It is not in the bushes now, Longarm."

"Having it and keeping it ain't quite the same thing, Angelita," Longarm said quietly. "It's a long way to the Rio Grande from where we're sitting right this minute. By now,

Diaz knows about them two *rurales* I had to shoot in San Antonio, and from what I heard about him, he ain't a man that wastes much time. I got more'n just a hunch he's already sent another bunch to track me down and get even with me."

"But it's you they're after, Longarm," Jorge pointed out. "Not us. They would know nothing about what we have found."

"You ain't looking at things real straight, Jorge," Longarm said. "I figured on the *rurales* following me, so I didn't bother to cover my trail here. I figured if the *rurales* caught up with me, I could handle whatever scrape I got into."

"If they follow you here, they will follow you away from here when you leave." Jorge shrugged. "Angelita and I will travel in another direction with the gold."

Longarm shook his head. "You still don't see what I'm trying to tell you. It was just an accident that them *rurales* run into me in San Antonio. They wasn't looking for me; they was after your uncle. They just hadn't had time to find him."

"But *Tio* Felipe is dead," Angelita said.

"How long you figure it'll take the *rurales* to pick up a trail from him to you?" Longarm asked. "And even if I didn't figure on leading the *rurales* here to you and Jorge, that's what I done, sure as God made little green apples. I'm real sorry it happened, but there ain't a way I can see to change anything now."

"What you say may be true, Longarm," Jorge said. "I had not looked at our situation the way you describe it."

"We're still alive now, Jorge!" Angelita said sharply. "And finding Santa Anna's gold has given us twenty-five thousand new reasons to stay alive!"

"Not meaning to run you and Jorge down, but you two ain't no match for Diaz's *rurales*, Angelita," Longarm said soberly. "And I don't aim to be responsible for you getting killed."

"Help us, then!" she snapped.

"What do you think I'd do? Leave you?"

"Oh, I don't know, Longarm. Finding the gold has changed everything," she replied.

"No, it hasn't!" Jorge said. "Longarm is right, though, Lita. The two of us alone . . . the *rurales* would swallow us without having to chew more than twice."

"You want to do as *Tio* Felipe was going to?" she asked. "Give the gold to the United States Treasury?"

"We would still get the portion Longarm promised him,"

Jorge said. He looked at Longarm questioningly. "Is that not true?"

"It's true enough. But before you can do anything with the gold, it's got to come outa that grave," Longarm pointed out.

"That is a small job." Jorge shrugged.

"Did you ever figure how much that gold's going to weigh, Jorge?" Longarm asked. "Twenty-five thousand ounces adds up to a lot of pounds."

"It will weigh . . ." Angelita closed her eyes to concentrate better. "It will weigh over one thousand five hundred pounds."

"I don't guess you got a wagon, have you?" Longarm asked.

Jorge shook his head. "No. Just a saddle horse for Lita and one for me."

"How about the people here in the settlement? Any of them got wagons?"

"No," Jorge answered. "They work on the farms nearby. Few of them have even a horse, but some have burros."

"What about the farms? How close is the nearest one?"

"Almost three miles," Jorge said.

"It's a pretty poor farm that don't have a wagon or two," Longarm said. He looked at Angelita. "You wouldn't be afraid of a few old dead bones, would you?"

"Of course not!" she replied indignantly. "But I would like to know what you are thinking, Longarm."

"What I got in mind is going out and finding a wagon and a horse to pull it while you and Jorge go dig up that gold," he said. "It's been three days now since I shot them *rurales* in San Antonio, and there's telegraph wires running just about anywhere you look these days. We don't know how much time we got."

"Where would you move the gold?" Jorge asked.

"To Houston first. I guess there's a bank there."

"You plan to put the gold into a bank?" Angelita gasped.

"Can you think of a better place for it?" Longarm asked her.

"But in a bank—" Angelita began.

Longarm interrupted her. "It'll be put there in the name of the U.S. Department of Justice, Angelita. Nobody can touch it but me or my chief. Don't worry. It'll be safe."

Silence followed Longarm's assurance. Jorge broke it. "I agree, Longarm. Your plan to move the gold at once is good." He stood up. "Come, Lita. You get our rifles and I will bring another shovel from the shed. We will dig up the bags while Longarm finds a wagon." To Longarm he said, "The name of the farmer you are going to see is Jenkins. Perhaps it would be best if you do not tell him why the wagon is needed."

"Don't worry, Jorge. I won't give away a thing, and I can be a pretty convincing talker when I got to be. If it's no more'n a couple or three miles to Jenkins's farm, I oughta be back here inside of an hour or so. Can you have the gold dug up by then?"

"With Lita helping, it will not take long."

"Don't try to bring it to the house. I'll drive the wagon out to where you're digging."

"But suppose you do not get a wagon?" Angelita frowned.

"Don't worry," Longarm assured her. "I'll get one."

When Longarm reached the Jenkins farm, he used the best argument he'd been able to think of during the short ride. He did not knock at the farmhouse door, but went first to the barn to look for a wagon. He found an almost new high-body Cleveland wagon that seemed to be in very good shape, and was inspecting it when the owner arrived, carrying a shotgun.

"You stand right where you are, mister," Jenkins said. He held the shotgun with its muzzle to the ground, but ready to bring up in an instant. "Who in hell are you, and what're you doing prowling around my barn?"

Holding his hands well away from his body, Longarm replied, "My name's Long, Mr. Jenkins, and I'm a deputy United States marshal. Be glad to show you my badge, if you'll guarantee to be careful with that scattergun while I reach in my pocket."

Jenkins hesitated for a moment, then nodded. "Go ahead. If you got a badge to show me, get it out."

Longarm took out his wallet and flipped it open to display his badge. Jenkins relaxed and said, "All right, Marshall Long. Now tell me what brought you here."

"I got a little emergency a few miles up toward the bayou, and I need a horse and wagon the worst way. I was looking at that Cleveland you got there—"

"Wait a minute, Marshal. I'll be bringing in my winter hay in a few days, and I'll need that wagon," Jenkins said.

"You'll have it back in a few days," Longarm replied.

Jenkins shook his head. "I'm sorry, but I can't run the risk of leaving my hay in the field. If anything was to happen and I didn't get it back—"

"Wait just a minute, now," Longarm broke in. "How much did that wagon cost you?"

"I paid sixty dollars for it two years ago."

"I guess you can buy another one for that now?"

"I guess," Jenkins nodded.

"And I'd imagine you got a pretty good wagon horse?"

"I hitch a mule to this wagon. Bit critter. It'll outpull a horse any day."

"What do you figure to pay for a big mule these days?"

"A real good one'll run as high as fifteen dollars."

"Suppose I was to give you a U.S. government voucher for seventy-five dollars?" Longarm asked.

"Hold on, Marshal!" Jenkins said. "I ain't offered to sell you my wagon or my mule, either."

"I ain't offering to buy 'em. What I was going to say is, I'd like to rent 'em for maybe three days. Now, I rent horses all the time, and I know what livery stables charge. I'd say two dollars a day is fair rent for a wagon and mule, wouldn't you?"

"Two-fifty'd be more like it," Jenkins replied.

"All right, let's say two-fifty," Longarm agreed. "Paid in advance. Now, if you was to rent me the wagon and mule, and something happened to either one of 'em, I wouldn't want you to be outa pocket. So say I give you a government voucher for seventy-five dollars. You can get cash for it from any bank or post office. If I don't get your wagon and mule back to you, you cash in that voucher and buy yourself a new rig."

Twenty minutes later, Longarm was sitting on the seat of the Cleveland wagon with his horse hitched to the tailgate, on his way back to the *casería*.

From the high seat of the wagon, Longarm could see farther than was possible on horseback. Even with the sun in his eyes as it descended toward the western edge of the treeless, coastal plain he had no trouble locating Jorge and Angelita. Turning the mule, he angled across the flat land in a straight line. Jorge was stamping clumps of surface sod on top of the newly filled excavation. Angelita stood to one side, the bags of gold in neat rows at her feet.

"Well, I see you got it all out," Longarm said as he reined

91

in beside them. "Now all we got to do is get it to Houston."

Jorge shook his head. "Angelita and I have talked of this while we were working, Longarm. We do not wish to follow the plan *Tio* Felipe agreed to. We will find a way to get all of the gold to our people in Mexico."

Longarm stared at the pair for a moment, then said, "I had the idea we'd made a deal, Jorge. I wasn't looking for you to pull outa it."

"No, Longarm," Angelita said. "Jorge and I did not agree to follow *Tio* Felipe's plan. Think back. You will remember that we only listened to you. We almost agreed, but never did we say we would give up the gold to your government."

Longarm frowned as he tried to remember exactly what had been said, and finally nodded. "I got to admit you're right about what you and Jorge done," he told Angelita. "We never did hit up a bargain."

"We don't expect you to help us any more, though," Angelita said quickly. "Now that you cannot deliver the money to your government, you would not want to be—"

"Wait a minute, Angelita," Longarm broke in. "I think you and Jorge are making a bad move, but that don't mean I'm giving up. I'll go along with you to the house. We can talk about it, and maybe I'll be able to get you to change your minds."

"We'll be glad of your company," Jorge told him, "but you will not be able to change our decision."

"That don't mean I can't try," Longarm replied. "But this ain't the time or place to argue. It's getting on for dark, and we better load them bags into the wagon and haul 'em to your house while we can still see some daylight."

Loading the gold took only a little time. The buckskin bags containing the coins had been oil-tanned and were still in good condition even after almost half a century in the damp earth. They took up a surprisingly small amount of space in the bed of the wagon after the three had lifted them into it. Though the job of loading had been short, the sun was beginning to redden into its twilight hue by the time they started for the *casería*.

An awkward silence rode with them. They sat shoulder to shoulder, Angelita between Longarm and Jorge, as the wagon made its ponderous way across the moist, yielding soil. Longarm had been thinking hard, trying to come up with an argument that would convince his companions to change their minds. He broke the ice by saying, "I don't reckon you'd want to keep all this gold in your house any longer than you got to."

"No," Jorge agreed. "As soon as we can, we must get it to a place where it will be safe."

"How you figuring to haul it to Mexico?" Longarm asked. "I imagine that's where you'll be heading."

"We have not talked about that yet," Angelita replied.

"Well, like you said a while back, it ain't my affair any more." Longarm shrugged. "But there's something about gold that makes people smell it out, so I'd say that's the first thing you better be thinking about."

They rode on, silent again, drawing nearer to the houses of the settlement in the orange light of the setting sun. They were within a mile or less of the houses when Jorge noticed that the *casería*, was unduly astir.

"Wait, Longarm!" he said, his voice worried. "Rein in!"

"What's wrong?" Angelita asked.

"Look at the *casería*," Jorge replied. "There is never so much movement between the houses at this time of day."

Longarm reined in and they gazed ahead. Men and women were walking back and forth among the houses.

"Something has disturbed them," Angelita said. "This is the time when they are usually inside, eating supper."

"You take the reins, Jorge," Longarm said. "I'll ride on ahead and see if I can find out what's got 'em all roiled up."

"No. They would not trust you." Jorge frowned. "Let me take your horse and go in front of the wagon."

"Take the horse and welcome," Longarm said. He reined in. "Just hand me my rifle before you ride off."

As Jorge took Longarm's rifle from the saddle scabbard and handed it up, he said, "If nothing is wrong, I will signal you to follow."

Jorge mounted the bay and started toward the *casería*. He had covered less than half the distance when a group of riders burst from the cover of the buildings and rode at a gallop toward him.

"They are coming after us!" Angelita gasped. She stood up and shouted, "Jorge!"

Jorge had not needed her warning. He was already wheeling the bay to start back to the wagon. The crack of a rifle shot, then another, shattered the still air of the gathering twilight.

Jorge bent forward over his horse's neck to present a smaller target and raced on toward the wagon. More shots came from the men chasing him. Longarm stood up and shouldered his Winchester, and Angelita was just reaching for hers when Longarm fired. He knew the oncoming riders were still out of range, but he counted the shot as a warning, to discourage them.

His shot had no effect. The pursuers kept their pace, but they were not gaining ground on Jorge. He was within a hundred yards of the wagon and the men chasing him were almost a hundred yards behind him when Longarm fired again. One of the pursuers dropped, but the remainder kept coming on. Angelita fired and missed.

Over his rifle sights, Longarm could now see the pursuers clearly, and he did not like what he saw. He told Angelita, "All them horses have got Mexican saddles. Get in the wagon bed, fast as you can move! Looks like the *rurales* have caught up with us!"

Chapter 11

Longarm grabbed Angelita's hand and helped her over the back of the wagon seat, then followed her into the cover of its high sides. He saw at once that there was enough space between the top of the sideboards and the bottom of the seat to allow them to slide their rifles into the gap. With the seat shielding their heads and the thick boards of the sides protecting their bodies, the wagon became a miniature fortress.

"Make your shots count," Longarm said. "The extra shells for my Winchester are in my saddlebags on the horse Jorge's riding. Once we empty our magazines, we're out of ammunition."

"I'm a good shot," she protested. "I'll do my share."

"Sure you will," Longarm agreed.

"Maybe not as good as you, though. Hitting that *rurale* at such a range was a miracle."

"I'd call it luck," Longarm said.

Neither of them had taken their eyes off the *rurales*, who were coming into normal rifle range now. Longarm slid his rifle into the opening between the seat and the top of the wagon bed and fired one shot, which missed. He held his fire, watching the deadly race between Jorge and the *rurales*, who had stopped riding in zigzags now that they were no longer under fire from the wagon. The *rurales* were slowly overtaking Jorge, but he was within fifty yards of the wagon.

Without turning his head, Longarm said, "We've waited long enough, Angelita. Start shooting now!"

While he spoke, Longarm had been sighting on one of the *rurales*, following his zigzag moves until he was sure that the man did not vary his pattern. He squeezed off the shot, and the man fell. Angelita found a target and fired. Her shot was low. She missed the *rurale*, but his horse went down, throwing the rider. Her second shot kicked up dust just short of the *rurale* as he was crawling to shelter himself behind his dead horse. Before she could get off another round, the *rurale* was behind the animal's carcass.

Jorge was now within a dozen yards of the wagon. He raised up in the saddle to look back, and an instant later flung his arms out, dropped the reins, and fell to the ground. Angelita screamed and lowered her rifle.

"Don't stop shooting, damn it!" Longarm snapped. "Jorge's safer on the ground than he'd be on his horse."

Slugs from the rifles of the four *rurales* remaining on horseback were buzzing around Longarm and Angelita now, thudding into the wagon's high sides, but the range was too great for the bullets to tear through the inch-thick boards. Longarm got the leading *rurale* in his sights, swung the muzzle of his rifle until he was certain of his aim, and squeezed the trigger. The man fell backward over his horse's rump.

Almost at the same time, Angelita fired and dropped still another of the attackers. The *rurale* whose horse she'd killed had left cover. He was running for the rifle he'd dropped when his mount went down. He reached the rifle and picked it up, and Angelita swung her gun to cover him when a rifle cracked and the running man fell forward on his face, his weapon spinning from his hands. Longarm looked beyond the *rurales* and saw a lone horseman galloping up. There was something familiar about the newcomer, but the remaining *rurales* were getting closer, so Longarm gave them his full attention.

There were now only two *rurales* attacking, and they had gone back to the zigzag riding pattern they'd used at the beginning of their onslaught. Longarm had not counted his shots, but he knew that he had only four or five rounds left in the Winchester's magazine. He tried repeatedly to anticipate the moves of the remaining *rurales*, but they had survived because they were expert horsemen who had mastered the technique of the zigzag movements that were foiling Longarm's efforts.

By now the strange rider was close enough to the *rurales* to take a more active part in the fight. He swung in a quarter-circle and rode at them from their flank. His move canceled the advantage their zigzag riding had given them over Longarm, in his head-on position. The newcomer's rifle cracked and one of the remaining *rurales* fell off his mount and lay still.

When his companion heard the shot and saw his flank man

drop to sprawl lifeless on the ground, he reined in. Longarm had been waiting for just such a chance. He triggered the Winchester. The last *rurale's* back arched and his body jerked when the slug went home. Then he slumped and slid to the ground while his horse continued to gallop ahead.

"*Gracias a Dios!*" Angelita said. "Now we can attend to Jorge. Hurry, Longarm! Let us see whether he still lives!"

Vaulting into the wagon seat, Longarm picked up the reins and geed the mule ahead. Angelita scrambled up to join him. For the first time, Longarm had a chance to get a good look at the rider who'd appeared from nowhere and played such a key part in swinging the fight's outcome. The man was now close enough for Longarm to see his face plainly.

"Watch what you say when that fellow riding up gets here," he cautioned Angelita.

"You know him?" she asked, taking her eyes off Jorge long enough to glance quickly at the newcomer.

"I sure do. His name's Will Travers and he's a Texas Ranger."

Facing Longarm, Angelita asked, "Is there going to be more trouble now?"

"Hard to say. All we can do is wait and find out."

They reached the spot where Jorge lay, and Longarm reined in the mule. Angelita jumped from the wagon with Longarm close behind. They bent over the young Montero's recumbent form. A bloodstain was spreading slowly up Jorge's shirt from his waist. Longarm pulled up the shirt. The ragged edges of an exit wound oozed blood just below his waist.

"It's a shallow wound," Longarm said. "I don't think he's badly hurt. But he's going to have to stay quiet for a while."

While he spoke, Longarm was tearing strips off Jorge's shirt. When Travers rode up, Longarm and Angelita were busy bandaging Jorge's wound as best they could. Travers dismounted and came to kneel beside them. He'd changed little, Longarm thought; the Ranger's tall form bore not an ounce of spare flesh, though there were a few more wrinkles framing his almost colorless blue eyes and thin lips.

"Howdy, Longarm," he said.

"Will." Longarm nodded. "I'd shake with you, only right this minute I'm a mite busy."

"I'll take the will for the deed," Travers said.

Longarm went on, "If you got any water in that canteen hanging on your saddle, we could use some."

97

"Sure." Travers got the canteen from his horse and handed it to Longarm. "Looks like I got here just about the right time. You and the lady'd done the rough work, and all I had to do was help you put on the finishing touches."

"We were right glad to see you, though," Longarm said.

"Oh, you were doing better'n holding your own," Travers told him. "Which is about what I'd've expected of you."

Longarm tucked the end of the last wrapping of bandages in place and stood up. Angelita stayed on her knees beside Jorge, cradling his head in her arms.

"Jorge's going to be all right," Longarm assured her. "His heart's beating good. He oughta be coming around pretty soon, if he didn't get a bang on his head when he fell."

"I'd imagine you'll want to put him in the wagon," Travers suggested. "It won't hurt him as much if we do it before he comes around. I'll just give you a hand."

"Me and Angelita can handle it, Will," Longarm replied quickly. "No use in you getting all bloodied up."

"It wouldn't be the first time," the Ranger answered. "And it's easier for three to lift him up than two."

Longarm saw no way to avoid it. He told Angelita, "You go and drop the tailgate so we can get him into the wagon."

When they began lifting Jorge into the wagon bed, Longarm kept his eyes on Travers. He saw the Ranger's eyes flick over the dirt-crusted leather sacks and widen in surprise, but Travers said nothing and Longarm offered no explanation. They laid Jorge in the space between the sacks and the side of the wagon, and just as they were trying to arrange his position to make him comfortable he regained consciousness.

Jorge's eyes opened. He moaned softly, then realized what was happening and asked, *"Los rurales, Angelita, que pasen?"*

"Todos son muerte," she replied. *"Y su herido no esta grave."*

"Just lay quiet while we get you to your house," Longarm told him. "We'll talk about what to do later on."

"We must talk now," Jorge gasped. "It will not be safe for us to go to the house. There may be—" He saw Travers for the first time, and stopped abruptly. Looking at Angelita, he asked, *"Quien es esto?"*

"A friend of Longarm's," she said. "He is a Texas Ranger."

Jorge began. "Has he come to—"

Longarm broke in quickly. "We ain't had time to find out

98

how it was he just popped up outa noplace." He said to Travers, "These folks are Angelita and Jorge Montero, Will. They live in that green house in the little settlement yonder."

"I've heard their names before." Travers nodded. "But, like you said, we can wait till later to talk."

Longarm looked at Travers, his face drawing into a thoughtful frown. "I got a hunch you know a lot more'n their names, Will. Am I right?"

"Like they say down along the Rio Grande, Longarm, *tal vez que si, tal vez que no,*" the Ranger answered. He waved a hand at the bodies sprawled on the ground, the horses wandering aimlessly, the little group of spectators who had gathered at the edge of the *casería*. "Before it gets too dark, I'll have to clean up this mess, but I'll get some of those people who've been watching to give me a hand. While I'm doing that, the best thing you can do is get your friends home. I'll stop in for a talk as soon as I've finished here."

Longarm had anticipated Travers's suggestion and had seen no alternative but to accept it. Putting the best face he could on the situation, he said, "That'll be fine, Will. And, while you're cleaning up, that big bay over yonder is my horse. If you'll keep an eye on my saddle gear and bring the horse along when you come to the Monteros' house, I'll be obliged."

"Sure," Travers replied. "We'll have a talk then."

After Travers had ridden off, Angelita told Longarm, "I do not feel comfortable going to our house now. There must have been a spy in the *casería* watching us for the *rurales*. If there was one, there may be others."

"I ain't one to say I told you so," Longarm said. "But you can see now why I been worrying."

"You were right, of course," Angelita admitted. "But what of the arrangements we had planned?"

Jorge told his sister, "You must see what I see, Angelita. We can no longer do as we had decided. Now we must do what *Tio* Felipe intended to."

"You sure that's what you want to do, Jorge?" Longarm asked.

"Yes." Jorge hesitated, then went on, "Angelita and I must talk privately, Longarm, if you do not object."

"Not a bit. She'll be riding back there with you anyhow, while I drive the wagon to your house." As an afterthought, Longarm added, "Don't worry about there being a *rurales'* spy running around loose, Jorge. With me and Will both here, there ain't nobody going to bother you."

While he was driving the mile or so to the *casería*, Longarm paid little attention to the low-voiced conversation between Angelita and Jorge in the wagon bed. He was having a silent conversation with himself.

Old son, Will Travers showing up is a right sure sign that things is getting a mite too tangled up for comfort.

That damn newspaper in San Antonio's to blame, of course. It give away the whole show: body, bones, and blood.

Not that there's anything wrong with Will. You and him got along most of the time when you joined up trying to catch Sim Blount, and chased the son of a bitch over half of Texas.

But Will's a Ranger before he's anything else and him showing up here means the state of Texas knows about Santa Anna's gold and aims to try to grab it.

And now that Will knows the gold's been found, he'll be doing his damnedest to make sure Texas gets it, just like you'll be doing your damnedest to hold on to it for the U.S. Treasury.

And you ain't found out a thing yet about them two Treasury agents somebody murdered, which is why you got sent here in the first place.

About the only thing you can say for this case, old son, is that you're going to have to play your cards real close to your chest and hope it don't get down to the point where you got no choice but drawing to a damned inside straight.

Longarm pulled the wagon around to the back of the Montero house and stopped under the shed roof of the stable. The back door of the house was open and sagging on broken hinges. Angelita gasped when she saw it.

"Someone has broken in!" she said.

"Likely whoever's been spying on you brought the *rurales* here first," Longarm said. "And they busted in to see if you'd brought the gold here yet. Don't worry about that now. Let's get Jorge inside and into bed, so I can try to fix up that bullet hole."

Inside, the house was a shambles. In the kitchen, cupboard doors yawned open, as did the door of the oven on the stove. The dining room had been hastily searched. Even the mattresses in both bedrooms had been slashed to see if anything had been hidden in their stuffing.

"Bastardos! Hijos de cabrones!" Jorge grated hoarsely when

he saw the damage as Longarm and Angelita helped him to his bedroom.

"Quietase, Jorge!" Angelita commanded. She'd found a pillowcase among the tangle of bed linen on the floor and was ripping it into strips for a fresh bandage. *No hay importancia. Vaminos ahorita, y no volveramos."*

Longarm understood the few key words he needed to grasp what she was saying, but he made no comment and asked no questions. He finished replacing the bandages and led Angelita outside.

"You got anything that'll ease Jorge's pain, maybe put him to sleep?" he asked.

"There is a bottle of laudanum somewhere, if I can find it."

"Look for it, then. I can't do much else for him. I'll go out and keep an eye on the gold if you'll look after him."

"Of course."

"Did I hear right when you was talking to Jorge?" Longarm asked. "You're figuring to leave here?"

"Jorge must have a doctor. You saw what I did when you put on the new bandage."

"It don't look good," Longarm agreed. "Still bleeding, and the place around the bullet hole's getting red."

"Besides—" Angelita's gesture took in the wreckage of the house. "I would not want to stay here now, even if we had a good reason. But will your Ranger friend allow us to leave and take Santa Anna's gold with us?"

"I'll know that better after I talk to him. And I figure it'll be better if me and Will talk private."

"But you will tell me at once what he says?"

"Why, sure. It'll help when I'm talking to him if you and Jorge make up your minds about the gold."

"Yes. I will talk with Jorge before he sleeps."

Longarm's talk with the Ranger was held late that night in the wrecked living room, after Travers had returned from his job of searching the bodies and saddlebags of the dead *rurales,* and arranging for the people of the *casería* to bury the bodies. By some quirk—either the *rurales* had been too engrossed in searching the house or else they had no taste for Maryland rye—the bottle of Tom Moore had survived the ransacking. Longarm and Travers sat side by side on the backless, armless divan, the whiskey bottle on the floor between them.

"I guess it's time for us to level with each other, Will,"

Longarm said, after he'd listened to Travers's account of his activities. "We done it before, so we oughta be able to do it now."

"Oh, I'm not forgetting we were on the same side before," Travers replied. "At least, we were until you took out with our prisoner and started for the New Mexico border."

"Now, don't forget, we'd agreed fair and square to go our separate ways and let the best man win. Besides, you gave me a real bad time when I tried to get Blount outa Texas."

Travers grinned. "I'm not carrying a grudge, Longarm. What happened before's over and finished."

"I'm glad to hear you say that, Will. Slate's clean, then?"

"Now, that depends. I know what's in that wagon out there."

"Oh, I could tell that right off. But I'm not as concerned about the gold as I am about that young fellow lying in there with a bullet hole through his guts, needing a doctor as fast as I can get him to Houston."

"You can take him to Houston any time you please, and I'll give you the name of a doctor there who's real good at treating gunshot wounds," Travers said, "on one condition."

"I know what you're about to say, but go on and say it."

"Sure you do. I get the gold to take to Austin. We've been hunting it ourselves, ever since we started investigating a murder case and found just by accident that the U.S. government was going to try to grab what by rights belongs to Texas."

"You mean the two Treasury agents that got killed? They're why I'm here, when you come down to it," Longarm said. "Billy Vail sent me to find whoever killed them."

"You don't have to worry about that," Travers told him. "If you hadn't shot those two *rurales* in San Antonio, we'd have had them either in jail or in coffins a day or two later. They're the ones who killed your Treasury men."

"Well, seeing as I saved you Rangers some trouble, I don't guess you'll balk at returning the favor," Longarm said.

"If you mean am I going to let you get away with those sacks of gold you've got in the wagon outside, you know damned well I can't do that, Longarm. The gold belongs to Texas, not to the U.S. Treasury."

"Look here, Will, I got a proposition for you, and I'll lay it out fair and square."

"Go ahead. I'm listening."

"Whoever that gold belongs to ain't something you and me

can settle between ourselves. We're way down on the bottom of the heap when it comes down to deciding something like that."

"Well, you're making sense so far." Travers nodded.

"Now, I got an idea that'll save us both a lot of grief. If I put that gold into a bank in Houston, what do you suppose would happen?" Longarm asked.

"Why, the Texas comptroller or the attorney general or the treasurer would go to court to get it for the state, of course."

"And if I let you put it in a bank, what'd happen?"

"I'd guess the U.S. Treasury would go to court." Travers stopped and chuckled. "By God, Longarm, you got an idea there!" Then he shook his head. "I don't know, though. There's an old saying about possession being nine points of the law."

"That don't apply if I put it in the bank in my name."

Travers stared at Longarm. "Wait a minute. If you were to do that, some little government lawyer that's not dry behind the ears might say you were trying to steal if for yourself. Hell, Longarm, it might even cost you your badge."

"Not if I come up with a good enough reason for doing it."

"Can you do that?"

"Not right this minute. I can by the time I get back to Denver, though. And it'd save you and me from getting into a wrangle over it right now."

Travers was silent for a moment. Then he said, "Well, if you've got the gall to do it, I've got the gall to go along with you. Let's shake on it!"

Chapter 12

"We're just about there," Longarm said over his shoulder to Angelita, who was riding in the wagon bed with her brother. Longarm could not see Jorge, but there was no need to look at him. Longarm had seen many wounded men, and when he'd checked the wound before they left he realized that the bullet which had passed through Jorge's body had done more damage than they'd thought. Jorge's need for the care of a skilled doctor was growing more urgent with each passing minute. "In another half mile or so, we'll be at the first houses," Longarm told Angelita. "How's Jorge holding up?"

"His fever is worse," she replied. "And the laudanum is wearing off. He moans more often."

"He'll be all right, though. When Will Travers saw he was going to have to stay back at the settlement another day or so and couldn't come along with us, he gave me the name of the best doctor there is in Houston."

"But Jorge is suffering so much, Longarm. I am afraid for his life."

"Now, quit fretting," Longarm said. He kept his voice calm, though he realized that Jorge was indeed in bad shape. "Will said this doctor is the best there is when it comes to looking after a man that's been gut-shot."

"I only hope we get there in time," Angelita sighed. "It seems that we've been traveling forever."

The progress of the heavily loaded wagon had indeed been slow. They'd left the *casería* at daybreak, as soon as the sky had brightened enough for Longarm to pick a course over the flat coastal plain. He'd pulled up twice for a few minutes to rest the mule, and they'd made another brief stop when Jorge had begun to stir restlessly, to allow Angelita to trickle another spoonful of laudanum down her brother's throat.

Now the sun hung directly overhead, and Angelita unfolded the wet cloth she'd kept on Jorge's forehead and rearranged its folds to cover his eyes as well. Ahead of them, between the wagon and the yellow waters of the narrowing bayou, Longarm saw the brown streak that marked the beginning of the graded road. He turned the mule to get on it as soon as possible, and with a firm surface under the wagon wheels the animal moved faster.

There were no street signs, but the clear directions Longarm had gotten from Will Travers enabled him to identify the turns that led him onto Brazos Street, and within minutes after they'd entered the little town, he was pulling up in front of the white two-story house that bore a sign: DR. S.T. WATKINS. OFFICE & SURGERY.

"I'll go get the doctor," Longarm told Angelita. "We'll need some help to get Jorge up the steps without jarring him."

A few moments after Longarm twirled the ratchet bell set in the door panel, the door swung open and Longarm glanced down what seemed to be a deserted hallway. An attention-getting cough drew his eyes down.

"Tell your daddy—" Longarm began, before realizing that the diminutive individual in the doorway was not a boy, but an exceedingly small man. His head came only halfway up Longarm's chest, but from his bearded cheeks and the white jacket he wore Longarm deduced that he must be Watkins. He said hastily, "I'm sorry. I reckon you're the doctor?"

"I'm Watkins. What's your trouble?" Without waiting for Longarm to answer, the doctor went on, "If you've just got a bellyache you can come in and wait while I finish my lunch."

"There ain't a thing wrong with me, Doctor. My name's Long, deputy United States marshal outa Denver. I got a gutshot man out there in that wagon, and Will Travers said you're the best doctor there is to take care of him."

"Travers, eh? And I suppose you want me to save this fellow so you can hang him? Why not just let him die peacefully?"

"This man ain't a prisoner," Longarm began. "He's—"

"Never mind," Watkins snapped. "If he has a belly wound, a few minutes can make a lot of difference. Bring him in. Or is he too badly hurt to walk?"

Longarm replied, "He's asleep. We been giving him laudanum since last night. But I'll carry him in for you."

"No, no!" Watkins said quickly. "I don't want his abdomen bending. Come along. There's a stretcher in my surgery."

Jorge moaned softly but did not regain consciousness when

105

they placed him on the stretcher and carried him down the long hall to the operating table that stood in Watkins's surgery.

"I want you two out of here," Watkins told Longarm and Angelita. "You can wait in the sitting room."

"How long will it—" Longarm began.

Watkins cut him short. "An hour, perhaps less."

"Will he be all right, Doctor?" Angelita asked.

"Madam, that's a final judgment, and only God can make it. But unless he's in worse condition than he seems to be, I think I can save him. Now, get out so I can go to work."

Longarm lighted one cheroot after another and Angelita sat telling the beads of her rosary for what seemed an interminable time before Dr. Watkins came in, wiping his hands on a towel. He was smiling, and they both felt better at once.

"Your young man will be all right," Watkins told Angelita.

"Can I talk to him?" she asked.

"Certainly not! He won't be conscious for another hour or more. And he can't be moved for three or four days. I'll keep him here in my convalescing room."

"But you're sure he's all right?" Longarm asked.

"Of course he is," Watkins replied impatiently. "The wound itself isn't bad; it's the infection of bruised flesh bullets seem to cause that kills from wounds of that kind."

"We better go find a hotel to stay in tonight, then," Longarm told Angelita.

"Come back just before supper time," Watkins suggested. "I think he'll be able to talk to you a few minutes then."

As they drove toward the business section, Longarm asked Angelita, "You got enough money to see you and Jorge through all this? Because if you ain't—"

"I have no need for more," she broke in. "The *rurales* did not find the hiding place Jorge fixed when they stormed through our house. But you are kind and thoughtful to offer, Longarm."

"I wasn't offering such a much, when you come down to it, but I figured if you needed some, there wouldn't be anything wrong with changing a few of them gold pieces into U.S. money. It'd just be a sorta advance on what you'll get out of the gold when all the smoke settles down."

"How long will it take to settle down?"

"There ain't any way to say, Angelita," Longarm replied. "Once the government starts winding out red tape, it seems like nobody's got brains enough to stop."

"I suppose it does not matter," she said, and shrugged. "Jorge and I have agreed to do as *Tio* Felipe intended. We will wait."

"It don't seem like there's much else to do," Longarm said. "The best thing we can do is go get settled into a hotel. Then, soon as I find a barbershop and get shaved so I don't look like a mangy saddle tramp, I'll haul these bags on down to the bank."

"When Jorge and I first came here with *Tio* Felipe, we stayed for the night at the Ashby House on Congress Street," Angelita told him. "They do not close their doors to the *gente*, as do some hotels in Texas."

"That's where we'll go, then. You can rest while I put the gold where it'll be safe."

After Longarm had explained to Cornelius Worsham, president of the Houston Commercial Bank, that he wished to deposit Santa Anna's gold pieces in a special account under his own name, the banker looked at him with a puzzled frown.

"Are you sure you have the authority to make this kind of deposit, Marshal Long?" Worsham asked.

"I ain't a bit sure, Mr. Worsham. The trouble is, I ain't got official authority to deposit the gold for anybody else," Longarm said. "You see, Chief Marshal Vail—he's my boss up in Denver—just sent me down here to find out who killed a couple of U.S. Treasury agents. He didn't figure on me turning up all them bags of gold."

"It strikes me that you could send a telegram to your chief in Denver and ask for the authority."

Before he replied, Longarm took out a cheroot and lighted it. He said blandly, "Well, now, Mr. Worsham, if I was to do that, Chief Marshal Vail would have to send a wire to the Justice Department in Washington, and then they'd likely have to find out from the Treasury Department whether they wanted to handle things that way, and the Treasury Department lawyers would have to sit down with the Justice Department lawyers, and I'd be cooling my heels here in Houston for a month or more while they made up their minds."

Worsham smiled. "Yes. I've experiences delays myself when government red tape has had to be unwound." The banker thought for a moment, then nodded. "Well, Marshal Long, I don't see any reason why we shouldn't accept your deposit.

107

We'll simply enter the deposit in your name with a notation that the ownership of the gold pieces may be a matter of dispute between the federal government and the state of Texas. Of course, you understand that you'll be the only person who can withdraw them when the dispute is settled. Is that satisfactory?"

"Suits me fine, Mr. Worsham. I said fair and square that the gold ain't mine, so you can see I ain't trying to put nothing over on anybody."

"Very well." Worsham nodded. "Now, how many of those gold coins did you say there are?"

"I don't recall that I said," Longarm replied. "Because what with fighting the *rurales* and all, and Mr. Montero getting shot, we ain't had time to count 'em."

Worsham took a deposit card from a pigeonhole in his rolltop desk and reached for a pen. "Our tellers would have to count them in any case, of if you'll just give me a round figure as an estimate, I'll have the deposit record entered accurately."

"Well, if I didn't get around to mentioning it before, there's fifty bags of twenty-peso gold pieces, and we figured there's about five hundred of 'em to the bag," Longarm said casually.

"Then your deposit would consist of—" The banker's hand stopped in midair. "Good Lord, Marshal! That totals a quarter of a million dollars in American money!"

"I expect that's a pretty close figure," Longarm agreed.

"But that's a small fortune!"

"I don't expect it's too big for your bank to handle, is it?" Longarm asked innocently.

"No, of course not! But, Marshal Long, I'm going to insist that you stay here and witness the counting."

"Why, I don't mind doing that a bit, Mr. Worsham," Longarm replied. "To tell you the truth, I'm sorta curious about how many of them gold pieces there is, myself."

With three tellers working at the job, the count of Santa Anna's gold was finished in a little more than an hour. Worsham handed the tally sheet to Longarm.

"Your estimate was very close, Marshal," the banker said.

"By our count, there were twenty-four thousand, seven hundred and eighty coins."

Longarm nodded. "I'm satisfied. Now, if you'll just hang onto that gold till it's settled who it belongs to, I'll be much obliged."

"Don't worry," Worsham assured him. "You're the only person who can withdraw it."

With the deposit receipt for Santa Anna's gold safely tucked away in his wallet, Longarm returned to the Ashby House, where Angelita had remained after they had signed in. She was waiting for him in the carpeted lobby, an anxious expression drawing her face into a frown.

"Was there trouble at the bank, that you were gone so long?" she asked.

"Not a bit. It just took 'em longer to count the gold than I'd figured," Longarm replied. "And I guess you're as hungry as I am by now. Why don't we find a restaurant and get ourselves a bite to eat?"

"Would it be too early to return to the doctor's, if we were to go there first, Longarm? I worry about Jorge."

"Well, the doctor said for us to come back before supper, and I guess it's about that time by now. Sure. We'll go see how he's doing first."

Dr. Watkins nodded reassuringly when he opened the door to Longarm's ring. "You haven't a thing to worry about, Miss Montero," he told Angelita. "You won't be able to talk to your brother—the anesthetic hasn't worn off yet. But come on down the hall and look at him, if you like."

Longarm and Angelita followed Watkins down the long hallway. He opened a door and beckoned for them to go in. The room was large enough to contain three narrow beds, and in one of them Jorge lay sleeping soundly. His face was pale but peaceful, no longer drawn with pain.

"You got him here just in time," the doctor said. "Another few hours and you'd have been too late. However, I'll have to keep him here for several days—perhaps even a week."

"As long as he's cured." Angelita smiled. "Time is not of great importance, now." Smiling happily, she turned to Longarm. "Suddenly I am very hungry. Let us go now and have our dinner!"

With Jorge and the gold both safe, dinner turned into an event. Midway through the meal, Angelita turned to Longarm and said, "I am happier tonight than I have been for many weeks, Longarm. Should we not celebrate by finishing our dinner with a bottle of champagne?"

"Well, I ain't tasted none of that fizzy stuff yet that'll hold

109

a candle to good Maryland rye, but if you'd like to have some, we sure can. And I don't imagine it'll hurt me none to drink a glass or two with you."

As they were drinking the last of the champagne, Angelita looked at Longarm over the bubbles that were popping on the surface of the wine in her glass. "I suppose you will not stay here longer, now that the gold has been found," she said.

"I can't stay, Angelita. I found out who killed the two Treasury men, and Santa Anna's gold's put away safe. Now I got to head back to Denver."

"But what about the rest of the gold?"

Longarm stared at her, his jaw dropping. "I guess I don't follow you. Are you saying we didn't dig up all the gold that Santa Anna buried?"

Angelita shook her head. "We found all the gold that was buried here. But that is not all there was."

"I never heard about there being more, except when you was telling about your grandmother and Santa Anna carrying some away with 'em when they started back to Mexico."

"That is what I am speaking of now," she said quietly.

"Now, they couldn't've got away with much, Angelita," Longarm said with a frown. "Gold's too heavy. The most they'd have been able to tote in their clothes was a hundred pounds or so apiece."

"That was only what remained after Santa Anna and my grandmother took the padding from the seats and seat backs of the carriage and put gold pieces in its place."

"How'd they find the time to do all that?"

Angelita shrugged. "I do not know, but Grandmother said that they worked at the job for many hours, hiding the gold and then putting the upholstery back in place."

"Your grandma never told anybody else about that?"

"I do not think so. Only my grandfather, of course, and my father when he was a small boy."

"And after they'd loaded as much as the carriage would hold they still had what we found left over?"

"Yes. You see, Santa Anna's plan was to carry all the gold with him when he went back to Mexico. And you saw how much they were forced to leave behind."

"What happened to the gold they took back to Mexico, then?" Longarm asked. "All of it was spent a long time ago, I suppose."

"You are wrong," Angelita replied. "Santa Anna was afraid of what would happen to him when he returned to the capital, with most of his army killed by General Houston's men and Texas lost forever. Mexico does not treat its defeated generals kindly, Longarm."

"You still ain't said what happened to the gold."

"That is because I am not sure."

"But you think you know?"

Angelita nodded. "Santa Anna did not carry the gold all the way to Mexico City. Somewhere he stopped and buried what he and Grandmother had hidden in the carriage and in their clothing."

"In Texas?"

"That is what I do not know, Longarm. All I am sure of is that the gold was hidden somewhere close to where he crossed, near where the Rio del Diablo flows into the Rio Grande."

"At the mouth of the Devil's River?" Longarm frowned. "But that'd be way north of Laredo."

"Yes, of course. Santa Anna's army marched back on the old military road that has long since been abandoned."

"So you think the rest of the gold's still hid someplace along the Rio Grande?"

"Jorge and I were planning to look for it after we found what was buried on the battlefield," she said quietly.

"And now you figure I oughta go with you and look for it?"

Angelita set down her empty glass. "No. I must stay here and take care of Jorge. He will not be able to travel for many weeks, I am sure. But you would not want to leave your job only partly finished, would you?"

"I ain't right sure that'd be included in my job," Longarm told her thoughtfully. "Except if word gets out that there's a lot more of Santa Anna's gold left hid someplace, it'd stir up another ruckus that I'd likely get sent back here to settle."

"My aunt, Doña Pia Belinda de Cruz, lives in a town called Guerra. It is near the place where the gold is supposed to have been buried," Angelita said. "She could be of much help to you, Longarm."

"I'm going to have to figure out what's best for me to do." Longarm frowned. "I was aiming to start back to Denver soon as Will Travers gets here. But I'll admit, you gave me something to think about. We'll talk about it more tomorrow."

111

Chapter 13

Under a cloudless evening sky which was turning into an unbelievable shade of blue by a full moon that made the night almost as bright as day, Longarm and Angelita walked slowly back to the Ashby House when they left the restaurant.

On the second floor, as Angelita unlocked the door of her room, she said, "You must think me ungrateful, Longarm. You have done so much for me, and I have not said thank you even a single time."

"What I done don't call for no special thanks, Angelita. It ain't no more'n what my job calls for me to do."

"No. It is much more. And I have no words to tell you how greatly I thank you," she replied softly.

"Well, you're sure more'n welcome. Now, we both had a long day, and we better turn in."

"I should be tired, I know," Angelita replied. "And I will be, I'm sure, when I go to bed. Good night, Longarm."

"Good night, Angelita. We'll talk about that other gold cache tomorrow."

Longarm watched Angelita go into her room and close the door. His room was just across the hall. He stepped to the door and entered it. Lighting a cheroot, he set about his methodical bedtime preparations. Hanging up his long black coat, he took his watch and derringer from their pockets and laid them on a chair beside the bed. He unbuckled his gunbelt and hung it on the bedpost, where the Colt would dangle close to his pillow and be within easy reach of his gun hand.

As Longarm turned away from the bed, his saddlebags and bedroll in the corner caught his eye. He stepped over and picked up the saddlebags. The bottle of Tom Moore, rolled up in his spare set of balbriggans for protection, was miraculously unbroken after having survived so many lumps and bumps. More important, it was still a quarter full. Closing his strong teeth on the cork, Longarm extracted it with a practiced twist of his wrist. He tilted the bottle and took a gurgling, satisfying swallow.

Shrugging out of his shirt, he levered off his boots and stepped out of his trousers and balbriggans in one swift move. Stretching luxuriously, he dropped the butt of his cheroot into the spittoon that stood by the bureau, turned out the coal-oil lamp, and crawled into bed.

On most nights, Longarm fell asleep the instant his head hit the pillow, but tonight sleep eluded him. *Old son*, he mused as he stared into the darkness, *maybe you took a step that's a mite too long for your legs when you stowed away that gold like you done today. And if you take out for the Rio Grande without telling Billy Vail what's on your mind, you could be stepping quite a ways further. But as long as there's some of Santa Anna's gold that ain't been found, there's going to be people after it, which means trouble all the way around. So you might as well buckle down and wind it all up and hand it to Billy Vail in a clean, pretty package.*

Longarm yawned and closed his eyes. He was drifting away to sleep when a quick tattoo of knocks on his door brought him instantly alert. Grabbing the butt of his Colt, Longarm stepped to the door and opened it a crack, shielding his naked body behind it. Angelita, wearing only a thin nightgown, her dark hair unbound and streaming down her back, stood in the dimly lighted hall.

"Longarm!" she gasped. "Someone has tried to kill me!"

"Wait just a second," Longarm replied. He reached for his coat and slid it on, then stepped into the hall.

"What happened?" he asked.

"I was asleep when a noise woke me up. I looked up and saw a man standing by my bed. He had a knife and was raising it to stab me. I rolled out of the way and when he saw that he had missed me, he left through the window."

"You stay here," Longarm said. "I'll go have a look."

He stepped across the hall. The door to Angelita's room was open. He peered through the door, his Colt held ready. When he saw no one, he went in. Moonlight streaming through the tall window opposite the door made the room almost as bright as the hall. The window curtains were swaying in the mild night breeze and he stepped over to look out.

There was no one in sight on the street, but the shed roof of the veranda that ran across the front of the hotel was only a few feet below the bottom of the window. Longarm could see how easily an intruder could have reached the window and climbed in. He looked at the bed. Its covers were thrown back and the sheet and mattress had been slashed in a long, straight cut.

Behind him, Angelita asked, "Did you see anyone!"

"Not a soul. The street's plumb bare. I don't guess you got a look at whoever it was?"

"No. The light was behind him." As Angelita spoke, Longarm turned to face her. With the moonlit window behind him, he could see the dark buds of her full breasts and the vee above her thighs through the thin fabric of her nightgown. She went on, "I could see him only as I see you now—a dark outline. But I saw the moonlight glittering on the blade of his knife."

"It'd be easy enough for somebody to've followed us here, or found out where we was, I guess," Longarm said thoughtfully. "But I don't imagine he'll be back tonight to try again. I'll shut the window and you can go back to bed."

"I do not think I would feel safe in this room tonight," Angelita said. "Can I come into your room, Longarm? I will sit in a chair, or—"

"You can sleep in the bed," he told her. "I'll curl up on the floor."

"I can't take your bed!" Angelita protested.

"It wouldn't be the first time," he said, taking her arm and leading her across the hall. "It don't bother me a bit."

At the door of his room, Angelita stopped. Longarm did not urge her to enter, but took a pillow from the bed and put it on the floor on the opposite side of the room.

"There ain't much reason for me to light the lamp," he told Angelita. "You come on in and go to bed. I'll lock the door. But there ain't nobody going to harm you now."

"As long as I am with you, I won't be afraid," she said.

When Angelita was in bed, Longarm closed the door, plunging the room into darkness. He stood at the door until his eyes grew accustomed to the dimness and made his way to the wall where he'd put his pillow. Still wearing his coat, he lay down. After the bed, the floor seemed hard, but not any harder than other floors on which he'd slept. Longarm felt sleepy now. He'd reached the stage measured in split seconds where wakefulness is replaced by sleep when Angelita spoke.

"Longarm."

Jounced back to wakefulness, he replied, "I'm right here. What's wrong?"

"Nothing is wrong, except that I cannot sleep now."

"You're still upset because of that fellow breaking into your room," Longarm told her.

"No. I just feel more alive than I have for weeks. I feel the way I did right after supper, when the champagne was making my blood tingle through my veins. I didn't really want our celebration to end when we finished dinner."

"There's a bottle of whiskey on the bureau," Longarm said, purposely being obtuse. "It's pretty strong stuff. It'll make you tingle again."

"You're teasing me now, Longarm," Angelita said. "I don't want a drink." Her voice dropped to a whisper. "You know what I want. Come to bed with me, Longarm. I need you."

"You're just upset," Longarm said. He was not surprised by her invitation. He had seen other women react in similar fashion after a long period when they'd been under great tension came to a sudden end. "You'll feel different in the morning."

"No. I'm old enough to know what I want, Longarm." She hesitated for a moment, then went on, "If you think I am just a young girl who knows nothing about men, you are wrong. I have been with men in bed before."

This time Longarm was surprised. He was familiar with the rigid, almost conventual seclusion in which girls of upper-class Mexican family were usually kept until they married.

When he did not reply, Angelita said, "Not many times, but a few. Does that make you think less of me?"

"Not a bit."

Longarm said nothing more, nor did he make any move toward accepting Angelita's invitation. In a few seconds he heard a rustling from the bed, followed by the soft sound of bare feet on the carpeted floor. He looked up and saw Angelita standing beside him. She was little more than a white shape in the darkness. He could see even less of her than he had in the moonlit room across the hall.

Angelita whispered, "You will not come to me, so I have come to you." She dropped on her knees beside him. "But we would find the bed softer."

Longarm obeyed his hunch, which told him that anything

115

he said at that particular moment would be wrong.

Her voice troubled, she asked, "Am I so ugly, with this big nose of mine, that you have no wish to touch me?"

"It ain't that, Angelita," he replied. "There ain't a thing wrong with your nose. You're a real attractive woman."

"But not attractive to you?"

"Now, that ain't what I said."

"Then what is wrong, Longarm?"

Longarm felt Angelita's hand wander over the fabric of his coat and slip inside. Her warm fingers touched his crotch, weighing and exploring.

Longarm could almost see the smile that he heard in her voice. "No," she said. "Nothing is wrong."

Angelita's fingers closed around him and squeezed in a soft caress. Longarm felt himself stirring. She leaned forward and let the tips of her firm breasts brush over his freshly shaven face, and he felt her shiver gently. Her hand was bringing him erect now, and from the manner in which her fingers moved Longarm was sure that Angelita had been truthful when she'd confessed that she was no stranger to men.

Longarm's hands found her breasts and his iron-hard fingertips rubbed their pebbled buds and firmly jutting centers. Angelita's hand closed convulsively around him and the intensity of her shivering increased as he continued to caress her with his hands. She bent forward and her lips sought Longarm's and found them. After a moment he felt her tongue thrusting, questing, and he opened his lips to it.

They held their embrace for a long moment, until Angelita stirred and began to unbutton Longarm's coat with her free hand. He sat up, carrying her slight body with him.

"You were right a minute ago," Longarm said. "We'll be a lot more comfortable in bed."

Longarm stood up, lifting Angelita with him as though she weighed no more than a feather. She released her grip on his shaft, now swollen and erect, and began unbuttoning the coat. They reached the bed. Longarm laid her down and shrugged the coat off as he straightened up.

Angelita looked up at him, her face a blur of white broken by the darkness of her eyes and lips. She stretched her arms up as Longarm knelt above her, spread her thighs, and sighed with ecstasy as she felt him sinking into her willing body.

"Que maravilloso!" she breathed.

116

Longarm sank down slowly, his engorged shaft going further into the pulsing warmth that surrounded it. He had not reached the full depth of his deliberate penetration when Angelita' hips began to twist. Her breathing faltered and grew gusty, and a smothered gasp came from her throat now and then.

Suddenly Angelita loosed a wild cry and lifted her hips to meet his. Longarm thrust hard in a final penetration and held himself deeply in her. Angelita squirmed beneath his weight, but he held himself pressed closely to her, not moving. As she continued to twist her hips her small shrieks sounded again, their tone sharper.

After a few moments Angelita's body began rocking against Longarm's hips. Her buttocks gyrated wildly and her throaty screams rose to a crescendo. Longarm tried to stroke, but her frantic thrashings defeated his efforts. After a moment he gave up his efforts to resume his rhythmic thrusts, and simply held himself deep inside her and waited for her spasms to subside.

Gradually, Angelita's body grew quiet, and her taut muscles softened. Longarm still did not move. A sigh of contentment rippled from her lips and she looked up at him. Even in the dimness he could see her lips moving.

"I could not stop myself," she said.

"Don't worry about it. Rest a minute," Longarm told her. He leaned forward slowly, lowering his full weight on her motionless, relaxed body.

"You will not grow soft if I rest?"

"No." He moved his hips for a moment. "Does that feel like I'm fading away?"

"Ah, no! You are still big and hard. But I do not want you to wait, Longarm. Now—start once more!"

Longarm needed no encouragement. He raised himself and then lunged with a sudden swift thrust that drew a gasp of surprise mixed with pleasure from deep in Angelita's throat.

Longarm kept lunging, driving with long, steady strokes. Angelita began trembling very soon. She responded to Longarm's powerful thrusts by heaving her hips upward, her slender body shaking with increasing urgency.

She was almost matching Longarm's rapid pace when her body seized its own control. She gasped and heaved in a tempestuous convulsion. Angelita's eyes squeezed closed and her throat worked as she tried to scream but found herself breathless, unable to make a sound louder than a whisper.

Longarm did not stop, but when he felt Angelita convulse and go limp he slowed the driving pace and thrust with a new and slower rhythm. She moaned, and her eyelids fluttered. Her arms fell away from their embrace around his chest and lay limp beside her. Then her breathing became more even and her eyes opened.

Looking up at Longarm, she said, *"Ay di mi!* Never have I felt this way, Longarm! I told you I had been with men before tonight, but now I know that never before was I with a man. They were only small boys compared to you."

"If you're tired, I can stop," Longarm suggested.

"No! I have been selfish. You must still have your pleasure."

"I'm having plenty of pleasure now, Angelita."

"You will have more, though, no?"

"I will have more, yes. And we'll share it this time."

Longarm did not hurry, but he did not hold back. He thrust with a slower rhythm until he felt Angelita's muscles tightening as she began to build. When she began responding to his long, firm lunges with a rhythm of her own, he matched the rise and fall of her hips with deep, steady thrusts until she was calling on him for more.

Longarm was building, too, and he was ready this time when Angelita's cries grew wild and her hips gyrated uncontrollably. He let himself go and began jetting. He kept up a slow stroking while he drained away, and when Angelita's body grew lax he no longer held the tension in his own muscles, but lowered himself to rest on her quiet, warm body.

"We sleep now, no?" Angelita whispered.

"For a while. But we got the whole long night ahead of us."

"You will not mind if I wake you?"

"Of course not. I might even do a little waking up myself."

"Whenever you wish." Angelita smothered a little yawn. "I think I would like to be waked up by you, Longarm, so do not wait too long."

Her last words trailed off into a murmur. Longarm lay quietly for a moment until the drowsiness that had left him earlier returned. Then he slept, too.

"But whoever it was didn't come back and try to get at the Montero girl again?" Will Travers asked Longarm.

"No. There ain't no doubt in my mind who he was, though," Longarm replied. "There's more *rurales* lurking around than the ones we cut down out by the settlement the other day, Will."

They were sitting in the Lone Star Saloon, a bottle of Tom Moore and another of Kentucky Dew Bourbon on the table between them. The Ranger had arrived in Houston shortly after noon and found Longarm and Angelita at Dr. Watkins's office. Jorge was recovering, but he was still weak, and the doctor had refused even to guess when he could leave his bed. Angelita had stayed with her brother while Longarm and Travers went downtown to talk.

"I found that out, Longarm," the Ranger said. "After you left I did a little bit of prowling and persuading. There was two *rurales* sent to watch the Monteroses about six months ago. They hid out in that little settlement up west on the bayou. My guess is it didn't take 'em very long to connect up the Monteroses with that Aguierre fellow in San Antonio."

"That'd be easy enough to do, I imagine," Longarm said, "seeing as he was their uncle."

"It took us a lot longer to find that out," Travers said, the corners of his mouth turning down. "Anyhow, to cut it short, a squad of eleven hand-picked *rurales* was sent across the Rio Grande not quite two weeks ago. You killed two of 'em in that fracas in San Antonio, and we got the rest the day before yesterday. So there's still two left."

"It'd've been one of them tried to kill Angelita last night, then," Longarm said. "Too bad I let him get away."

"Hell, it wasn't your fault. But it won't take 'em long to find out that gold's safe in a bank vault, now. There's not much way to keep a thing like that from being talked about in a little town like Houston."

"Talk never hurt nobody, Will." Longarm put down his empty glass and lighted a long, slim cheroot. "I'd sooner they talked about the gold that's been found than what's still left to find."

"Maybe you better explain that." Travers frowned. "I had the idea those bags you had in the wagon was all the gold that'd been buried out along Buffalo Bayou."

"It was, as far as I know. As far as Angelita and Jorge know, too. At least, that's what they say, and I believe 'em. But it seems like Santa Anna was smarter'n old Sam Houston gave him credit for being. Angelita says the story in her family is that Santa Anna got away from that battlefield with about as much gold as he left behind. Had it hidden in his carriage."

"What happened to it, then?" Travers asked.

"That's something I still got to find out, Will. All I know right now is that it's supposed to be hidden someplace along the Rio Grande."

Travers whistled softly. "That takes in a hell of a lot of territory. The Rio Grande's a long river."

"Sure. Angelita narrowed it down for me, though. The rest of the gold's supposed to be someplace close to the mouth of the Devil's River."

"That'd put it right smack in the middle of the free zone." Travers frowned.

"What the devil's a free zone, Will?"

"It's a strip along the border that old Juarez set up years ago, when he was trying to stir up more trade with the U.S. Any kind of goods can be shipped through the free zone from one country to the other without paying taxes or customs duty."

"I guess folks live in it, too?"

"Oh, sure. There's a good-sized town called Guerra right about the middle of it, close to the mouth of the Devil's River."

"You ever been there?" Longarm asked.

"More times than I care to count. As far as the Rangers are concerned, it's a damn big headache."

"I don't see how that could be, if it's like you said—just a place for shipping goods back and forth across the border."

"You'll understand when I tell you the rest of it. The free zone don't belong to Mexico or to us. Mexican law, U.S. law, Texas law—none of 'em apply in it. So every damn outlaw on the run heads there, because the law can't touch him. It's the way I guess the frontier used to be—tooth and claw, every man for himself, and the devil take the hindmost."

"Sounds like it must be quite a place," Longarm commented. Then he added, "I guess I'll get to find out for myself soon enough, Will, because that's where the rest of Santa Anna's gold is supposed to be."

Chapter 14

Since the previous day when he'd crossed the Nueces River
west of the little hamlet of Uvalde, Longarm had followed what
remained of the old Mexican army road. The military highway
had been abandoned thirty years before when a more southerly
route had been chosen for a new road, but long stretches of it
were still passable. The old road ran east-west in an almost
straight line, veering only when it was necessary to avoid the
base of one of the low-rising tan limestone bluffs that rose to
the north of the arid, flat, featureless plain.

Longarm could discover no changes in the climate or terrain
of this section of Texas since he'd visited it several years
previously. Once he'd left behind the moist air of the well-
watered plateau on which San Antonio stood and started his
ride across the sunbaked Nueces Plain, the air grew dry. High,
fluffy clouds no longer rode the sky and the sun beat down
with a baking heat.

Allowing for small variations in bulk and height, the bluffs
on the north of Longarm's path all looked alike. The only signs
of life on the plain to his right were an occasional small lizard
scurrying among a few scattered tufts of grass as yellow as the
soil itself. The only color came from a few clumps of prickly
pear; some of these were still in flower, and bore pinkish-red
buds atop the spiny clusters of their oval, olive-green leaves.
Everywhere else monotony reigned.

When he'd tried in Houston to buy a railroad ticket to his
destination, Longarm had discovered how isolated West Texas
was. There was a railroad far to the north at El Paso, and
another far to the south at the Gulf of Mexico, but between
the two railway lines the Rio Grande made a sinuous southward
sweep of a thousand miles, and Longarm's destination was
almost exactly in the center of that stretch of river.

"There's not much reason for anybody to want to put a railroad in there," Travers had pointed out when Longarm complained. "All the people who live in that part of the state wouldn't fill two passenger coaches. And there wouldn't be any freight to haul—nothing but gravel and sand and cactus, and we've got plenty of all three just about everyplace else in Texas."

"You'd think some damn fool would build one, though," Longarm replied. "Especially with that free trading zone you were telling me about real close to midway of the river."

"Oh, that was set up when the ox carts used the army road," Travers explained. "About all Texas amounted to then was a few towns that grew up around the mission churches between the southern end of the river and San Antonio."

"I guess things ain't changed much since I was in those parts a few years back," Longarm said. "I'll go like I did the last time—get me a cavalry horse from the army remount station at Fort Sam Houston and put in five days on horseback getting to where I got to go."

With four days of his trip behind him, Longarm was more than glad to break his long ride at Del Rio, on the Texas side of the Rio Grande. Small and crude as the town was, it had a boardinghouse where he could sit at a table and eat food that hadn't come from his saddlebags, sleep in a bed with a mattress and springs instead of a bedroll spread on the hard ground, and soak off the crust of sweat and travel dust in a bathtub.

To Longarm's way of thinking, though, the best thing about Del Rio was that when he reached it his trip was almost over. A short day's ride along the riverbank would take him to his destination: Guerra, the merchant town near the center of the free zone.

When he saw Guerra silhouetted across the Rio Grande in the declining sun the middle of the following afternoon, Longarm gaped with surprise. He reined in the cavalry horse and stared while he took out a cheroot and touched a match to it.

Old son, he said to himself, *it sure don't look like you'll suffer much in that place. A town that big is bound to have just about anything a man could look for to keep him comfortable.*

Seen from the Texas side of the river, Guerra was imposing indeed. It sprawled in a natural depression a short distance beyond the Mexican side of the Rio Grande, and from the high bank on the Texas side Longarm looked down upon the town.

In its center rose the ornate twin towers of a massive church built from blocks of cut limestone. Streets radiated from the square in which the church stood and though Longarm could see few people moving on them, he knew the siesta hour was just ending; the streets of any town down this way were seldom busy until much later in the afternoon.

Most of the houses facing the streets were built from the same cut-limestone blocks that formed the walls of the church. A number of the houses were two stories high, and a few rose three floors. Even looking into the sunlight, Longarm could see the carved doorways and window arches decorating the facades of the more imposing structures.

Interspersed between the mansions there were smaller houses, some of stone, others of adobe bricks. On the outskirts, forming a wide belt around three sides of the town, was the inevitable huddle of small shacks—*jacales*. Beyond the huts there were corrals and sheds. Huge freight wagons stood in some of the corrals, though he saw horses and mules in only a few of the enclosures. Most of the sheds bordering the corrals looked to be in need of repair, and a few had decayed to the stage where repairs would be almost impossible.

At the point where Longarm had stopped the Rio Grande ran deep, its roiling currents yellow-green, but a few hundred yards upstream its surface rippled gently and the water's color faded to the brownish yellow that marked shallows. On each bank, deep ruts left by the wheels of countless laden wagons indicated a ford. Toeing the horse ahead, Longarm crossed into Mexico.

Not until he'd reached the outskirts of the town did the realization sink in that many of the houses which had looked so imposing from a distance were uninhabited shells, with doors missing or sagging open, and no glass in their yawning windows. The adobe houses were in better shape. Most of them appeared occupied, though the plaster on many was scabbed and broken, and some of the empty ones were already crumbling to reintegrate with the soil from which their bricks had been made.

In the town, the number of people on the streets had not increased. Longarm reined in beside the first man he saw and asked, "Where'll I find the Cruz house?"

"*Lo cual Cruz?*" the man asked in turn. "*Hay tantos nom-*

brado Cruz como los dedos on mis manos."

"Doña Pia Belinda de Cruz," Longarm told him.

"Ah, esto Cruz." The man pointed to a three-story house half a dozen doors down the street and on the opposite side. Separated by the walled enclosure of a high adobe fence, the house rose like a fortress above its more modest neighbors. *"La casa de Doña Pia,"* he said.

"Gracias." Longarm nodded.

He toed the horse toward the house the man had indicated, noting as he drew closer that it was in better condition than most. There were a few small cracks in the high adobe fence, but the portion of the house visible above the tall wall showed signs of recent repairs having been made to the pillared arches of ornate carved stone that framed the doors and windows. Reining in at the gate which pierced the surrounding wall, Longarm found the latch handle after a moment of fumbling. He walked up the flagstone path leading to the house and tugged at the bell pull that protruded from the wall beside the massive timbered door.

After having waited with dwindling patience for several minutes, Longarm was reaching for the pull to ring again when the door swung open. The tiny, bent woman in the maid's uniform who opened it took her time inspecting his travel-stained and well-worn clothing. She crinkled her face into a frown and asked, *"Que quieres, hombre?"*

Longarm touched the brim of his hat. "A man down the street told me this is the Cruz house," he said.

"Si. You look for who?"

"I'm looking for Doña Pia Belinda de Cruz."

"Es la casa de ella. Y su nombre?"

"Long. Tell her Angelita and Jorge Montero sent me."

When she heard the Monteroses' names the woman's wizened face cracked into a smile. She opened the door wide to reveal a long wide hallway with a floor of tiles laid in a checkerboard pattern. *"Ah, Angelita y Jorge! Entrese, señor!"* she cried.

Longarm followed the ancient maid from the hall through the carved double doors into a large room. Having just come in from the bright sunlit street, his eyes adjusted slowly to the room's dimness. The maid indicated a small chair that stood against the wall and gestured for him to sit down. Then she vanished.

Gradually the room's details began to register as Longarm's eyes adjusted to the light. He saw that the chair he sat in was one of several dozen that stood in a neat line along three sides of the room's walnut-paneled walls. The wall opposite the door was made up of three floor-to-ceiling windows draped with curtains of embroidered silk. The light trickling around the edges of the drapes was the only source of illumination in the huge chamber.

By now Longarm's eyes could make out other details. Massive matching tables of mahogany were paired in the center of the room on a mellow-hued Oriental carpet that covered almost the entire area of the marble floor. At each end of the room, a single high-backed armchair sat on a low platform. A crystal chandelier hung from the center of the high frescoed ceiling, and at intervals along the walls there were sconces with silken shades to filter the light of the candles they held.

Old son, he told himself, *Angelita ought to've told you what you was going to run into here. This damn room looks like one of them pictures of royal palaces over in Europe. If Angelita's aunt can afford a place like this, her family sure don't need none of Santa Anna's gold!*

Now that he had reached his destination, Longarm's earlier impatience had faded. He settled back in the fragile little chair and made himself as comfortable as possible while the minutes ticked away. At last he heard footsteps on the tiles of the hall floor. A woman swept past him, ignoring him as though he did not exist, and with the tiny wizened maid following her went regally to one of the tall armchairs on its dais.

Longarm got only a fleeting glimpse of Doña Pia Belinda de Cruz as the two went past him. He had time only to glance at her face, but in the brief moment he could see her face he noted that she had a refined and smaller version of the hawk nose that seemed to be a family characteristic.

She was tall and bore herself erect. Her hair was light, but he could not tell in the dim light whether it was blonde or gray, as her head was covered by a black lace mantilla. Her dress was long and light in color, and made of some silken fabric that rustled as she moved. The skirt was full, the bodice tight. She sat down and for a minute or so the maid bustled around the chair, arranging the folds of her mistress's full skirt. Finally satisfied, the tiny, stooped maid came back to Longarm.

"*Ahorita, Doña Pia recebete,*" she said, beckoning to him

125

to follow her. Scurrying to keep a step ahead of his long legs, she led Longarm to the dias. With a half bow, she said, *"Doña Pia, presente a usted el Señor Long."*

Longarm was somewhat at a loss. He did not know whether he was expected to speak first or to wait for the woman on the dais to acknowledge his presence. Doña Pia solved his problem.

She nodded, extended a hand, and said, *"Bienvenido, Señor Long. Mi casa es suyo."*

Longarm took the extended hand in his own big, hard palm. "Glad to make your acquaintance, Doña—" He stopped and smiled at her. "I guess I don't rightly know how many of your names I'm supposed to use when I talk to you."

"Doña Pia will be quite satisfactory," she replied. "And I am pleased that you have called with news of Angelita and Jorge." Her voice was was soft and her English totally unaccented. She said to the maid, *"Servimos, Luisa."* When the maid scuttled away, she sighed and said to Longarm, "Bring a chair, Mr. Long, and please sit here beside me so that we can talk comfortably."

A bit bewildered by the abrupt change that had followed his extremely formal reception, Longarm obeyed. When he'd settled into the chair that he brought from the wall beside the dais, out of habit he reached for a smoke and had the slim cheroot out of his pocket before realizing what he was doing. He hesitated a moment, then pushed the cheroot back into the pocket.

"Please, light your cigar if you wish, Mr. Long. And you may light my *cigarillo* at the same time, if you will be so kind."

Doño Pia produced a thin gold case from a fold of her full skirt and took from it a cigar or a dark cigarette, slimmer than Longarm's and a bit longer. She held it between her slender fingers while he flicked a match across his thumbnail, then puffed it into life when he held the flame for her before lighting his own.

While lighting their cigars, Longarm took the opportunity to study his hostess. He was no stranger to the artifices women use to accent their youth and hide their age, but Doña Pia's face had been so expertly made up that Longarm was baffled when he tried to guess her age; she could have been thirty or fifty.

Her face was thin rather than broad, and the prominent family nose appeared much smaller when she faced him squarely than it had looked in profile. For a moment Longarm thought that he had not seen her face clearly when she'd passed him. Then his sharp eyes told him her secret: the shade of powder she used on her nose was a bit darker than that on her cheeks.

Doña Pia's cheekbones were high, their contours masked by rouge and powder skillfully applied. Her eyebrows had been accented, for they were much darker than her silver-blonde hair, and her eyelashes were darkened and emphasized with artful lines above them to frame her violet eyes. Her rouged lips were full, her chin's square lines, like her nose and cheekbones, minimized with artful touches of cosmetics. The skin of her neck was smooth and unlined, and the low, square-cut neckline of her dress pulled her full breasts together and caused them to bulge prominently above the fabric.

"I hope this formality in our introduction hasn't bothered you, Mr. Long," she said with a wry smile. "You see, Luisa gets upset when she isn't allowed to follow the old-fashioned routine my mother taught her. At her age, it's easier just to let her do what she's accustomed to than it is to try to change her ways."

"Well, I'll tell you the bedrock truth, Doña Pia," he replied. "I wasn't quite sure what I'd got into—this big place you got here and all."

"Yes. This house has that effect on strangers," she said.

"Angelita didn't tell me what to look for," Longarm went on. "All I had to go by was your name and the name of the town."

"How is Lita?" Doña Pia asked. "And Jorge? I have so few relatives left alive that I treasure each one, but I'm especially fond of those two."

"When I left East Texas, they was doing all right. Jorge got himself shot when we..." Longarm paused, still a bit unsure of his hostess, and went on quickly, "we had a little brush with some renegades. But he's going to be fine. Angelita, she's staying back there to look after him."

Doña Pia had made no effort to hide her close scrutiny of Longarm while he'd been speaking. She said now, "Mr. Long, I don't believe in wasting words. You did not come to Guerra for a social call, to report on the health of my niece and nephew. Let's consider that we have finished with the formalities. Suppose you tell me what has really brought you here."

"I'll be glad to," Longarm replied. "I like straight talk my-

127

self. First off, I better tell you I'm a deputy United States marshal, even if that don't mean a thing on this side of the Rio Grande." He took out his wallet and flipped it open to show the badge pinned in it. "Now, I reckon you know—"

Longarm was interrupted by Luisa's return. The maid set a large silver tray on the table. The tray was crowded; it held a silver teapot and china cups, a cream pitcher and sugar bowl, and an assortment of bottles and glasses. She stood at the table, looking questioningly at her mistress.

"We will continue in a moment," Doña Pia told Longarm. "Would you care for tea, Mr. Long? Or a glass of sherry? Or a sip of tequila or brandy? I'm sure there's American whiskey as well, if that's what you prefer."

"I think I'll stick to my usual," Longarm said. "Whiskey."

"Tu oigale, Luisa." Doña Pia said to the maid. *"Y a mi, amontillado."* Turning back to Longarm, she said, "You do not have to worry about Luisa. She knows a few words of English, but even if she understood what we were saying, she would repeat nothing she might overhear."

Luisa brought them their drinks, the sherry in a thin fluted glass, the whiskey in a cut-glass tumbler. Doña Pia dismissed her with a wave, faced Longarm again, and raised her eyebrows inquiringly.

"I was about to say that I imagine you know more about Santa Anna's gold than I do," Longarm said.

"Perhaps so," she agreed. "You mentioned that Jorge had been wounded. There must have been fighting, then, and I suppose it was connected with their search. Were they successful?"

"They dug up a bunch of gold pieces out along Buffalo Bayou, where Santa Anna and Sam Houston fought that battle. Trouble was, a bunch of Diaz's *rurales* jumped us when—"

"You say 'us,'" she broke in. "Were you with Jorge and Angelita, then? And fought against the *rurales?*"

"Why, sure. Them *rurales* was after me as much as they was after your kinfolks, Doña Pia. I'd had to kill a couple of *rurales* a few days before that, when they tried to ambush me in San Antonio. And that wasn't the first time me and the *rurales* locked horns. I've tangled with that outfit a few times before, and so far I've always beat 'em."

"Then you are one with us!" Doña Pia exclaimed.

"Now, wait a minute!" Longarm cautioned her. "I got a

128

duty that comes first. I was sent down here to keep Texas from grabbing Santa Anna's gold away from the U.S. Treasury."

"If you are not with us, you are against us!" she exclaimed angrily. "The gold belongs to its finder after so many years!"

"Now, I didn't come here to argue the law with you, Doña Pia," Longarm said quietly. "I'll leave that to the lawyers and judges. I don't stand to make or lose a penny myself."

"I apologize, Mr. Long," she said. "I spoke hastily."

"I don't take offense, ma'am. But, going back to why I come here, Jorge and Angelita told me there's another bunch of them gold pieces someplace around here. From the way they talked, you know where they're hidden."

Doña Pia shook her head. "They were wrong, Mr. Long. I do not know where the gold is hidden, nor does anyone else. No, Mr. Long, you have come on a fool's chase. If part of Santa Anna's gold was ever here, I am afraid it will stay lost forever."

Chapter 15

Longarm did not respond at once. He raised his glass, and though his nose told him the whiskey it contained was bourbon, he took a swallow. Then he said, "Now, I can take what you just told me two ways, Doña Pia. Either you don't think there was any of Santa Anna's gold around here, or you believe it was hidden here and somebody's already found it."

"Mr. Long—I suppose I should call you Marshal Long—" Doña Pia began. "Which do you prefer?"

Longarm realized that Doña Pia was playing for time in which to decide how much of her story to tell him, or whether to tell him anything at all. "It don't matter all that much," he said. "I got a sorta nickname a lot of folks call me, and I answer to that as good as I do to my right name."

"Would you mind telling me what it is?"

"Longarm."

"Ah, of course!" Doña Pia smiled. "I'm familiar with the phrase it's taken from, but I won't repeat it because I'm sure you hear it so often that it bores you. But your nickname has a ring which pleases my ears. Would you be offended if I should call you Longarm?"

"Not a bit."

"I think I will like you, Longarm. You have my permission to call me Pia."

"Well, thanks, Pia. It's nice we can get friendly so quick." In spite of her gesture, Longarm decided he'd allowed her to stall long enough. He said, "You still ain't answered my question."

Her voice sober now, Pia said, "I will tell you two things, Longarm. The first is that I know positively that a great deal of the gold Santa Anna and my mother brought back from Texas was hidden close to Guerra. The second is that the gold will not be found, because today there is no way to find where they hid it."

"Maybe you better explain that," Longarm suggested.

"Of course. But first..." She produced her gold case and took out another *cigarillo*. She held it to her lips, and Longarm flicked a match into flame to light it for her. "It is a long story, I'm afraid," she mentioned. "Would you like to fill our glasses again before I begin?"

When Longarm returned from the table with their replenished glasses, he said, "Since it was your mother with Santa Anna, I guess you'd know about the gold better'n most."

"I'm sure I do. But even I do not know enough to find it."

"You've looked, I guess?"

"Many times. But I did not begin looking early enough to defeat *El Rio del Diablo.*" She saw the question in Longarm's eyes and said, "You're not familiar with the river that flows into the Rio Grande just north of the town."

Longarm shook his head. "No. Like I told you a minute ago, I been down here to the border on some cases before, but I never got this far north. The only thing I know about the Devil's River is its name."

Her face serious, Pia said, "The river is treacherous, Longarm. It earns its name. Far to the north, where it begins, it fills quickly when there is heavy rain. The riverbed is cut through stone in the high northern plain, and fills so swiftly that the stream overflows its banks and becomes like a small ocean. Then it roars south through deep gorges and when it reached the soft soil near the Rio Grande the force of its current cuts new channels and fills the old ones."

"I've seen rivers do the same thing in other places." Longarm nodded. "A stream like that ain't one you'd be safe in using for a landmark. And, from what you said a minute ago, I reckon that's what Santa Anna and your mother did."

"Yes. That was the first mistake they made," she replied. "The second was burying the gold at night and depending on their memories to guide them when they returned to dig it up."

"You don't have to go into the rest of it," Longarm told her. "You say you're sure the gold's out there someplace around the mouth of the Devil's River. That's all I need to know."

Pia frowned and asked him, "You plan to look for it in spite of what I've told you?"

"As long as I'm here, I figure I might as well."

"But what you propose is not possible. Others have tried—I myself have tried and failed," she protested.

"I don't guess one more try's going to hurt, then," Longarm said quietly.

For a moment Pia said nothing, then she shrugged. "Very well, Longarm. It will do no harm, as you say."

Longarm stood up. "Now I know I'm going to be here a while, it's time I go find me a place to stay."

"Why, you will stay here, of course, as my guest."

"Now, Doña Pia, I ain't going to impose on you."

"You are not imposing." She waved a hand, indicating the huge room. "There are seventeen bedrooms in this house, Longarm. I occupy only one. The rest stand empty, ready to be used. In the stable there are stalls for thirty horses. My carriage pair and saddle horse use three."

"Well, it don't seem like I'd get underfoot or crowd you none if I accept your invitation, so I will, and thank you for it."

"De nada, Longarm. There is another good reason for staying here, as you would have discovered if you had tried to find a room. There is no inn, no place for travelers to sleep, except perhaps a blanket on the floor in some peon's hut." She sighed. "You have not looked closely at Guerra yet, I am sure."

"No. I rode right straight to the square as soon as I crossed the river."

"Did you notice nothing as you rode down our streets?"

"There's sure a lot of empty houses, if that's what you're getting at," he replied.

"Guerra is dying, Longarm."

"It didn't seem like a busy place, I grant you."

"Even a few years ago it was different. The houses were all filled, the great ones as well as the hovels. A dozen inns were always crowded with travelers. The wagon trains went out, often as many as twenty or thirty each day, bound for Tucson and Santa Fe and San Antonio, and as many came in each day with fresh goods from Chihuahua, Monterrey, and Durango. Guerra was the trading center for all of Mexico."

"I'd guess the railroads had a lot to do with wagon hauling falling off," Longarm said thoughtfully.

"They had everything to do with it. When it became cheaper to pay duties on goods and ship them by rail than to hire the men and feed the livestock so they could avoid the customs

132

duties by shipping from the free zone, Guerra began to perish."

"I got to admit I wondered about all the empty houses."

"There are a few who still live in the big houses. Some of them stay because they are no longer rich and cannot afford to leave." She shrugged expressively. "Some of us stay out of sentiment."

"That sentiment wouldn't have anything to do with Santa Anna's gold in your case, would it?" Longarm asked.

"No. I have a better reason for staying. My husband stood with Lerdo against Diaz. He was killed in the battle of Tecoac, when Diaz defeated Lerdo. Diaz is *tipo Indio*, Longarm. He has a thirst for revenge on anyone who has ever acted or spoken against him. He never forgets an enemy, or an enemy's widow."

"So you stay here to keep from reminding Diaz that you're still around," Longarm said.

"Of course. And there are things I can do here to help our cause. I pass messages between my friends in the capital and the ones who have fled to your country, and I hide those trying to escape the *rurales* and Diaz's evil *Fuerza Secreta*. I keep busy."

"Well, I don't expect I'll be here more'n a few days, but as long as all of Santa Anna's gold still ain't found, it's going to cause trouble. So I aim to try my hand at finding it."

"I will help you all I can," Pia promised. She stood up. Longarm noticed with surprise that she was almost as tall as he was. She said, "Luisa will take you to a bedroom, and my stable boy will attend to your horse and bring up your saddle bags. It is an hour yet until dinner. Luisa will call you."

Longarm followed Luisa up the stairway. The bedroom into which she ushered him was only a third the size of the room where he'd talked with Pia, but it was still unusually large. She busied herself drawing the heavy draperies, letting a flood of light into the room. Longarm looked from the canopied fourposter bed to the full-length mirror set into one of the walls, to the heavy polished bureau and clothes press and the upholstered chairs that stood against the walls.

Old son, you ain't used to this kind of fancy fixings, he told himself, comparing the room with his usual surroundings in Denver, his boardinghouse room with its water-stained wallpaper, tattered window shades, and threadbare carpet. *But it'd sure be nice to get used to 'em,* he thought ruefully.

Luisa turned from the windows and asked, *"Quiere afetida,*

señor?" She drew the edge of one hand down her wrinkled cheeks as she spoke.

"A shave?" Longarm frowned. He felt the stubble on his chin, rough even though he'd gotten a barbershop shave in Del Rio the day before, and was sure the suggestion had originated with Doña Pia rather than the maid. He shook his head and said, "Now that'd be nice, but you don't need to bother. I got a razor in my gear."

"Pues, mira, señor." The tiny maid scuttled to a door in one of the walls and opened it. *"Bano, señor. Hay agua fria y calor. Quiere algun mas?"*

Longarm shook his head. "No, thanks. I'm sorta used to looking out for myself."

When the maid left, Longarm made a more detailed inspection of his new surroundings. The room had the strange, unidentifiable air of one that has been kept ready for occupancy but has been long unused. The windows overlooked the courtyard and stables of the house, and Longarm could see that they had the same look of disuse he'd noted in the room. He watched while the stable boy led his horse in, placed it in one of the stalls, and started toward the house carrying his saddlebags.

To have something to do while waiting for the saddlebags, Longarm wandered into the bathroom. It was a symphony in marble and gold. Thick white towels were folded over golden rods, gold faucets were fitted to the oversized bathtub and sink, which were made of the same polished gray-veined white marble that covered the walls and floor, and even the toilet was enclosed in a square marble base.

Yes, sir, old son, there wasn't nothing too good for whoever it was built this place. he thought as he ran his hand along the smooth surface of the sink. *They was rich enough to get the best, but chances are you'd feel real uncomfortable trying to live up to all these fancy fixings.*

Longarm's inspection was interrupted by the arrival of Luisa with his saddlebags. He dug out his razor and soap and his clean pair of balbriggans. While shaving, he ran water into the tub. He was leaning back, soaking luxuriously, when he ran his hand along one side of the tub. His fingers encountered a rough spot and he examined it curiously. An area twice as large as the palm of his hand was covered with odd, wavering lines that had been scratched into the hard marble. The scratches formed no letters or design, but seemed to be inscribed at random.

Now, who'd want to do a thing like that? he asked himself. *Outside of one little spot, this whole fancy room's as good as it was when it was brand new. And somebody done it on purpose, too, like maybe they had a new diamond ring and wanted to see was the diamond real. Well, if that's what it was, they sure found out. A diamond's about all that'd cut this hard marble in here.*

Dismissing the scratches as the work of idly curious hands, Longarm finished his bath, dressed, and waited for the summons to dinner.

Pia was waiting for him when Longarm came down the stairs in response to Luisa's summons. Offering him her arm to escort her into the dining room, she said, "We will have a very simple meal, I'm afraid."

"I ain't got fancy tastes, Pia," Longarm replied. "Just meat and potatoes is plenty good enough for me."

"We will have a bit more than that," she told him, subtly guiding him to the door that led to the dining room. "Salad and soup and dessert are needed to make meat and potatoes into a suitable dinner."

They entered the dining room, a long narrow chamber with a table capable of seating twenty persons on each side. Places for two had been set in the center on opposite sides. Pia indicated that she would take the place nearest the door. Longarm seated her and moved around the end of the long table to take his own seat.

Pia picked up their conversation where she'd left off. "I'm sure you'll enjoy your meal. Thanks to my mother's training, Luisa is an excellent cook."

"Right about now I'd settle for most anything," Longarm said. "I just had a bite in the saddle at noon, and it's been a long time since then."

Though Longarm was no salad lover, he found himself enjoying the sliced *aguacate* and tiny tomatoes, seasoned with a touch of oil and vinegar into which a pinch of *chili molido* had been stirred. The soup was chicken broth with a few shavings of *chiles verdes*, and with it came crisply fried *tortillas de maiz* cut into bite-sized triangles.

Luisa was just removing the soup plates when a knock

135

sounded at the door. She looked at Pia, who nodded, and, without taking the plates, the tiny housemaid hurried into the hall. She had no sooner left the room than Pia looked at Longarm, her face drawing into a worried frown.

"I'm sure I know who that is," she said, "and I'm afraid I made a very bad mistake."

Before Longarm could reply, a man's loud voice came from the hall. *"Al lado, mujer! Quiero habla con Pia!"*

Pia pushed her chair back as the thudding of boot heels sounded on the tile floor of the hall. Longarm moved to stand up also, but she flicked her hand in an imperious gesture which he interpreted as a command to remain seated. Longarm had not put on his gunbelt. He slid his hand to his lower vest pocket where his derringer rested and hooked a thumb into the pocket.

Pia turned to face the door as a bulky man stepped into the room. He stopped short when he saw Longarm. Longarm sized the newcome up in a single glance. The unexpected visitor was not a Mexican of the upper class; he had the square face, blunt nose, and thick lips of what Pia had earlier called *tipo Indio*, and wore a heavy untrimmed moustache.

He wore the tan *charro* jacket with ornate gold embroidery that Longarm instantly associated with the *rurales*. His hat was not the high-crowned, decorated sombrero with upturned brim that Diaz's rural police force favored, but was flat-brimmed with a low, peaked crown, bare of any mark of rank. Longarm could not see his legs, but from the sound his footsteps made he guessed that the newcomer was wearing flare-legged *charro*-style pants and high-heeled boots. The visitor and Pia stood with eyes locked for a moment. Then the man turned his baleful stare on Longarm.

Before the newcomer could speak, Pia said quickly, *"Lo siento muchisimo, Leon. Olvide que invitate a la cena anoche."*

"Pero no olvides el Yanqui!" the man snorted.

"Momentito, Leon!" she snapped. *"Esta mal tiempo por disputamos. Y por favor habla en Inglis. El señor Long no habla Espanol."* Before the angry man could erupt again, she turned and said to Longarm, "Marshal Long, may I introduce Captain Leon Salazar. You two should have much in common. Captain Salazar is the chief of the free zone's police."

Longarm stood up. With a poker face, he nodded and said, "Howdy, Captain Salazar. Glad to make your acquaintance."

Salazar's angry frown did not vanish when he returned

136

Longarm's nod, and he did not reply to the greeting. In excellent English, he said to Pia, "I do not like to have a servant tell me I am an unwanted guest in your home, Pia!"

Her voice as brittle as his, she replied, "I have already apologized for my unfortunate oversight, Leon. I told Luisa that Marshal Long and I were not to be disturbed at dinner. I did not mean to shut you out. I simply forgot that I had invited you before the marshal arrived."

"I do not like it that you forget me, either," Salazar said sharply.

"Please, Leon," Pia said, "take off your hat and join us. We have just begun our dinner. I'm sure Marshal Long would enjoy talking with you."

Salazar removed his hat but made no other move. His eyes were fixed on Longarm, a frown growing on his face. After a long moment of silence, he asked, "Long? You would be perhaps the marshal of the United States who is called Longarm?"

"Some of my friends call me that," Longarm replied, his voice levelly noncommittal.

"I am sure there would not be two United States marshals who have the same name and the same—" Salazar stopped and his frown deepened as he sought for the word and failed to find it. He shrugged and went on, "The same *apodo*."

"Nickname, Leon," Pia said quickly.

Without taking his eyes off Longarm, Salazar gestured that she was to stay silent. As though she had not interrupted, he went on, "You are known to me, Long. There are few of us in the *rurales* to whom your name is not known."

"You're a *rurale*, then?" Longarm asked.

Salazar shook his head. "Not at present. As Pia told you, I am chief of Police in the free zone. *El Presidente* did not think it appropriate for one holding the office to be part of any other of our forces."

Pia said, "Leon, since you have already started talking with Longarm, please sit down. I will have Luisa set you—"

Salazar turned to her, his face purple with suppressed anger. "Do not trouble yourself. I will not sit at the same table with this Yankee murderer." He turned and his boot heels rang down the hall, their clangor punctuated by the slam of the front door.

Her eyes wide, Pia looked at Longarm. "What have you done to the *rurales* that Leon should become so upset just by learning your name?" she asked.

"I tangled with the *rurales* a few times, Pia," Longarm said. "Might be it was just luck, but I come out on top every time we locked horns."

Pia looked at him and smiled, but the smile quickly gave way to a thoughtful frown. Her voice grave, she said, "I am afraid I have made a serious mistake when I forgot I had invited Leon to dine. He is your enemy, Longarm, and Leon Salazar is no man to have against you when you are in the free zone."

Chapter 16

"Salazar don't bother me a bit, Pia," Longarm said quickly. "He wouldn't be the first enemy I've had."

"Don't underestimate him," Pia warned. "The free zone is small, only four miles on each side of the river and twenty miles along its banks. And there are few people in Guerra now."

"Meaning that I'll stick out like a sore thumb?"

Pia nodded. "You would find it easier to avoid Diaz in Mexico, where you can find places to hide, than to evade Salazar in the free zone. Where is there for you to hide here?"

"I ain't figuring on hiding from Salazar. I won't set out to make trouble for him, but if he fights me, I'll fight back."

"I wish I could have found a way to fight him," Pia said angrily. "But if I do not stay on good terms with Leon, I will destroy my usefulness to our people."

"I figured that was why you played up to him."

"Let's not talk of that now, or of Leon. We hadn't really begun our dinner when he interrupted us, by the way. Sit down, Longarm, and let's talk of other things while we eat."

"There's one thing has got my curiosity roused up," Longarm said. "I'd like to talk about it, if you wouldn't think I was getting too personal."

"I'll tell you if I think it is. Go ahead."

"Tell me about your mother, Pia. How she got hooked up with Santa Anna and how your folks came to build this house here."

"Mother's affair with Santa Anna is ancient history by now, Longarm. So many people know about it that talking about it doesn't bother me a bit. Let me call Luisa to finish serving dinner, and I'll tell you the whole story."

After they'd started eating again, Pia began talking without waiting for Longarm to prompt her. "My mother was French," she said. "Gabrielle Michaux was her name. Her father was a minor official at the French embassy. She met Santa Anna when he was a dashing young army officer who couldn't afford to marry. She became his mistress—and, as she warned me many times, a man does not marry his mistress. But they stayed together until he became president of Mexico for the first time."

Longarm asked, "The first time? Was he president twice?"

"Oh, he was president of Mexico three times before he died a few years ago. But that's not part of my family's story, because when Santa Anna became president the first time, politics made it very inconvenient for him to have a French mistress."

"So, being a politician, he had to get rid of your mother?" Longarm's remark was more a statement than a question.

"Yes," Pia replied. "He arranged a marriage—and, though he and Mother hadn't had any children, I was born less than a year after Mother's wedding. My brother was born two years later. I had no children, but my brother had Angelita and Jorge."

"I don't mean to be interrupting all the time, Pia," Longarm said. "But unless your mother and brother had something to do with you being here, tell me about what happened to you after you got married. You came here with your husband, I guess?"

Pia nodded. "Of course. The de Cruz family had always been merchants and traders. They moved to Guerra right after Juarez opened the free zone and made a great fortune here. My husband Raoul added to it, before the railroads came. But surely it takes only one look at this house for you to see that."

"It's quite a place," Longarm said. "But go on, Pia. I won't butt in again, I promise."

"That doesn't bother me. I'm quite interested to know why you're so curious."

"I might hurt your feelings if I tell you the truth, and it ain't my way to lie about things."

"I can control my feelings, Longarm, and I'd rather hear an unkind truth than a kindly lie."

"What I been wondering ever since Salazar left is whether you owe him or he owes you."

Pia did not reply for several moments. Then she said, "I'd ask that question, too, if I were in your place. And I cannot answer you, for I am not sure myself."

"Salazar's bound to know how you feel about Diaz."

"Of course he does. I make no secret of that. But Diaz is a name we rarely mention to one another."

"Does he know about Santa Anna's gold?" Longarm asked.

"I think not. Mother would not talk about it outside of the family. Besides that, she has been dead for almost ten years. And, though she visited here often, Salazar did not come to Guerra until four years ago."

"You can't be sure, though?"

"If he does know of the gold, he has never mentioned it to me, or even hinted that he knew."

"How many people here in Guerra do you know, Pia?"

Pia's brow wrinkled in thought. After a moment she said, "Very few. Old Andres Roybal might know—his family came early to the free zone. The Sandovals—no, I do not think so. If a Sandoval thought there was gold buried close by, they would still be digging after fifty years, trying to find it. And those are the last of the early trading families who have not left Guerra."

"Well, if I'm real careful when I go out looking around the mouth of the Devil's River, maybe nobody's going to tumble to what I'm after," Longarm said.

"When will you start looking?"

"No use wasting time. I aim to ride out there tomorrow."

"I will go with you," she said quickly.

"Now, Pia, there's no use you taking a chance of getting your friend Salazar all riled up."

"I don't belong to Leon Salazar, Longarm," Pia said. "And I owe him nothing. If I try not to annoy him, it's only because I can't afford for him to be openly hostile. And there is a very good reason for me to ride with you. I know the countryside, and it's strange to you."

"I ain't going to argue about it, Pia. I'll be right glad to have your company, as long as you're sure you won't be hurt none by going with me."

When Longarm and Doña Pia rode out of the courtyard of the de Cruz mansion, the sun was already well up in the sky. When they'd completed their plans at the dinner table, it had been Longarm's idea to leave at dawn, but Pia had insisted that to make such an early start would be pointless.

"We have so little distance to go that it is not worth the

141

discomfort of riding with the sun in our faces for an hour," she said. "Let us leave at a more civilized time, Longarm."

Looking at Pia's smooth white skin glowing across the table from him in the soft candlelight, Longarm had agreed without argument. They'd eaten an early breakfast, and had sat over coffee, Pia puffing one of her pencil-thin *cigarillos* and Longarm one of his slim cheroots, until she gave the signal to leave. When she decided the time had come to ride out, the morning had warmed considerably. Longarm left his heavy coat behind and Pia dressed lightly too, anticipating the warmth of the afternoon when they would be returning.

After splashing through the ford across the Rio Grande, Pia had turned her sleek mare north. For half an hour they'd followed the east bank of the big river. Once Guerra in its low saucerlike valley was out of sight, they rode across a plain that had no landmarks except the slow-flowing river. From the banks on both sides the land stretched in a seemingly endless expanse of plain. It was a treeless land Longarm saw, virtually free of vegetation aside from an occasional clump of prickly pear growing atop a small hillock only a few inches high.

"If the whole country around here's like this, I can see why somebody who'd buried something would have a hard time finding it again," Longarm commented. "A map wouldn't be much good unless it was marked off by counting paces from the river."

"Unfortunately, Mother and Santa Anna couldn't do that in the dark," Pia said. "And when you see the Devil's River it will be even plainer why the gold they buried has not been found, even after so many years."

"I guess there ain't any more landmarks where the Devil's River flows into the Rio Grande?"

"None except the little channels at the mouth of the Devil's River," Pia said. "And they change each year, as I told you."

They rode on. Ahead, Longarm saw that they were approaching an area where the land was broken, the horizon line jagged now instead of being almost straight. "That'd be the Devil's River we're coming to, I guess?" he asked.

"Yes. We can't see its valley yet, but we'll get to the edge of it in just a few miles."

Another quarter of an hour of steady, unhurried progress brought the valley into sight. Longarm could see the seamed sloping walls of the *barranca's* north side. The yellow soil was gullied, serrated by wind and water into low hillocks, round and oval and serpentine, the valleys between the rises still dark in shadow. When they reached the point where the flat plain slanted down into the riverbed, he got his first sight of the Devil's River.

Here at its mouth the river was not a single stream. It ran through the floor of the *barranca,* which Longarm's practiced eyes told him was at least two miles wide. Upstream some five or six miles it curved, but the point at which the river was split into rivulets was downstream from the curve. The valley's side sloped gently enough, but it was cut and gullied as badly as the opposite side, which he had already seen from a distance. Still, the horses had little trouble covering the slope to the bottom.

At its bottom the valley flattened out, but the floor had been carved even more deeply than on the sides by water and wind. It was cut and seamed by a score of more rills of widely varying size that flowed like the strands of a web woven by some insane spider. Between the streams there were miniature islets. Some of these had tops big enough to accommodate the foundations of a house; others were so small that a man would be forced to balance like a tightrope walker in order to move along them.

"Now you will understand why I told you that searching for the gold here is a hopeless task," Pia told Longarm as they reined in and looked down at the scrambled maze.

"It's a mixed-up chunk of ground, all right," Longarm said, looking down.

"Remember, Longarm, this is only the way we see the valley today," she reminded him. "Tomorrow a rainstorm may fall on the plateau and flood the river to the north. When the rushing water sweeps down and fills the valley, where we are now may lie below the surface. Then, as the water flows away into the Rio Grande, the current will have changed the shapes of those little islands, and they will not be at all as we see them now."

"I guess a horse can wade down there where a man can't," Longarm said thoughtfully, gazing at the riverbed.

"None of the *rias* are deep now," Pia told him. "It will be as easy to ride among them as it was to cross the plain coming here from Guerra."

"Let's try it, then," he said, toeing his horse ahead. "I don't expect to find anything, but I sure ain't about to ride off till I've had a closer look."

For a short distance, where the surface currents of past floods had cut only shallow grooves into the valley wall, they had easy going. Halfway down, the soil underfoot was of a finer texture, and it crumbled in places under even the lightest touch. The hooves of their horses slipped and the animals broke stride, lurching and sliding on the treacherous footing.

When they reached the floor of the gorge the going was easier. It was at least level, and most of the rills between the islets were shallow. Now and then one of the horses would balk when it stood knee-deep in a stream and pawed and found no bottom ahead. Then they would be forced to turn and move along the bank until they found a spot shallow enough to wade.

"You sure hit the mark when you said the Devil's River came rightly by its name," Longarm told Pia at one of the stops they made to rest the horses. "I'd hate to get caught in it when it's brim-full."

"Some have been caught," she replied. "Here at the mouth the sky may be fair when there is a great rain falling on the plateau. Then the water comes down at great speed, in a high wall, and neither man nor horse can withstand it."

A quarter of a mile further on, they came to proof of the river's worst nature. Pia was riding in the lead. Her horse shied, and when she'd quieted the animal she motioned for Longarm to ride up to her. She pointed to the ground. Half a skull, the round eyeholes and triangular nose hole showing, glistened whitely above the surface of the ocherous soil.

"Someone too brave or too foolish," she said. "He will cross no more rivers."

"I don't guess there'd be any way of finding out who he was," Longarm said, gazing at the skull.

"No. Or where he came from or when he drowned," Pia said. "It would be useless to bury him. The next flood would uncover him again. He has been claimed by the river, Longarm, the way Santa Anna's gold was claimed so many years ago."

"I'm beginning to think you're right, Pia," Longarm replied as he slid his foot from the stirrup. "But I'm going to take a closer look around, just to see if I run into anything that might show who he was and where he started from."

He levered himself up on his left foot and was bending forward and turning to swing his right leg over the saddle, so the bullet that was intended for his heart missed its mark. The slug scored the flesh of his left shoulder-blade before tearing a shallow wound through the deltoid muscle just below his shoulder.

Before the sharp crack of the rifle had reached their ears, Longarm was lying flat on the ground and Pia was swinging out of her saddle. She dropped facedown on the ground, too, and they lay motionless, waiting for a second shot.

"Just lay quiet," Longarm said. He twisted his neck, trying to locate the sniper, but saw nothing. "Whoever fired that shot might think he got me. He would've, too, if I hadn't been moving just at the right time."

"Could you tell where it came from?" she asked. Lying as they were, with Pia on Longarm's right, she did not see the blood beginning to stain his shirt.

Ignoring the pain in his shoulder, Longarm said, "All I'm sure of is that it came from down toward the mouth of the river."

"Whoever fired it must have followed us from town."

"Maybe, maybe not. It could've been somebody who saw us when we forded the Rio Grande."

"Who knew you were coming to Guerra?" Pia frowned.

"A whole passel of folks. Angelita. Jorge. A Texas Ranger named Will Travers. God knows who else."

"Perhaps the *rurales*?" she suggested. "You told me there were two left of the squad that had been sent to Texas. They can use the telegraph lines as easily as a Ranger could."

"I don't guess it'd've been much of a trick for them to've found out where I was headed," Longarm agreed. "But I've had too many men trail me not to've learned how to spot 'em. And I'm sure as anybody can be there wasn't anybody dogging my tracks out of Houston."

"I know of no one in Guerra—" Pia began, then stopped short and stared at Longarm.

"Except Salazar," Longarm finished for her.

"Yes. But I can't believe it would be Leon, in spite of the scene he made last night."

Longarm grinned mirthlessly. "Nobody in the *rurales* would balk at backshooting me, Pia. Salazar could've told somebody; they'd have had time to pass the word along. I guess there's a *rurales* outfit at that little bunch of shacks across the river from Del Rio?"

"Villa Acuna?"

"If that's its name."

145

"There is a *rurale* stationed there, yes."

Longarm lifted his head and shoulders and strained his eyes, looking at the area from which the rifle shot had come. There was no sign of movement downstream.

"You stay where you are," he told Pia. "I'm going to scout around a little bit."

"Are you sure it's safe?"

"Safe as it'll ever be. Whoever the bushwhacker was, he's likely gone by now. I tumbled off the horse like he'd got me."

"Then it's safe for me to go with you," Pia said.

"No, it ain't."

Disregarding his wound, Longarm rolled under his horse as he spoke, to reach his rifle in its saddle scabbard. When he was between the two horses, he sat up and took another look around, but he still saw nothing. He got to his feet and slid the rifle out. Pia saw his shoulder for the first time.

"You did get hit!" she exclaimed, leaping to her feet.

Longarm shifted his rifle to his left hand, gritting his teeth when he closed his fingers on its barrel. He grabbed Pia's arm, pulled her down again, and squatted beside her.

"It's shallow—nothing more'n a scratch," he said, clumsily levering a shell into the Winchester's chamber. "And it's just about quit bleeding. I can still handle my rifle."

"I'll have to put a bandage on you. With a fresh wound like that, you can't just get up and walk around."

"It wouldn't be the first time," he told Pia, "and likely won't be the last. It's all open land between here and the Rio Grande. I'll take my chances of getting off the first shot."

"But, Longarm—"

"Never mind. You just set right where you are till I get back. I won't need to go far."

Keeping his eyes moving, scanning the rough valley floor for any sign or flicker of movement, Longarm dodged from one islet to another until he reached a rivulet too wide to leap and too deep to wade without going over his boot tops. He saw nothing. Satisfied the ambusher had gone, he turned back to join Pia.

She was waiting for him with some strips of cloth in her hand. "I don't suppose you saw anyone?" she asked, and when Longarm shook his head, she held up the strips of cloth. "I tore these off my petticoat," she told him. "Now take your vest and shirt off and let me bandage that wound."

146

This time, Longram did not object. His movement combined with the friction of his shirt against the bare wound had started it bleeding again. He slid his arms free of his vest after moving his watch into the pocket with the derringer, and stripped off his shirt.

"You're right," Pia said. "It's only a scratch. I'll put a good bandage on when we get back to Guerra."

"Sure," Longarm said absently. He followed the train of thought in his mind to its logical end and said to Pia over his shoulder, "That could've been somebody that spotted me just by accident, I guess. But we got to think about something else. It might've been somebody that's found out we're looking for Santa Anna's gold."

Chapter 17

Propped up in the bed by two exceedingly large and tightly packed feather pillows, Longarm puffed the cheroot he'd just lighted and looked out the window. It framed nothing more than a patch of sky, a rectangle shirred with thin clouds lighted pink by the sunrise. An hour ago, he'd awakened suddenly in the gray dawn with the nagging feeling in his mind that he'd seen or thought of something significant the previous day, but hadn't understood it. But, though he'd mentally retraced each step and recreated each move he and Pia had made, whatever had caught his eyes or had lodged in his mind stubbornly refused to surface.

Still belaboring his memory trying to recall whatever lost thought or observation had eluded him, Longarm rolled on his side to reach for the bottle of whiskey that sat on the small table beside the bed. He rolled back very quickly as the shifted weight of his body resting on his left side sent a stabbing pain through his wounded shoulder and arm.

Damn the backshooting son of a bitch! Longarm said to himself. "But it's your fault, too, old son," he muttered aloud. "You lost your smarts and didn't remember to keep an eye on your backtrail."

"Don't blame yourself, Longarm," Doña Pia said from the doorway. "Perhaps if I hadn't been along, if we had done less talking and looked more carefully as we rode, we would not have been taken by surprise."

"Saying that don't make me feel no better, Pia. I acted like a damn tenderfoot yesterday, and I got what was coming to me."

Pia came into the room. "Do you feel better this morning?"

"There's not a thing wrong with me that a drink of whiskey and a bite of breakfast won't fix up."

"Luisa is bringing your breakfast. And I will pour your whiskey into a glass so you do not have to drink from the bottle like a *peon.*"

"I guess maybe I'm not any better'n a *peon,* Pia. When I'm on the trail or by myself, I drink from the bottle a lot."

"On the trail it is permissible. In this house, no."

She handed him the glass she'd filled. Longarm downed a healthy swallow and though he missed the bite of his favorite rye, even bourbon was better than no whiskey at all.

After a puff on his cheroot, Longarm said, "I don't need to have Luisa bring me breakfast like I was an invalid. If you'll just turn around a minute, I'll slip into my clothes and—"

"No," Pia said sharply. "You must stay in bed today."

"Now, damn it, Pia, I ain't hurt all that bad. I been shot before."

"Yes. I saw the scars of your wounds when I was bandaging you yesterday."

"And I know how I feel," Longarm finished. "Besides, I aim to go back out there to the Devil's River soon as the sun's high enough and see if I can pick up the trail of whoever it was that potshot me. I oughta done that yesterday, but the tracks will still be fresh."

"You should not ride a horse today," Pia said. Her tone showed that she knew the protest was a formality, an admission that she was giving up the argument.

Luisa came in carrying a loaded tray. She cleared the table beside the bed and put on it a plate holding two thin steaks, a saucer covered with a napkin, an empty cup, and a porclain pot.

"Desayuno," she announced, and turned to go.

"Wait, Luisa," Pia said, and turned to Longarm. "Suppose I have Luisa bring my breakfast up here. Would you mind?"

"You know I wouldn't mind a bit, Pia. I'll eat along slow and give you time to catch up."

"No need for that. I have only coffee and a *bizcocho.*" To Luisa she said, *"Trajerse aqui mi desayuno, Luisa."* She pulled a chair up to the table and sat down. "If I can't persuade you to stay here in bed, at least I can go with you. And this time, I will also carry a rifle."

"This time you'll stay right here, where you'll be safe. It ain't that I don't appreciate you offering to go, but if there's any more shooting out there, you might get hurt."

"Shooting doesn't scare me, Longarm," Pia said. "I've been through revolutions, remember. And if you should get into a gunfight, you're not in shape to fight back very well."

"I'll have my Colt. And I can handle a rifle pretty good, even with my left hand sorta crippled."

"If you're thinking I'm one of those women who doesn't know one end of a gun from the other, you're wrong. I'm a good shot. I'd feel better going with you than staying here waiting for you to come back."

"I had in mind you doing something here that might help more than if you went along."

"What's that?"

"Keep an eye on Leon Salazar for me. If he rides out toward the mouth of the Devil's River, follow him at a safe distance and when you get close to the riverbed let off a couple of shots in the air to let me know he's come after me."

"You think it was Leon who shot you yesterday?"

"I'm trying not to make up my mind until I got some proof one way or the other. Would it make you feel bad to spy on him?"

"No. His office is on the next street over, toward the cathedral. I can watch it from one of the rooms on the third floor without Leon knowing anything about it."

"It'd be a real big help," Longarm said.

Pia hesitated for only a moment; then she nodded. "Very well. I'll watch his office. And if he starts somewhere, I'll do my best to follow him without letting him see me. If he does, I can make up some excuse he'll accept."

"I'll be right grateful, Pia." Longarm looked at the food. "I guess I'll start eating before them steaks get plumb cold, if you don't mind. Now that everything's settled, I got a pretty good appetite."

Longarm waited until the morning clouds had been burned away and the sun was casting its light clearly on the ground before starting back to the river valley. He rode unhurriedly, turning in the saddle now and then to scan his back path and make sure he was not being followed. He did not take the trail along which Pia had led him the day before, but zigzagged back and forth from the bank of the Rio Grande in wide vees that he was sure would lead him across the hoofprints of a rider who was riding parallel to that well beaten trail.

For the first half mile the ground was marked fairly heavily with the hoofprints of a number of horses. Longarm had no trouble identifying the prints left by his cavalry mount and the blooded mare Pia had ridden. They overlaid the older prints and their impressions were clean, with sharp edges, while the edges of the impressions made earlier had been eroded by the wind, and were frazzled and crumbling.

A bare half mile from the juncture of the two rivers he found the first fresh prints made by another rider. They were the only new ones, other than those of the horses he and Pia had ridden. The fresh tracks came up from the bank of the Rio Grande and overlaid those made by himself and Pia.

So far, so good, old son, Longarm mused as he studied the tracks of his unknown assailant's horse. *Here's where the back-shooting bastard picked you up yesterday. But where's the hoofprints his horse made getting away?*

Backtracking on the ambusher's trail gave Longarm the answer. As he rode down the gentle slope to the Rio Grande, he found the hoofprints made by the bushwhacker's horse returning from the Devil's River. The prints marking the rider's flight after the shooting were deeper and spaced differently, in the pattern made by the hooves of a galloping horse. They were close to the water's edge, and reentered the Rio Grande at the point where the tracks of the same rider had crossed from Mexico to the Texas side of the stream.

Now, Longarm was sure that he had a clear picture of the moves made by the bushwhacker. Avoiding the ford across the Rio Grande at Guerra, the unknown man who'd shot him had crossed closer to the mouth of the Devil's River. Logic told Longarm that the shallow spot used by his assailant to ford the Rio Grande must be known only to those living in or near Guerra. Once on the Texas side of the Rio Grande, following Longarm and Pia into the bed of the Devil's River would have been easy.

Whoever used that Rio Grande crossing must've been somebody like Salazar, old son, Longarm told himself as he studied the spot where the tracks disappeared into the water. *Or maybe a rurale or maybe just an outlaw on the prod that seen us riding along and figured on picking us off for the sake of what cash we might have and our horses and guns. Hell's bells, it could've been damned near anybody in country rough and raw as this place is. But after what all's happened since you got on the trail of*

151

Santa Anna's gold, the chances are whoever taken that potshot knew who we were and what we were after.

Still without a clue as to his attacker's identity, Longarm rode up the bank from the Rio Grande and picked up the beaten trail to the Devil's River. He followed the path he and Pia had taken the previous day. He still was not quite sure what he was looking for, but the hunch that had been in his mind when he woke up was too strong to be pushed aside.

By the time Longarm reached the place where the skull was lying half buried in the gravelly sand, he was almost convinced that he was on a fruitless search. He dropped the reins of the cavalry horse and let the animal stand while he dismounted. Looking down at the bleached dome of the weatherworn skull, he slid a cheroot from his vest pocket and touched a match to it, still gazing upstream, looking for something he might have seen during the few minutes before the sniper's shot tore into his shoulder.

To the north, just before the river disappeared behind the curve in the canyon through which it ran, he could see the point at which the stream began to split. Downstream, the dancing reflections from the bright morning sun defined the main channel and showed where a wide vee of land divided the river into two smaller streams. As the floor of the canyon grew steadily wider, the single vee became two, then three, four, and finally, as the current cut new channels in the soft, gravel-studded soil, the river was divided into the spiderweb of islets and tiny rivulets that surrounded the spot where Longarm stood.

Well, if you seen something up that way yesterday, old son, you sure as hell don't see it now, Longarm thought, releasing a puff of tobacco smoke to dissipate in the morning air. *But you rode this far trying to find what you might or might not've seen yesterday, so there ain't much point to turning back without trying the rest of the way.*

Accustomed as he was to gauging distances by eye, Longarm estimated that the curve in the river was a good three miles upstream. He swung into his saddle and nudged the horse ahead, letting it pick its own footing through the maze as it moved slowly up the riverbed. The sun was past mid-morning now, and against the brilliant sky the east wall of the river's broad canyon was case into deep shadow.

Longarm saw the silhouette of the approaching horseman break the sharply defined line of the canyon's rim. By the time

152

the rider's shoulders were outlined against the sky, Longarm had slipped his Winchester from its saddle scabbard and had the horseman squarely in his sights.

He waited, the weight of the rifle straining his injured shoulder as the seconds passed. The newcomer was not carrying a rifle in his hands, and Longarm could not see the butt of the other man's weapon silhouetted either in front of the saddle or behind it. He began to relax even before the oncoming rider waved at him, and dropped his rifle muzzle when he saw the other man's arm raise to greet him. Longarm returned the wave. With a breath of relaxing tension, he sheathed his own rifle and reined the cavalry dun over to the canyon's wall to greet Will Travers.

"I'm glad you recognized me when you did," The Texas Ranger grinned as he pulled in his horse at the end of its stiff-legged slide down the canyon wall to the riverbed. "But I figured you was smart enough not to pull the trigger on a man who didn't have his own gun out and ready."

"You'd've been safe enough thinking that most times, Will," Longarm replied, extending his hand as Travers reined in beside him. "Only I got backshot yesterday while I was poking around down in this canyon, and I'm not in much of a humor to take a chance today."

"Most anybody else would've shot the minute they saw me," Travers said.

"Maybe I would've, too, if I hadn't seen how you had your saddle scabbard fixed. I was ready to trigger one off if I'd seen your rifle butt sticking up in front of you or behind you, the way the *rurales* carry their saddle guns. But I remembered the Rangers carry 'em the only sensible way, so I sorta figured it was you about a minute before I was sure."

For the first time, Travers noticed the stiff manner in which Longarm was carrying his left shoulder. "Looks to me you just sorta got scratched yesterday," he said. "You get the man that done it?"

"No such luck. I didn't even get a shot off at him."

"Would you know him if you saw him again?"

"See him? Hell, I never seen hide, hair, nor powder smoke of the backshooting son of a bitch! But I'll sure as hell find' him if I stay here."

"I gather you've got some idea about who it was, then?"

"Oh, I got a pretty wide spread of choices, Will, but none

153

of 'em certain. It could've been a fellow named Salazar; he's the law in this free zone here. Or it could've been a *rurale* out prowling after me. As long a time as it took me to get here, I figure they've had plenty of chance to spread the word about what happened back at Buffalo Bayou. Or it might've just been some outlaw on the prod, figuring to get traveling money."

"Well, it looks like you're stirring things up, the way you always do." Travers commented, pulling out his sack of Durham and starting to roll a cornhusk cigarette.

"You got to stir the batter if you want to see hotcakes in the pan," Longarm commented. "And I'm sorta glad to see you, even if I can guess what you've come for. I'd say the state of Texas is figuring that if any more of Santa Anna's gold turns up on this side of the Rio Grande, they want it."

"That's right, as far as it goes," the Ranger agreed. "But there's a little bit more to it this time. Seems like the state treasurer got real riled up at the way you deposited all that gold in the bank in Houston, so that you're the only one who can touch it."

"Why, hell, Will, that's the deal we made when we talked about the best way to handle it," Longarm said.

"Sure it was. But I wasn't going to risk my badge by even letting on I had any part of a deal with you."

"I can't say I blame you for that," Longarm replied. "There wouldn't be much sense in both of us being out of a job."

"Now, I didn't mean that the way you took it, Longarm!" Travers protested. "If push comes to shove, I'll tell my chief we fixed that up between us."

"Oh, I ain't worried about you doing the right thing, Will."

"Anyhow," the Ranger went on, "I got sent down here to the border to sorta ride herd on you and see that you don't slip off into Mexico and have that deposit transferred to the other side of the river."

"Now, you don't think I'd be fool enough to do a thing like that, do you?" Longarm asked.

"Of course I don't! But the state treasurer don't know you the way I do, Longarm. I guess, according to the way he looks at things, he's just doing his job."

"Well, both of us know the gold in that Houston bank's safe until Texas and Washington get their minds made up about who it goes to," Longarm said. "So you're welcome to stick

154

around and see nothing happens to me till I can sign it over to whoever finally gets it."

"And that part of it's out of our hands," Travers said. He surveyed the maze of rills that flowed through the bottom of the river valley and asked, "Is this where the rest of the gold's supposed to be buried?"

"Someplace around here," Longarm said. "Trouble is, nobody seems to know exactly where."

Condensing his story as much as possible, Longarm told the Ranger what had occurred since he'd arrived in Guerra.

"So you see, Will," he concluded, "if that gold's still someplace in this messed-up chunk of ground, we got about as much chance as a snowball in hell to find it."

"You wouldn't be out here right now unless you had some idea about how to go about finding it," Travers suggested.

"Maybe. There's something floating around in the back of my mind that I can't bring up, Will. I figured I'd give myself a day or two to nosey around a little, but if I don't come up with something pretty soon, I'm inclined to give it up as a bad job."

"I'll stick to it as long as you do," Travers said.

"Sure. I'll tell you what. We can look some more, then go on back to Guerra before it gets dark. This lady that's putting me up has got a house big as all outdoors, and I don't imagine she'll balk much at putting you up, too."

Travers frowned. "Guerra's across the river, Longarm. I've got strict orders to stay on this side of the river."

"But if you want to make a fine point of it, Guerra's not in Mexico now, any more than this place where we're standing is in Texas. We're in the free zone, Will."

"Free zone or not, Guerra's across the Rio Grande, and I can't go across it."

"Now, Will, you and me both know orders don't mean all that much when we're in the field," Longarm said. "You chief's like Billy Vail; he's got sense enough to know that a man in our situation can't go too close by the book."

"If this was any other case, I'd say you're right. Not this time, though. My chief took the train down from Austin to Houston to give me my orders on this case, and he didn't leave me any room to maneuver. If I don't stay on this side of the river my ass is in a sling that I can't get it out of."

"Now, that's a hell of a note!" Longarm said. "Send a man out on a case and tie him down so he can't work the best way there is to handle his job. Damn it, Will, when you said you was sent down here to keep an eye on Santa Anna's gold, I begun counting on you to give me a hand finding it."

"I'm real sorry, Longarm," the Ranger replied. "But it looks to me like you've just got one choice. Handle it by yourself, the way you always do."

Chapter 18

Longarm did not answer for a moment. He lighted a fresh cheroot and, after puffing it into life, said thoughtfully, "You know, Will, maybe that ain't such a bad idea, you staying here at the Devil's River. You can sorta ride herd on this place while I'm in Guerra trying to make sure Pia's not just putting us through some kinda turkey trot."

"You think she's been lying to you?"

"Let's say I just ain't real sure what I believe yet."

"After what you've told me, Longarm, I don't see that we've got much of a chance to find that gold."

"Hell, there's a chance of anything happening. I didn't think we had a chance to find anything at Buffalo Bayou. But I got an idea the gold's around here someplace."

"Find it or not, my orders don't give me much leeway," the Ranger said. "I'll have to stick with you until the gold's found, or we both decide it never will be."

"You said you was going to have to camp here at the river, Will. You ain't changing your mind, are you, now you know how everything stacks up?"

"No. Why? Are you in a hurry to get back to Guerra?"

"I better start back pretty soon. Whoever it was put that slug through my back yesterday left some tracks down by the Rio Grande that I want to follow, if I can. I'll stay here till you pick a campsite, so I'll know where to find you when me and Pia come back tomorrow."

Travers's camp was soon established, on a ledge just below the rim of the wide *barranco* through which the many rills of the Devil's River ran into the Rio Grande. Within an hour, Longarm was back on the Texas bank of the Rio Grande, studying the river at the point where the escaping bushwhacker's hoofprints disappeared into the water. Even though the flow of the Devil's River into the bigger stream was divided into a number of small trickles, their crosscurrents were enough to keep the Ruo Grande roiled. A foot or so from shore, its silt-covered bottom could not be seen through the murky brown water.

Just sitting here looking won't get you across, old son, he told himself. *Riding down to the ford at Guerra and coming back here on the other bank might save getting your butt wet, but by the time you got back it'd be too dark to see anything, so go ahead and give it a try.*

At the spot where Longarm guided the cavalry horse into the water the Rio Grande was almost two hundred yards wide, the bank on the Mexican side having been scoured away by the current flowing in from the Devil's River. Longarm kept a light hand on the reins, trusting the horse to feel for the bottom with its forefeet. The animal moved cautiously, pawing ahead with its leading foot before putting down its weight. Then, a hundred yards from shore, with two hundred yards more to go, the horse balked.

Longarm glanced down. His stirrups were only inches above the swirling surface of the opaque water, and the horse was standing with its legs half submerged. Twitching the reins to start the animal downstream, Longarm nudged it with the toe of his boot. The mount hesitated a moment, then obeyed. It plunged ahead, and in the next instant was swimming.

In the saddle, Longarm was hip-deep in the warm water. Its sand-laden current plucked at his feet. He wriggled his boots out of the stirrups and rolled off the horse's back. Floating beside the animal, he locked his left hand into the open arch at the front peak of the McClellan saddle, with the reins gripped between his palm and the saddle arch.

He saw that the horse was swimming with the current, not across it. With his right hand, Longarm pulled the off-side rein and put the animal on a course that would take him directly to the bank. The horse began to churn toward shore. Longarm wasted neither time nor energy swearing at himself for his bad judgment, but gave his full attention to guiding the horse.

Less than sixty yards of water stretched between him and the swimming horse and the sloping sandy bank ahead when Longarm saw a rider coming toward him. The horseman topped the rise beyond the riverbank and headed for the stream. The late afternoon sun glinted on the gold threads of the embroidery that ornamented the high-peaked, wide-brimmed sombrero and waist-length *charro* jacket the man had on. Even at a far greater distance, Longarm could have identified him as being one of Diaz's *rurales*.

During the few seconds that passed between the time Longarm saw the rider and the time the *rurale* saw him, Longarm decided what course he would take. He slid his hand across his chest and gripped the butt of his Colt. The *rurale* reined in a few yards from the water's edge. Longarm did not recognize him, but he saw recognition in the grim smile that formed on the *rurale's* moustached face even before the man called him by the name the *rurales* had given him after his first brush with them.

"*Que buena suerte!*" the *rurale* said. "*No echarse como ayer, Brazolargo! Su cabeza es vale lo que peso!*"

While he was speaking, the *rurale's* hand darted forward and closed around the rifle in his saddle scabbard.

Longarm saw the man's finger seeking the rifle's trigger as its muzzle cleared the scabbard. Before the *rurale* could shoulder the rifle, Longarm brought his Colt out of the water and fired.

In the split second between the time the *rurale* got his hand on his rifle and the time Longarm's slug went home, the triumphant grin on the man's face changed to a stare of surprise.

His dying reflex closed the *rurale's* finger on the trigger, and his rifle barked. The slug kicked up a cloud of sand at the water's edge as the man pitched from his saddle and lay still. The horse snorted when its rider toppled, but it did not bolt.

Longarm held his Colt out of the water until he felt his horse lurching when its feet found the river bottom. He kept his eyes on the fallen *rurale* until he reached the man's side and made sure he was dead.

Well, old son, he said to himself, *that makes one less* rurale *you got after you now. And you'll have—*

Hoofbeats thudding on the Texas side of the riverbank drew Longarm's attention from the dead *rurale*. He stepped over to his horse and freed his rifle from the clinging wet scabbard. While the sound of the hoofbeats grew steadily louder, Longarm snapped the rifle's muzzle sharply downward to clear the barrel of water and led his horse up the sloping bank to its crest. Standing beside the animal he waited, his eyes fixed on the opposite bank.

His wait was a short one. The rider's head topped the slope of the bank. Longarm grunted when he saw the man's flat-brimmed hat appear over the crest. He'd seen that hat before, on the head of Leon Salazar.

Salazar's rifle was in his hand, resting across the saddlehorn. He saw Longarm and the sprawled form of the dead *rurale* and started to raise the rifle. Longarm brought up the muzzle of his Winchester. Salazar brought his own rifle level, but held it as he would a pistol, without shouldering it.

"Don't move, Long!" Salazar shouted. "You are my prisoner now! I arrest you for the murder of *rurale* Cruz Arredondo!"

"You better cool off and find out what happened before you talk about arresting anybody, Salazar," Longarm replied. He kept his voice level and raised it only enough to be sure it would carry across the wide river. "This *rurale* friend of yours was getting ready to shoot me. I killed him to keep him from killing me."

"You killed him while resisting arrest! Cruz was—"

Longarm broke in, "Hold on, Salazar! You know damned well he didn't have no authority to arrest me here in the free zone." When he saw Salazar hesitate and let the muzzle of his rifle sag an inch or two, Longarm pressed his point home. "You told me the other night nobody but you and your men's got any authority here, Salazar! Now, you was close enough to hear the shooting. You heard two shots, didn't you?"

After a long silence, Salazar said reluctantly, "Yes. The shots were very close together."

"Sure they were!" Longarm agreed. "But you'll find a slug from this *rurale's* rifle in the riverbank, and if you'll look close you can see me and my horse are still dripping wet. Your friend figured to potshoot me while I was still in the river."

"And I'll back up what Marshal Long says," Will Travers announced, suddenly rising from the ground behind Salazar. "I heard the shooting, too. That's what brought me here."

Salazar was obviously rattled. "You are who?" he asked.

"My name's Travers, and I'm a Texas Ranger. If you don't want to take my word, it won't be a bit of trouble for me to show you my badge."

"No, no, I take your word," Salazar replied quickly, his careful English shattered by Travers's surprise appearance.

"Well, Salazar?" Longarm asked. "You going to argue some

more?" Longarm's tone was not threatening, and he did not bother to point out what Salazar knew quite well: that the odds favored Longarm and Travers.

"Perhaps your story is true, Long," Salazar said after a moment's thought. "Since Cruz Arredondo is dead, and you and your friend both live, I have no choice but to accept it." Then, with a little return of his usual bluster, he added, "But I do not have to forget what you have done. And Cruz has other friends in the *rurales* who will remember."

"I don't doubt that a minute, but it don't bother me a bit," Longarm replied. Now that he could afford to relax, he reached by habit into his vest pocket for a cheroot, but his fingers found only disintegrating shreds of soaked tobacco. He shrugged off his disappointment and gestured toward the body on the sand. He asked Salazar, "I guess you'll take care of your friend's body?"

"Yes, of course," Salazar answered quickly. He looked from Longarm to Travers, gestured toward the Rio Grande, and said, *"Con permiso?"*

"Sure." Travers nodded.

Salazar replaced his rifle in its scabbard and started his horse toward the river.

Longarm called to Travers, "I'll ride on into Guerra, Will. But after I've dried my clothes and got the sand outa my boots, I'll be coming back." Then, to make sure the Ranger understood that his remark had been for Salazar's benefit, he added, "I'll get back about the time we fixed up a while ago."

"That's good," Travers called back. "I'll be looking for you then."

Salazar's horse was in the river by now, and Longarm waited to mount his own. He saw Salazar turn his horse upstream, the animal moving along a submerged sandbank with its legs little more than fetlock-deep. He watched until he saw where Salazar turned the animal toward shore, marking in his mind the location of the unmapped ford. When Salazar had crossed without getting his boots wet, Longarm mounted quickly and rode away with a wave to Will Travers, who still stood watching on the opposite bank.

Back in Guerra, Longarm rode into the stable yard behind the de Cruz mansion and turned the cavalry horse over to the stable boy for attention. Carrying his rifle, he went in through the back door. Pia came to meet him in the hallway, her eyes

161

growing wide when she saw the condition of his clothes.

"Longarm!" she gasped. "Did you fall into the river?"

"I didn't exactly fall, but I sure been in it. Lucky I left my saddlebags here. At least I got dry underwear and another shirt I can put on."

"Luisa will dry the rest of your clothes. You'll need a bath, too. If you've been in the Rio Grande, you'll find when you take your clothes off that you're covered with sand. And I'll have to put a fresh dressing on your shoulder."

"Now, Pia, you don't have to go to a lot of trouble," Longarm protested. "I'll just change what I got on underneath. My outside duds will dry on me."

"Nonsense! Come into the kitchen and have a good stiff drink of whiskey while Luisa fills the bathtub. And I want to hear what happened to you. I saw a *rurale* ride up to Salazar's office about two hours after you left, and a few minutes later they galloped off together too fast for me to follow. I suppose they had something to do with you getting into the river?"

"You could say they did. But look here, Pia, if it's all the same to you, I'll just step outa my boots here and go on upstairs where I can get a cigar outa my saddlebags. The ones I had in my pocket got ruined."

"Go ahead, Longarm. I'll bring your drink to you."

Longarm had finished his drink, but his cheroot was only half smoked and his story still unfinished when Luisa came in from the bathroom to announce that his bath was ready.

"You should get in the tub while the water's still warm," Pia said. "You can hand Luisa your clothes. Take off the old bandage, too. I have the material for a fresh one, so I'll stay in here and get it ready while you tell me the rest."

Stretched out in the marble tub, hot water lapping the brown curls on his chest, Longarm finished his abbreviated account of the events at the river.

"And that's about all there is to it," he concluded. "Will Travers is going to give us a hand when we go back out there tomorrow. They say three's a lucky number, so maybe we'll have better luck."

"We will need it," Pia told him. "While I was watching Salazar's office from the floor above, I looked toward the bluffs north of the river. There is a storm raging up there, Longarm. If it is a bad one, with much rain, the river will rise, and by tomorrow night the high water will flood the mouth." ·

"You're sure the high water won't get to the mouth until late tomorrow, though?"

"Quite sure. I have seen this many times since I have been here. Even a very great rain cannot raise the water faster."

Longarm was suddenly aware that Pia's voice was much louder than it had been before. He turned his head and saw her standing in the doorway, strips of white cloth in her hand.

"I think you are not a man who has false modesty, Longarm," she said. "It will be easier for me to put on this fresh bandage while you are in the tub, if you don't object."

"If it don't bother you, it won't brother me, Pia."

"I have tended the wounds of many men. You will not be the first one I have seen naked." Pia came to the side of the tub and took a towel from the stack that lay folded on a small bench. She said, "Sit very straight now, Longarm. Before I put on the bandage, I must dry your shoulders and back."

Pia leaned over the tub and blotted the drops of water from Longarm's chest. She did not look at his broad shoulders and chest while she worked, but kept her eyes locked on his. She moved behind him and Longarm felt her soft hand on his shoulder as she dried his back.

"Now lean forward," she said. "I must look closely at the wound to see how it is healing."

Longarm leaned forward. His new position brought his face close to the rim of the tub, and the patternless maze of scratches was only inches from his eyes. He stared at them absently, very conscious of the gentle warmth of Pia's hands as she felt his back and shoulders in the area of the wound.

"Your arm must still be sore," she said.

"Just a mite. When I twist it, mostly."

"Both wounds are healing well," she assured him. "Now, sit on the side of the tub, so that I can put the bandages on."

Longarm sat as she directed, his feet and legs still in the tub, his back to Pia. She held a pad of cloth on the shallow crease across his shoulder blade, and quickly wrapped the strips of cloth around his chest to hold the pad in place. Then she wrapped a bandage around his upper arm to protect the scabs on the puckered holes where the rifle bullet had passed through.

"You are a very healthy man, Longarm," she said. "Already a scab has formed to protect your flesh, and there is no inflammation, so the wound should heal quickly. But you should not move your arm too much. Perhaps I'd better finish drying you."

"You're doing the doctoring, Pia," Longarm told her. "I'll go along with whatever you say."

"Stand up, then, and I will finish drying you." Pia's voice was no longer lightly brisk and matter-of-fact. It was strained and came hoarsely from her throat.

Longarm rose to his feet, but did not turn around. Pia patted his buttocks and the backs of his legs with the towel, and now her movements were slower, the drying no longer a matter of impersonal care, but more like a caress. Longarm felt himself stirring and beginning to swell in anticipation of Pia's next request.

She did not ask him to turn to face her, but reached around his slim waist with one arm, put her hand on his hip, and pulled gently until he turned in response to the pressure of her palm.

"Ah, yes," Pia sighed as she gazed at Longarm's burgeoning erection. "You are very healthy indeed, Longarm. Much healthier than I thought you would be."

Pia no longer made a pretense of drying Longarm. Her hands went to his groin. She hefted him in her palms, encircled his shaft with her soft fingers, lifting it while pressing gently. Longarm looked down, and saw only the top of Pia's head, her silver-blonde hair gleaming, as she bent to press her lips to his swelling flesh. He felt the moist warmth of her tongue on his shaft, almost fully erect now, and then he was engulfed, her lips pulling at him eagerly as she took him deeply into her mouth.

For several minutes Longarm said nothing. When Pia's busy lips and tongue had brought him fully erect and ready, he told her, "It ain't that I don't enjoy what you're doing, Pia, but you oughta be ready for a little bit more than that about now."

Pia released him and looked up, her eyes shining, her moist lips parted in a smile. "Of course I am. I was just getting you ready to invite me," she said.

Longarm stepped over the rim of the tub and lifted Pia from her knees. He fumbled at the back of her dress, trying to find a fastener, but Pia shrugged his hands away. She tugged the end of the knotted ribbon that gathered the dress at her throat, and when she dropped her arms the dress slid from her shoulders. She wore nothing beneath the dress.

Pia's body, like her unlined face, did not betray her age. Her ivory skin was taut and flawless. Her breasts stood high and, despite their fullness, were only slightly pendulous. The rosettes that accented them were as pink as the blush of a soft sunrise, the tips protruding from their centers a darker pink. Her waist swooped in like an hourglass above generously spreading hips, and the tuft of her pubic brush was as silvery-gold and finely textured as the hair on her head.

Longarm picked her up and carried her into the bedroom, dim in the last light of the fading day. He lowered her to the bed and lay down by her, but when he turned and moved to press himself against her, Pia put her hand on his chest and shook her head.

"Lie back," she said. She encircled his rigid shaft with her soft hand and went on, "You are so big, and it has been such a long time since I have been with a man, that I must take you only a little way at a time. You do not mind?"

"Of course not." Longarm lay back and looked at her. "You do whatever pleasures you the most, Pia."

"This, I think, will please us both," she said, straddling his hips with her thighs and crouching above him.

For a moment, Pia contented herself with rubbing his swollen tip on the soft, moist lips that nestled beneath her tuft of gold. Then she held his erection in place while she lowered her hips a bit before letting herself sink slowly down. She stopped when he had gone into her, and a gasp of delight bubbled from her lips. Deliberately, with many pauses, took him in deeper and still deeper, until their bodies met. For several moments Pia neither moved nor spoke; then she began rocking her hips in a slow, steady rhythm. She looked down at Longarm.

"Ah, yes," she whispered. "For too long I have missed the hardness of a man filling me. Will you stay hard for me until I make up for the time I have lost?"   .

"I'll do my best, Pia."

"Two, three, four times?"

"More than that, if you want more."

"Oh, I will want more!" Pia said happily.

"Go ahead and take your pleasure. And I'll stay with you till you've had your fill," Longarm promised. "Even if it takes all night."

Chapter 19

Dawn's first gray hues were stealing around the edges of the heavy window drapes when Longarm awoke. He sat up and looked around. Pia lay beside him, still asleep, a soft, satisfied smile on her full lips. Moving quietly to keep from rousing her, he slipped from the bed and dug into his saddlebag for a cheroot. Flicking a match into flame across his iron-hard fingernail, he lighted it. Ignoring the summons of his night-filled bladder when the long slim cigar was drawing well, Longarm went to the window and pulled the heavy curtain aside.

Guerra was just waking. A few scattered windows shed the soft yellow glow of kerosene lamps. Looking to the north, he found that the bulky rise of a two-story house just down the street cut off his view of the distant limestone bluffs. All that he could see was the sky, and he realized that he would not be able to get a good look at the bluffs until sunrise, and then only from the windows of the third floor.

By now the demand of his bladder could no longer be ignored. Longarm went into the bathroom and stood beside the marble-cased toilet to let the night's accumulation drain away. The fresh balbriggans and shirt that he had never put on the evening before lay neatly folded on the bench beside the tub, where Luisa had placed them.

Sitting down on the bench, Longarm shoved his feet into the legs of the longjohns and bent down to pull them higher. His eyes were level with the rim of the tub, and in the dim light the scratches on the marble lining it stood out sharply white. He glanced at them idly and was standing up to pull the suit up his body when the nagging ghostly thought that had been recurring for the past two days suddenly took on a recognizable shape.

Frowning, Longarm bent over the bathtub and studied the

166

scratches closely. For the first time he saw a familiar pattern in them, and saw at the same time a dot in the pattern, which he had not noticed before. Without waiting to slip his arms into the sleeves of his balbriggans, Longarm hurried into the bedroom and leaned over the bed.

"Pia!" he said softly. "Pia! Wake up! There's some questions I got to ask you!"

"What is it, Longarm?" she asked. She started to yawn, and covered her mouth quickly with her hand. When the gaping had ended, she said, "Is something the matter? Your face—"

"Never mind that," Longarm said. "Can you remember who's used this bedroom, Pia?"

"Why, certainly. This was the bedroom my mother favored when she came to visit us here in Guerra after I married Raoul. I tried to keep it for her use until she died, and since then—"

Longarm interrupted her. "That's mainly what I wanted to know," he said. "And, when your mother was here, I'd imagine she used to go out to the Devil's River and look around and try to remember where she and Santa Anna had hidden their gold?"

"Of course. Several times. I went with her out there at least once during almost every visit she made here." Pia was frowning now. "Why are you asking me this, Longarm? There are many unhappy memories in my life that I try to put aside, to forget, and your questions are bringing back one of them."

"I'm sorry, Pia, but I got to ask you. Just put up with me a minute or two longer, will you?"

"Very well." Pia sighed. "I'm sure you have a good reason."

"I have," Longarm assured her. "Now, I bet your mother had a nice diamond ring she wore most of the time."

"Yes. It was one given her by Santa Anna when he was first elected president, soon before they parted." Pia's eyes were no longer sleepy now. "Why do you ask such questions about her, Longarm? What have you thought of?"

Again Longarm ignored her question. "Were you with your mother when she died, Pia?" he asked.

Pia shook her head. "No." She pressed her lips together and sat silently for several moments before going on. "That is one of the unhappy memories I spoke of. My mother died here, Longarm—in this house, in this very room. She had arrived for a visit while Raoul and I were away, at the de Cruz ranch in Nueva Rosita. Only Luisa was with her when she died."

Pia's voice was trembling now and her lips were white. "I do not wish to talk of it, Longarm," she said.

"It's real important, Pia. Just one more question."

"I have—" Pia stopped, then said, "One more, then."

"What did Luisa tell you? When you and your husband got back here, I mean."

"Luisa sent a messenger to the ranch. We rode through the night and got here the next afternoon. My mother was in her casket, then, in the salon. Luisa told me that she had been here, in this room, while Mother bathed. She heard some small noises and called to see if Mother wished something, and when she got no reply, Luisa went in and found her dead in the bathtub. She called the doctor, but—" Pia stopped suddenly and shook her head vigorously. "No. No more, Longarm. I will say nothing else until you tell me what all this means."

"It might not mean much, Pia, but if I'm right, the last thing your mother did was to draw a map to show you where she and Santa Anna hid them gold pieces."

"A map? But where? How?"

"There ain't any way I can prove a bit of this, Pia, but here's what I figure must've happened. Your mother had been out to look at the Devil's River, and she got some kind of clue to where they'd buried the gold. Maybe there'd been some new flooding that put the riverbed the way it was years ago, or something like that. Then when she got back here, and was taking a bath, she started feeling faint. Maybe she didn't figure she was going to die, or maybe she had some sorta hunch she was. But she scratched a map with her diamond ring in the marble inside the tub, figuring you'd find it and understand what it was."

"How can you be sure, Longarm?" Pia frowned.

"I can't. I told you that. But if you'll go take a look at the scratches, you'll see they show the way the Devil's River forks out down below that bend in the canyon. There's the big fork first, and then downstream from it the little forks. At least, that's what I take the marks to be. And about midway down from the top of where the first fork starts, there's a dot dug into the marble. I'm betting that's where the gold was buried."

"I must go and look!" Pia said, her violet eyes glowing excitedly. "Come with me—quickly!"

Pia hurried into the bathroom, Longarm following her. They bent over the tub and stared at the scratches in the marble.

"Yes!" she exclaimed. She put her finger at the top of the crudely scratched pattern and traced the lines. "I can see it, too! The first fork here. The next forks here and here. And here is the dot."

"You think I figured it right, then?" Longarm asked.

"I'm sure you did. And to think how often I've looked at those scratches and turned my head aside. I have always believed that, after she was seized by her fatal attack, Mother made them when she tried to lift herself from the tub. She was leaving me a last message, was she not, Longarm?"

"She must've been," he agreed gravely.

"Then the gold must be there!" Pia said excitedly, pointing to the dot. "Come, Longarm! We must hurry and find out."

"Ain't you forgetting something?" Longarm asked.

"Oh, I will put my clothes on before we go, of course," Pia said with a smile. "Just as you must."

"I wasn't talking about our clothes, Pia. I meant the rainstorm you said was going to flood the mouth of the Devil's River."

"Now that we know where to dig, we will have time. The high water cannot get to the mouth before sundown, Longarm."

"You're sure about that?"

"Of course. I have seen it happen for many years."

"We better get a move on, then," Longarm said. "After that sand-scrubbing in the Rio Grande that I didn't want yesterday, I don't feel much like getting another one in the Devil's River today."

Longarm and Pia reached Travers's camp soon after sunup. The Ranger had just finished eating breakfast, and while he wiped his skillet clean and drained his final cup of coffee, they told him of the map and showed him a copy of the crude lines which Longarm had made before he and Pia set out.

"Are you sure you've figured out where that gold's buried, Longarm?" Will Travers frowned when Longarm had finished his explanation.

"Now, Will, if you're looking for an ironclad money-back guarantee like a patent-medicine quack promises, I can't give you one," Longarm replied. "But it all hangs together, as near as I can tell."

Waving her hand toward the upper end of the broad canyon cut by the rills of the Devil's River, Pia demanded, "If the gold is not here, where is it? If the gold pieces had been dug up, some of them would have been spent or passed from hand to hand. How could my friends and I not have heard about that?"

"Well, now, ma'am, I'd venture to say there's some things happen in Mexico that your friends don't hear about," Travers suggested.

Pia shook her head. "You know nothing about the plotting and spying that goes on in my country, Mr. Travers. Those of us who are tyring to rid Mexico of Diaz and his corrupt followers have as many informers as does Diaz himself. Be sure we would have heard."

"There's only one way we're going to find out if the gold's still there or not," Longarm said quietly. "And that's to take these shovels me and Pia brought along and start digging at the place marked on that map. And we better get started right quick if this place is going to get flooded around sundown."

"I guess you're right, Longarm," the Ranger agreed. "So, if you're willing to get a bunch of blisters on your hands, I'm as game as you are. Soon as I get saddled up, we'll go to work."

Skirting the bottom of the *barranca's* wall to save the slow task of weaving among the maze of little islets and rills on its wide floor, they soon reached the point below the curve where the river first split into two streams. They waded their horses across the nearest of the two watercourses to the point where the river divided. There they reined in and sat looking at the narrow triangle of land that lay downstream.

It was less than half a mile long and perhaps five or six hundred yards wide at its base. The sharp point of its upper vee split the Devil's River into two separate, smaller streams, which flowed along the sides of the triangle. Downstream, these in turn divided, one forming two still smaller streams, the other forming three. The crisscrossing and intermingling of these five and the even smaller rills into which they divided served to define the base of the triangular island.

"I guess you and me better do the heavy digging, Longarm," Travers said. "If that bullet wound don't bother you too much."

"I can dig also," Pia volunteered. "Perhaps not as fast, but I will help, of course."

170

"You'll be more help standing watch, Pia," Longarm told her. "My shoulder's all right. I might not be able to keep up with Will, but I'll get along."

"I did not come to watch someone else work!" Pia protested.

"Keeping an eye on the river upstream's as important as digging," Longarm told her. "I know you said that flood ain't going to get here before sundown, but I'd still feel better if you'd ride up by the bend in the canyon, just in case."

"No, Longarm," Pia said firmly. "Later in the day, when there is real danger of the flood crest pouring in, I will gladly be the sentry. Now, there is enough work for all three of us to do here, and I intend to do my share."

Travers had been looking over the spit. He said, "That's a pretty good-sized chunk of real estate for the three of us to tackle. I hope that X on your map is in the right place."

"It may not be," Pia warned. "I have seen this place many times, and always the streams seem to flow in different channels. The floods widen some and fill others."

"Well, all we can do is start where the map's marked," Longarm said, looking at the copy of the bathtub map. He led the way downstream until they reached the midpoint of the triangle's eastern side, dismounted, and paced off half the distance to its center. "This is right close to the middle, I'd say. Come on, Will. Let's give it a try."

Within a few minutes the still air was broken by the scrape of steel on gravel and the thud of shovelfuls of dirt being thrown aside. Longarm and Travers worked back to back, just far enough apart to keep their shovels from clashing together.

Luckily for the inexperienced diggers, the soil for the most part was fairly loose sand mixed with stones that ranged from pea-sized to those as big as a man's fist. Now and then a stretch of adobe dirt was encountered, and had to be broken with hard jabs of a shovel. Occasionally a rock as big as a man's head had to be lifted out of the growing excavation.

Still, it was slow work, and the increasing heat as the sun climbed higher did not make the work any easier. Both Longarm and Travers were sweating profusely. By the end of two hours they had managed to open a ragged hole a bit more than a foot deep and eight or ten feet in diameter. By common consent, Longarm and Travers stopped and leaned on the handles of their shovels.

"How deep do you think that gold was buried?" Travers asked.

"Not very." Longarm turned to Pia. "You got any idea how deep?"

She shook her head. "No. But Mother and Santa Anna were working at night, I suppose by lantern light. They couldn't have buried it much deeper than two or three feet."

"We've got a way to go, then," the Ranger said. "But it seems like the deeper we go, the harder this dirt gets."

At high noon, when they knocked off to eat the cold *burritos* Luisa had packed into Longarm's saddlebags, the sun was beating down mercilessly and the excavation was a bit more than three feet deep. They sat at the edge of the gaping hole, munching the beans wrapped in *tortillas*, and between bites flexed their cramped fingers.

After a few minutes of silence while they took the edge off their hunger, Longarm said thoughtfully, "You know, we been going at this all wrong."

"If you know any easier way to dig a hole, I'd sure like to hear about it," Travers told him.

"That ain't what I'm getting at, Will," Longarm replied. "We ain't even certain this is the right place to dig."

"But this is where the dot showed on the map," Pia said.

"Sure. But that map was made a lot of years ago, Pia. You said yourself a while ago that floods and the current can make a lot of changes in a lot shorter time than that."

"You sound like you're getting ready to spring an idea on us," Travers told Longarm. "Go on, get to the meat of it."

"What we oughta do now is branch out."

"You mean, to make the hole larger around?" Pia frowned.

Longarm shook his head. "The way we're working now, we could dig clear on down to bedrock, and if the gold's a foot or so away from the side of this big hole, we'd never know it was there. Besides that, we're running out of time."

Travers surveyed the expanse of the still unbroken surface. "It's a bigger job than we figured. Pia, you know this river better than any of us. How much more time do you figure we've got to work in?"

Pia glanced at the sun, almost directly overhead. "Four hours, perhaps five. The floodwater is by now halfway here."

"Well, Longarm, if you've got a new idea, now's the time to trot it out," Travers said.

"We might not be any better off if we try this scheme that popped into my head," Longarm cautioned them. "But it looks to me like what we need to do is dig a bunch of ditches that'd start from the sides of the hole we got and go off maybe ten or fifteen feet from it in all directions. They wouldn't have to be any wider than a shovel blade."

"Now, that's the best idea I've heard yet," Travers said. "Why didn't you come up with it before we dug a hole big enough to bury a couple of cows in?"

"I suppose there's times when none of us ain't real bright, Will," Longarm replied. "But if you think it's a sound scheme, let's try it out."

"Since we have only two shovels, I will mark lines for you to follow," Pia volunteered. "If we don't find anything as we dig across the spit, we can dig other ditches at right angles to the first ones. That way, we'll be sure nothing will be missed."

Longarm and Travers set to work again. Digging the narrow trenches was no easier than had been the job of excavating the single big hole they'd already dug, but it seemed to go faster. Within the next two hours, they put down half a dozen narrow slits, a yard apart and ten feet long. The trenches covered about half the perimeter of the big hole.

"We don't seem to be doing any better this way than we were just putting down one hole," Travers observed when they stopped for a rest. "I'm beginning to get the idea there's nothing here to find."

"We can't say that until we have finished all the trenches," Pia told him. "I would not like to see us stop with the job only half done."

"Nobody's said we're going to stop, Pia," Longarm told her. "What bothers me is that it's getting late. If the river floods before we've dug up this whole island, we'd have to wait till the water goes down and start all over again."

"Let's get back to work, then, instead of talking about it," Travers suggested.

It was Travers's spade that hit the box an hour later. He said nothing to the others for several minutes after the blade grated against wood. He prodded and chopped with the tip of the spade's thin blade, and only after his efforts had chipped away a few splinters to reveal the bright grain of solid oak did he call to Longarm and Pia.

"I don't want to put out any false alarms," the Ranger said

173

quietly, "but I think maybe I've found something."

Longarm and Pia rushed to the ditch, where the Ranger stood hip-deep. They saw the strips where the spade had taken thin bites out of the wood, and stared for a moment without speaking.

"Sure looks to me like you hit pay dirt, Will," Longarm said. He spoke as unemotionally as Travers had. "But let's do a little bit more digging before we get all worked up."

Longarm took his spade a foot or so beyond the end of the narrow trench Travers had been digging and started a trench at right angles to the first. Pia got into the trench behind Travers and began scraping away the loose soil that remained around the corner of the box.

"We've surely found it!" she exclaimed as she brushed away the last crumbs of soil from the corner. "What else could have been buried in a place such as this?"

Longarm quit digging long enough to step out of the trench he'd started, to come and look at the cleared section of what was certainly a large oak box. A flick of motion against the bright afternoon sky caught his eye. He stopped and looked up at the rim of the *barranca*.

Four horsemen were riding along the rim from the direction of the Rio Grande. They were still half a mile away, but Longarm did not need a closer look to recognize the gold-embroidered *charro* jacket and flat-brimmed hat worn by Leon Salazar.

Stopping in his tracks, Longarm said quietly to his companions, "It looks like we found Santa Anna's gold, all right. Now all we got to do is figure out how we're going to keep it."

174

Chapter 20

"That's Leon!" Pia gasped when she saw the four riders.

"I recognized him," Longarm said.

"Leon could not have known we were here," Pia said. "He may not be looking for us at all."

Longarm shook his head. "He ain't here but for one reason, Pia. I told you what happened out here yesterday. As for him knowing about us being here, I'd imagine he started keeping an eye on your house right after I got to Guerra, so after his lookout told him we'd left it wouldn't take much figuring for him to know where we'd be heading."

"And this time, he's brought some help with him," Travers put in.

"What's your idea, Will?" Longarm asked. "Parley, or just start shooting?"

"It'll come down to shooting in the end, so I don't suppose it matters much how we start out," the Ranger replied.

"I'd say that's right," Longarm agreed. "But when it comes down to shooting, I don't like being the one that starts it."

"We can afford to give Salazar the first shot," Travers pointed out. "It'd look better in our reports if we did."

"Suits me. I don't give a damn who gets the first shot, as long as we get the last one." Longarm took his eyes off the approaching horsemen long enough to say, "Pia, you better get in the hole before Salazar's bunch comes too close. Stay on this side. You'll be safe there. Even from the rim they won't be able to put any slugs in that hole."

"But what will you do?" Pia asked. "I am not a coward, Longarm! Even if I have no gun, I want to stand with you!"

"Taking cover won't make you a coward," Travers told her.

"Longarm and me will be in that hole with you as soon as Salazar and his bunch get in easy range."

Reluctantly, Pia stepped into the large round hole they'd dug before Longarm's idea of trenching had resulted in discovery of the oaken chest. She did not crouch down in the excavation, but stood waist-deep, watching the approaching riders.

Before he was within easy rifle range, Salazar halted his men. They pulled their horses together in a close group, and it was obvious to Longarm and Travers that they were planning the strategy to be used in an attack. The conference lasted only a few minutes; then two of Salazar's riders slid their mounts down the sloping *barranca* wall and started across the floor of the wide gully. While Salazar stayed in position, the fourth rider began moving ahead along the edge of the drop-off.

Longarm grunted. He told Travers, "Salazar's got smart, Will. You see what he's aiming to do."

"Sure. Come at us from four sides at the same time. We've got to raise up above the edge of the hole to shoot, and there's four of them to the two of us."

"Looks that way," Longarm agreed, his eyes following the two horsemen who were splashing across the floor of the *barranca*. "This ain't going to be a turkey shoot, like we figured."

"We've still got the edge," Travers pointed out. "Those two coming across the river bottom can't get up to much of a gallop, with the ground all busted up the way it is."

"You got any druthers which side you take?" Longarm asked.

"Nary a one. Have you?"

"Nope. Except I've got more to pay Salazar for than you have. If it's all the same to you, I'll take the wall side, and you look after the floor."

"Good enough," Travers agreed. "And we'll give them the first shot."

"Oh, sure. Billy Vail will have an easier time smoothing down the pencil pushers in Washington if he can say whatever I'll get blamed for was just self-defense."

"Longarm, how can you be so calm, with Leon and his men getting ready to attack us?" Pia asked.

Longarm did not reply at once. He was watching the rider on the rim of the *barranca*. The man had ridden past them by now and was still moving. As he returned his attention to Salazar, he said, "No use to get all nerved up, Pia. Once you

176

get on a mean horse, all you can do is ride him till he quits bucking."

Salazar had his rifle out now. Longarm saw him drawing a bead on the excavation and snapped, "Duck down! The shooting's about to start!"

Longarm ducked himself just as Salazar's rifle cracked. A slug whistled over the hole and threw up dirt when it struck the ground a foot beyond its edge.

"That what we've been waiting for," Travers said calmly. He stood up, scanning the floor of the *barranca* in one lightning glance to locate his two targets. The riders were approaching at right angles, one from the south, the other from the west. The Ranger dropped his head below the edge of the excavation as their bullets buzzed above the space he had just occupied.

Longarm was concentrating on Salazar. The leader of the attackers was advancing slowly, just edging off the bottom of the *barranca* wall and onto its floor. He was carrying his rifle ready to shoulder, and when he saw Longarm, he brought the gun up and fired quickly. Salazar's aim was ruined by the speed with which he had to trigger his shot, for the slug tore into the earth fifty feet away from the hole.

Bullets from Salazar's men were pocking the dirt now. Both Longarm and Travers kept their heads down until a bullet whizzed into the hole and thunked into the raw wall of dirt exposed by their digging.

Longarm realized instantly that only a rifleman on the *barranca's* rim could have fired the shot. He let Salazar wait and turned his attention to the horseman who'd passed a few minutes earlier. A quick glance gave Longarm the man's location, and when he raised his head above the edge of the hole a few seconds later he had his rifle ready. A split second was all Longarm needed to take aim. He triggered the Winchester and as he was dropping back into the shelter of the hole he saw the man beginning to topple from his horse.

Will Travers was occupied with the men riding toward them across the river bottom. They kept firing as they came, but the roughness of the ground, cut by dozens of small rills, spoiled their shooting. When he saw how ineffective his adversaries' shooting was, Travers took his time. He stood up, bringing a staccato burst from the oncoming riders, and cut their firing off with two fast, well-aimed shots.

Over his shoulder, Travers said to Longarm, "If you got the

177

one on the rim, then Salazar's the only one left to worry about."

Longarm stood up to join Travers. Salazar had seen the same thing the defenders had. His force wiped out, the Mexican turned his horse and started toward the mouth of the river.

"He's damn near outa range now!" Longarm said angrily. He scrambled out of the hole and started for his horse. Over his shoulder, he called to Travers, "You and Pia keep on digging, Will. I'm going after Salazar!"

Salazar had a start of a quarter of a mile on Longarm, but the cavalry mount had been resting and was fresh, while Salazar's mount was showing the effects of its gallop from Guerra. Under Longarm's urging, the cavalry horse ate up the distance. Salazar had not reached the mough of the *barranca* before Longarm closed enough of the distance between them to be in rifle range.

Salazar kept looking back, and when he saw Longarm closing so rapidly, he realized that he must made a stand. He wheeled his mount and brought up his carbine. Longarm had only a few seconds to rein in when he saw Salazar begin to turn his horse. He wrapped the reins around his left wrist and hauled back with all the force he could exert.

A pang shot through his wounded shoulder, but Longarm paid no attention to it. The horse showed its cavalry training by thrusting out its forefeet and skidding to a halt in little more than its own length. Longarm was squeezing his rifle's trigger while Salazar was still aiming. The Winchester's slug sent Salazar cartwheeling from his saddle before his horse could stop.

Salazar landed in a heap on the canyon floor. Longarm levered a fresh cartridge into the Winchester's chamber, but saw that he would not need it. He waited for a moment, watching his downed adversary for some sign of movement, but Salazar lay still. Turning the horse, Longarm started bakc toward the spit.

As short as the fracas had been, it had cost valuable time. The sun was dropping low in the sky by the time Longarm reached the hole. Travers and Pia were once again shoveling dirt off the oak box and had more than half of it uncovered.

As he reined in beside them, Longarm asked, "Pia, how much longer you guess it's going to take for that flood water to get here?"

Pia stopped shoveling long enough to look at the declining sun. "Another hour," she said. "Maybe a bit more. It is very late, Longarm."

"I'll spell you digging while you ride up and look," Longarm said, starting to dismount.

Pia shook her head. "No. You are already mounted, Longarm. It would waste time. After you reach the bend, you can see a mile or more upstream. You go and see what the river is doing."

"You know the country better'n I do," Longarm began. "And I can move more dirt than—"

Travers interrupted him. "She's right," he said. "You don't need to know anything about the country. Quit interrupting our digging, and go look!"

Longarm wasted no more time in argument. He started up the canyon toward the bend, almost two miles from the spit. He could see no signs of an impending flood. Upstream from the split, the current flowed normally enough, and when he reached the point where it entered the canyon the stream danced along in its narrow channel between the high, rocky walls.

He got to the bend and rounded it on the precarious trail that ran along the bank. When he looked upstream his jaw dropped, and for a moment all thought that all was well. Beyond the curve the canyon ran almost straight for four or five miles. For a moment Longarm thought that he was looking at another curve in the walls ahead. Then his eyes began to pick out the details of the vista, and all he could do was stare in amazement.

Between the walls of the narrow canyon, a solid wall of water was rushing downstream. There was little debris by which the speed of the water's advance could be gauged. A few sparsely leaved bushes and much less often an uprooted clump of prickly pear appeared briefly on the face of the towering wall of brown, frothing water.

Clusters of white foam floated on the surface ahead of the water wall as its unpredictable currents swirled around and were broken by the rough stone of the canyon's walls. For a hundred yards or more ahead of the main flood wall, a hump rolled along the river's surface as the pressure of the onrushing flood pushed the slower-moving river in front of it.

Longarm wasted no time; he knew he had none to waste. He watched the approaching wall of floodwater long enough to get an idea of the speed at which it was moving before turning the horse. The animal stepped gingerly as it turned, for the shelf on which the trail ran was barely wide enough to allow it to reverse its direction. Not daring to risk a gallop on the precarious shelf, Longarm kept prodding the horse to walk faster as he made his way back to the *barranca*.

"Maybe we've got as much as two hours," he told Turner and Pia when he reached the hole. "If we don't get that box dug up and get outa this place by then, we're in real trouble."

"You can see we have it almost uncovered," Pia said.

"We could go faster if the damn thing wasn't too heavy for us to move," Travers added. "Pia and me tried to shift it, but we couldn't budge it."

"Let's all three of us try," Longarm said, swinging out of the saddle and joining them in the hole.

Except for one corner which was still buried, the box was standing free. It was was made from inch-thick oak, and along its top edges Longarm could see the heads of the huge hand-forged nails that had been used in making it. The box was smaller than he'd expected it to be, though, only about a yard square and a foot deep. In spite of its modest size, even when Longarm added his efforts to those of his companions they could not budge it from spot where it rested.

"I ain't surprised," Longarm told the others as they stood gazing at the case. "If what Angelita told me was right, there's as much gold in that box as what we took out of the ground at Buffalo Bayou, and it weighed around fifteen hundred pounds. That's three-fourths of a ton, the way I learned to cipher when I was a tad going to school back in West Virginia."

"You had the gold loaded in a wagon by the time I caught up with you," Travers said. "How'd you manage to lift it?"

"We were lucky there, Will. That gold was all in bags, and we carried it one bag at a time."

"Then perhaps we can break open the box and carry the gold as you did there," Pia suggested.

"That might work," Travers agreed. "There's only one thing wrong with your idea, Pia." He pointed to the big nail heads. "We don't have any tools that'd open it. Our shovels would snap in a mintue if we tried to pry that top off with them."

Longarm said, "There's something else wrong with trying to move the gold a little bit at a time. It took us better'n an hour to move all them bags just a few feet at Buffalo Bayou, Pia. The time it took didn't matter much because we didn't have a flood coming at us like we got here."

"There's no way to get hold of this damn box!" Travers said, kicking the sturdy oak side of the case. "What we need is a block and tackle to lift it and an ox team to haul it."

"Will and I talked of using our horses," Pia said, "but we have no rope."

"I didn't figure the reins and straps and such that we could get from our saddle gear would stand the load," Travers added. "Too bad we're not a bunch of cowhands. If we were, we'd have lariats strong enough to stop a running steer. They'd do—"

"Hold on!" Longarm broke in. "I recall seeing lariats on a couple of the horses them fellows with Salazar was riding. Maybe we ain't whipped yet. Will, you and Pia go on and finish getting that box free from the dirt, while I see if I can catch us a couple of them nags."

Longarm soon found that spotting the horses was easy, but catching them without a lasso was another matter. He rode up to the first horse, expecting to pull his own alongside the animal and grab its loose reins. Half broken, half wild, as Mexican horses frequently were, the riderless animal allowed him to come almost close enough to reach its trailing reins before moving away.

After a half-hour of persistent effort, Longarm caught one of the horses. By using the lessons he'd learned in taking the first, a second horse was captured in half the time. The second animal had a braided leather lariat looped on one of its saddlestrings.

Leading the two animals, Longarm started back to the hole. When he reached the bottom edge of the spit, he noticed for the first time that the water in the maze of rills that flowed below it was appreciably deeper. The surface of the water was only an inch or so below the top of the soil now. He looked ahead, and at the mouth of the canyon saw the first indication of how small a margin of time they had. A hundred yards upstream from the spit the river rose in the hump he'd seen rushing down the canyon only minutes in advance of the flood wall.

"We got just about fifteen minutes to get that box slung between these horses and start out of here," he told Pia and Travers. "If we take any longer than that, we'll be lucky to get out ourselves."

"We've been watching the water coming up and wondering if we were going to make it," Travers said. "But the sides of the box are clear all around, so all we've got to do is lash it on the horses and head for high ground."

Grabbing the lariat, Longarm jumped into the hole. He and Travers quickly found the center of the lariat and formed the braided leather strands into a twin-loop sling. With their bare hands they clawed away the dirt below the sides of the chest and slipped the loops over it. As fast as they worked, by the time they had the sling on the chest and were ready to bring up the saddle horses, there was almost a foot of water in the bottom of the pit, and the entire surface of the spit was covered by the fast-rising water.

Longarm looked for the hump he'd seen earlier. It was gone now, and he realized that once outside the confining walls of the canyon the water had spread. His hope that they would get out safely suddenly revived.

"Pia, mount up fast!" he commanded. "Will, while Pia holds these two horses I brought back, you and me can hitch the ends of the lariat around their saddlehorns."

Longarm and Travers led the horses into place and handed the bridles to Pia. They were working in calf-deep water now. Longarm stole a glance upstream while he and Travers were wrestling the horses into position. The flood wall had reached the mouth of the canyon and was just beginning to spill into the *barranca*. As it poured out of the narrow canyon onto the broad expanse of the shallow valley the water spread, filling the *barranca* from wall to wall, and Longarm had no way of knowing how much more remained pent up in the canyon.

"Shake a leg, Will!" Longarm urged as he took the slick wet lariat and began throwing a clove hitch over the high Mexican-style horn of the saddle. "And hitch that lariat tight! Once we start off, it ain't going to be safe to stop, and there's noplace we can come back to."

"Don't worry about my hitch!" Travers snapped. "Take care of your own! I cowhanded before I joined the Rangers, and I'll match my hitch to stand up to anybody's."

Wading knee-deep, the water-washed bottom treacherous under their boot soles, strange currents grabbing at their legs, Longarm and Travers got to their horses and jumped into the saddles. They nosed their mounts up to the rump of Pia's horse and each man took the reins of one of the Mexican horses.

Maneuvering carefully, they walked their horses into place beside the pair hitched to the gold.

"Pick a trail for us, Pia," Longarm called. "Angle down from the canyon, and we'll try ot get out of the *barranca* at that gentle slope just past Will's camp. Just take it slow and easy, and we'll make it all right."

As the strange little cavalcade moved slowly toward the wall of the *barranca*, there were times when Longarm wondered if he was going to have to eat his optimistic words. The bottom was treacherous, constantly shifting as the water from the flood wall spread over the valley floor, cutting new channels in the soft bottom, swirling around the legs of the straining horses.

Before they'd covered half the distance to the safety of the wall, the horses were belly-deep, and the swirling currents were twisting the heavy box of gold like a child's top. Pia's horse almost went down once when it stepped in a hole gouged by some freakish current, and all the mounts lurched like camels as they moved across the uneven bottom.

At last they reached the safety of the *barranca* wall, and mounted to the ledge where Travers had pitched camp. The wet horses, their legs trembling from fatigue, stood exhausted as the three dismounted.

"We will go to Guerra now, won't we?" Pia asked. "I know we will all feel better after a hot bath and in dry clothes."

"I guess we can make it, if we take it slow," Longarm said.

"You better count me out, Longarm," Travers said. "I told you I had orders not to cross the Rio Grande."

"But your case is closed, Will," Longarm protested. "A man's got a right to get cleaned up after he's been up to his belly button half the day in cold, murky water."

"Not if he's in Cap'n McNelly's Ranger company, he don't!" Travers retorted. "Besides, you won't get that box of gold to Guerra the way it's lashed up. Remember, everything weighs a lot less in water than it does on land, and these horses are just about blowed now. Let that box stay right where it sets tonight and come get it with a wagon tomorrow."

"I think Will is right, Longarm," Pia said. "If he cannot go to Guerra, and will look after the gold tonight . . ."

Longarm nodded slowly. "I guess you got a point, Will. You don't mind me riding in with Pia, do you?"

"I figured you to. Go on. I'll be all right."

"Sure." Longarm moved to the horses that were still hitched to the gold box and started removing the lariat from their saddles.

"What d'you think you're doing now?" Travers asked with a frown.

"Why, I aim to turn these horses free, Will. I don't know who they belong to, but they sure ain't mine. And I'm damned if I'm going to let anybody call me a horse thief!"

Watch for

LONGARM AND THE CUSTER COUNTY WAR

sixty-first novel in the bold
LONGARM series from Jove

coming in December!

LONGARM

Explore the exciting Old West with one of the men who made it wild!

___06953-1	LONGARM ON THE SANTA FE #36	$2.25
___06954-X	LONGARM AND THE STALKING CORPSE #37	$2.25
___06955-8	LONGARM AND THE COMANCHEROS #38	$2.25
___07412-8	LONGARM AND THE DEVIL'S RAILROAD #39	$2.50
___07413-6	LONGARM IN SILVER CITY #40	$2.50
___07070-X	LONGARM ON THE BARBARY COAST #41	$2.25
___07538-8	LONGARM AND THE MOONSHINERS #42	$2.50
___07525-6	LONGARM IN YUMA #43	$2.50
___07431-4	LONGARM IN BOULDER CANYON #44	$2.50
___07543-4	LONGARM IN DEADWOOD #45	$2.50
___07425-X	LONGARM AND THE GREAT TRAIN ROBBERY #46	$2.50
___07418-7	LONGARM IN THE BADLANDS #47	$2.50
___07414-4	LONGARM IN THE BIG THICKET #48	$2.50
___07522-1	LONGARM AND THE EASTERN DUDES #49	$2.50
___06251-0	LONGARM IN THE BIG BEND #50	$2.25
___07523-X	LONGARM AND THE SNAKE DANCERS #51	$2.50
___06253-7	LONGARM ON THE GREAT DIVIDE #52	$2.25
___06254-5	LONGARM AND THE BUCKSKIN ROGUE #53	$2.25
___06255-3	LONGARM AND THE CALICO KID #54	$2.25
___07545-0	LONGARM AND THE FRENCH ACTRESS #55	$2.50
___07528-0	LONGARM AND THE OUTLAW LAWMAN #56	$2.50
___06258-8	LONGARM AND THE BOUNTY HUNTERS #57	$2.50
___06259-6	LONGARM IN NO MAN'S LAND #58	$2.50
___06260-X	LONGARM AND THE BIG OUTFIT #59	$2.50
___06261-8	LONGARM AND SANTA ANNA'S GOLD #60	$2.50

Available at your local bookstore or return this form to:

JOVE
Book Mailing Service
P.O. Box 690, Rockville Centre, NY 11571

Please send me the titles checked above. I enclose _____. Include 75¢ for postage and handling if one book is ordered; 25¢ per book for two or more not to exceed $1.75. California, Illinois, New York and Tennessee residents please add sales tax.

NAME _____

ADDRESS _____

CITY _____ STATE/ZIP _____

(allow six weeks for delivery.)

☆ **From the Creators of LONGARM** ☆

The Wild West will never be the same!

____ LONE STAR ON THE TREACHERY TRAIL #1	07519-1/$2.50
____ LONE STAR AND THE OPIUM RUSTLERS #2	07520-5/$2.50
____ LONE STAR AND THE BORDER BANDITS #3	07540-X/$2.50
____ LONE STAR AND THE KANSAS WOLVES #4	07419-5/$2.50
____ LONE STAR AND THE UTAH KID #5	07415-2/$2.50
____ LONE STAR AND THE LAND GRABBERS #6	07426-8/$2.50
____ LONE STAR IN THE TALL TIMBER #7	07542-6/$2.50
____ LONE STAR AND THE SHOWDOWNERS #8	07521-3/$2.50
____ LONE STAR AND THE HARDROCK PAYOFF #9	06234-0/$2.25
____ LONE STAR AND THE RENEGADE COMANCHES #10	07541-8/$2.50
____ LONE STAR ON OUTLAW MOUNTAIN #11	07526-4/$2.50
____ LONE STAR AND THE GOLD RAIDERS #12	06237-5/$2.25
____ LONE STAR AND THE DENVER MADAM #13	07112-9/$2.50
____ LONE STAR AND THE RAILROAD WAR #14	07133-1/$2.50
____ LONE STAR AND THE MEXICAN STANDOFF #15	07259-1/$2.50
____ LONE STAR AND THE BADLANDS WAR #16	07273-7/$2.50

Available at your local bookstore or return this form to:

 JOVE
Book Mailing Service
P.O. Box 690, Rockville Centre, NY 11571

Please send me the titles checked above. I enclose _____. Include 75¢ for postage and handling if one book is ordered; 25¢ per book for two or more not to exceed $1.75. California, Illinois, New York and Tennessee residents please add sales tax.

NAME_____

ADDRESS_____

CITY_____ STATE/ZIP_____

(allow six weeks for delivery.)

54